LUCKY
FEW

Also by Kathryn Ormsbee
The Water and the Wild

LUCKY FEW

Kathryn Ormsbee

SIMON & SCHUSTER BFYR

NEW YORK • LONDON • TORONTO • SYDNEY • NEW DELHI

SIMON & SCHUSTER BFYR

An imprint of Simon & Schuster Children's Publishing Division

1230 Avenue of the Americas, New York, New York 10020

For information about special discounts for bulk purchases, please contact Simon & Schuster Special Sales at 1-866-506-1949 or business@simonandschuster.com.

The Simon & Schuster Speakers Bureau can bring authors to your live event. For more information or to book an event, contact the Simon & Schuster Speakers Bureau at 1-866-248-3049 or visit our website at www.simonspeakers.com.

Jacket design by Laurent Linn

Interior design by Hilary Zarycky

The text for this book is set in ITC Berkeley Old Style Std.

Manufactured in the United States of America

First Edition

2 4 6 8 10 9 7 5 3 1

Library of Congress Cataloging-in-Publication Data

Names: Ormsbee, Katie.

Title: Lucky few / Kathryn Ormsbee.

Description: First edition. | New York : Simon & Schuster Books for Young Readers, 2016. | Summary: Homeschooler Stevie Hart meets Max, a strange boy who is obsessed with death, but what starts off as fun together begins spiraling downward when Stevie's diabetes sabotages her fumbling romance with Max, and her best friend, Sanger, announces she is moving out of state.

Identifiers: LCCN 2015019889 |

ISBN 9781481455282 (hardcover) | ISBN 9781481455305 (eBook)

Subjects: | CYAC: Home schooling—Fiction. | Death—Fiction. | Love—Fiction. | Friendship—Fiction.

Classification: LCC PZ7.O637 Lu 2016 | DDC [Fic]—dc23

LC record available at http://lccn.loc.gov/2015019889

To Annie—
my first word,
only classmate,
sister, hero, and friend

ACKNOWLEDGMENTS

Acknowledgments! I suck at these in person. Whenever I talk about someone who has given me invaluable encouragement, insight, and guidance, I inevitably get choked up. Luckily, these acknowledgments are in print, but if you'd like, you can imagine me sobbing violently as I write them.

Stevie, Sanger, Max, and I owe a lot of thanks to a lot of people; without them, this story simply wouldn't have been told. First, my Super Agent, Beth Phelan, who believed in and championed this book like none other. Thank you for cluing me in to the fact that lanyards are not a universal sign of preppiness and for helping me get a grape out of a toaster that one time. Your dogs are awesome. You are awesomer.

My magnificent editor, Zareen Jaffery—I stand in awe. Thank you for asking all the right questions, even when they were really tough and occasionally gory. And a great big thank-you to everyone at Simon & Schuster BFYR: Mekisha Telfer, who kindly answered all my stupid questions; Laurent Linn, whose design skills are like whoa; and the numerous others who worked to get this story into the world. Endless thanks to the supremely talented Carlo Giambarresi for the breathtaking artwork and to Katharine Wiencke, copyeditor extraordinaire.

I've lived with some top-notch roommates during my writing years, and I'm thankful to each one of them for dealing with

Hermit Mode when deadline season came around. Thanks to Rachel, for keeping me fed with delish baked goods; Kayla, for our late night walks; Sandra, for our *Gilgamesh* translation dates; Danielle, for the *New Girl* breaks; Celine, for tickling me into going out on weeknights; and Ashley, for all the "Gasp, me too!" conversations over macaroons.

A special thanks to all my Austin friends who explored and laughed and gabbed with me—especially Sasha, fellow *Mad Men* enthusiast and owner of THE cutest handbags, and Anita, whose tales of paranormal activity kept me up late at night.

Thank you to all my Twitter buddies—psst, Ash and Jen, HI!—and to the members of the talented Fearless Fifteeners, who've reminded me that I am not alone when I feel like a floundering mess in the way of book things. Seoling and Kristen—you make my heart go boom, boom; I couldn't ask for better writing pals or friends. Kathryn, critique partner o' mine, you have a great name; thank you for the sharp suggestions.

Thank you to the professors of the Samford English department, who challenged and enlightened me—all under the watchful eye of Virginia Woolf's portrait.

I wouldn't be standing or sane were it not for my friends. Badger, my fellow fangirl—because of you, I now know the joys of a "fir real" Christmas tree. Little Miss Shelly Twin, thank you for allowing me to spew my book news on you in a Cambridge waffle shop all those years ago. Soup, you are the smartest

Ravenclaw and nicest soprano. Katherine, you send me texts that make me cry in the best possible way. Hilary Friend, thank you for quoting *Teen Girl Squad* when I need it most. Sara, I will never forget your FAVORITE MOON or your Ron Swanson Otter. Nancy, you fill my life with giggles and fun facts; let's go back to Gloucester Road soon, okay?

Destiny, my A+ critique partner and part-time dinosaur—thank you for being a Slytherfriend.

Katie Carroll, my fellow adventurer—I can't include a picture of a cute woodland squirrel, but imagine one right HERE.

Thank you to my fabulous extended family for the love and support. Thank you, Matt and Annie, for being you; I still think you're the coolest couple around, even though you moved thousands of miles away from me.

Thank you to Hal Ashby for directing a film that changed my melancholy teenage life. I'm still melancholy, but happily so.

Thank you, readers! I am so lucky (*ba dum tsh*) to have my words read by YOU.

And to my parents, Lindell and Susan Ormsbee—thank you for homeschooling me. You raised me to be a confident and independent thinker; props for not going totally berserk in the process. I love you.

Mithridates, he died old.

—A. E. Housman, *A Shropshire Lad*

One

For a dentist office receptionist, she had stunningly bad teeth. The ocher stains on her enamel were a mystery of Sherlockian proportions. What was the culprit? Was it years of coffee consumption? Tobacco use? Or some other foul substance equally capable of corrupting a pearlescent smile?

"Do you need a school excuse?" she asked.

I was far more interested in the answer to my dental whodunit than the answer the receptionist awaited. I was about to tell her something she wouldn't like and wouldn't understand.

"No," I told her.

I said it politely.

"I think both you and your cousin do," she said.

"Yeah, I'm pretty sure we don't."

The receptionist inched a blue square of paper across her desk.

"Come on, honey," she said, like she was coaxing a naughty dog out from under the porch.

No choice was left to me.

I was forced to drop the H-bomb.

I said, "We're homeschooled."

Bad-Teeth Receptionist blinked at me. Then she asked the question I got asked about seventy percent of the time upon H-bomb impact:

"Oh, sweetie, don't you miss being around *people*?"

I was used to this. I was well versed in the homeschool stereotype. I understood that this receptionist was probably thinking, *Lordy, she's Amish and doesn't have a cell phone and lives with fifteen inbred kinfolk.*

What I wanted to tell her, but never would, was that the realm of the home educated was a many-splendored, multi-faceted thing. There was nuance. There was diversity. She couldn't just slap a single, all-inclusive label on my forehead. She had to choose from an *assortment* of labels. If she wanted, she could pick from the list I had personally compiled in the ninth grade. I had divided the homeschooling population into four clean categories, as follows:

Blue-Jean Jumpers

The most common stereotype associated with the home edu-cated. You know, families of seven or more. The standard issue of dress for boys is jeans two sizes too big, Velcro sneakers, and button-up plaid shirts (we're talking the original hipsters). Girls wear long blue-jean jumpers, and when they want to get super insane, they choose the jumper with the embroidered sunflowers on the front. They are bound by some cultish church law to never cut their straggly blond hair or expose their ankles. The kids all look slightly soulless, like something out of *Children of the Corn*. They're so painfully shy, they can't place their own fast-food order—if their parents even believe in fast food. They attend church five days a week, don't own a television, and live on a farm with chickens. The mom makes killer homemade monkey bread. Commonly sighted at:

Church

Home

The homeschool co-op

Granolas

Hippie folk who are conscientious objectors to the public education system. Usually upper-middle-class progressives who drive a Prius or, better yet, a tandem bicycle. They live on a strict Paleo diet. They compost. Favorite fashion choices include Birkenstocks, homemade beaded necklaces, tassels, and tie-dye. A typical school day involves "field trips" to the backyard and to the local herbal remedy shop. Commonly sighted at:

Whole Foods

Anti-war demonstrations

Urban organic farms

Last-Chance Charlies

Mom and Dad have no clue what to do with their problem kid. After Charliekins got expelled from his third school, they figured they'd give homeschooling a spin, because if all else fails, do it yourself, right? Zero to 0.5 percent parental supervision. After parents leave for work, Last-Chance Charlie lapses into a pot-induced Netflix-slash-World-of-Warcraft binge. He texts his public school friends throughout the day to make them jealous of his unchecked autonomy. Dresses in baggy black jeans and one of thirty unwashed action hero T-shirts. Will eventually be booted to a school in Virginia or else run off to live with his gaming bro in the next county over. Commonly sighted at:

Comic cons

Gaming stores

Curb outside the local liquor store

Normal Types

The kids who are just trying to get a decent education. The most diverse pool yet, this reasonably normal lot chooses homeschooling for a variety of reasons. Maybe they've been zoned for a bad school district and are unable to afford private tuition; or the parents are geniuses better qualified than public school teachers; or maybe the kids are professional models, actors, or Olympians with erratic schedules. The normal types dress in whatever Gap says is in vogue. More often than not, they're high scorers on their SATs. Commonly sighted at:

Normal places

(like the dentist's—

NOT their parents' basement)

It irked me that this fourth category got lumped in with all the others. Brand yourself a homeschooler and you'd branded yourself a sheltered, narrow-minded prude for life. That's why I was loath to ever let on my true H-word identity. Not that it mattered there, in Dr. Kopeck's Lasting Smiles office. I didn't care that the stained-teeth receptionist was judging me.

But maybe I did.

A little.

Bad-Teeth Receptionist had asked me a question about my level of social interaction, and so far I wasn't making a great impression. I'd already exceeded the socially acceptable span of time between the asking of a question and the answering.

I had nothing to lose.

I leaned across the desk and looked slowly to my left, then slowly to my right.

"I miss people so much," I said. Then I shifted in closer and whispered the words *"Help me."*

I bugged my eyes meaningfully at the receptionist. In response, she emitted a low, warbling sound.

As she warbled, I trotted from the waiting room out to Mom's idling sedan.

I took shotgun. My cousin Joel was sprawled in the backseat, holding an ice pack to his jaw. His gangly legs were propped against the window in an odd, bendy way that looked like a yoga move gone wrong.

"You'll probably want to hoof it out of here," I told Mom. "That lady might be calling CPS on you."

"Oh God," groaned Mom, though she was smiling. "What did you do?"

"I told her I stay locked in my bedroom and I'm only fed one packet of Top Ramen per day."

"Huh," said Joel. "Sounds like college."

"Funny," I said, "I don't remember you going to college."

"Inconsequential." Joel tipped his chin proudly. "You wear shirts with the Eiffel Tower and shit on them, and you've never been to Paris."

"Language, Joel," Mom said, though it was more of an observation than a reprimand.

She pulled the sedan out of the parking lot.

"So," I concluded, "we may want to change dentists."

"I can't take you anywhere."

"Yeah, I know. That's the problem, remember? I don't get out. You lock me in my bedroom."

Joel moaned. He mushed his ice pack closer to his jaw.

"You are an infant," I informed him.

"It *hurts*," Joel whined, hovering in falsetto territory. "Oh sweet Lord, the pain. You wouldn't know. You've never had a root canal."

"Maybe because I clean my teeth with something other than Dentyne Ice."

"Cut it out, both of you."

Mom cranked up soft rock radio, effectively drowning out our bickering with the wails of Enrique Iglesias.

I propped my sneakers on the dash and watched cars crawl past as we joined the swarm of morning rush hour traffic on southbound I-35. I was in no particular rush to get back home. I had a trig test that morning. Mom would plunk down twenty questions on the breakfast room table, and the only thing I'd be able to sort out was where to write my name.

And yes, I realized that writing my name at the top of my tests was unnecessary, but it's the little things that make you feel like a normal sixteen-year-old.

I couldn't sweet-talk Mom into delaying the trig test. I'd already postponed my American Government quiz the previous week, and Joel had been in top academic form lately, so I couldn't deflect by pointing to him, the once perpetual scapegoat.

There had been a time when I could one-up Joel in every subject, bar none. My scores were always higher, my goal chart always fuller. Once, Joel was the very picture of Back-the-Hell-Off-Couldn't-Care-Less-Adolescent. And as long as Joel was in worse academic shape than I was, I could stay out of the heat. Then, in his junior year, Joel got serious about getting into UT-Austin, which resulted in a pretty impressive SAT score and a lot of backslaps from formerly concerned family members. I was happy for Joel and all, but his success meant my failures were more noticeable. I was going to bomb that trig test, and I was going to have to endure Mom's unadulterated wrath.

My phone lit up just as we were pulling into the carport. The screen flashed a selfie of me and my friend, Valerie
Borkowski. Our cheeks were squished together, Valerie's lips
forming the traditional fishy pout.

"This is important," I told Mom. "About tonight."

Mom waved her acquiescence, cut the engine, and got out
of the car. I answered the phone.

"Are you alone?"

Valerie's voice was taut and papery—the voice of someone
about to have a good cry.

I glanced back at Joel. He'd fallen asleep, legs still crossed
in an awkward gangle, ice pack drooping off his cheek.

"Good as," I said. "What's wrong?"

There was a whimper. Then a wheeze. Then a full-out sob.
I yanked the phone away from my ear and jabbed frantically at
the volume, lowering it to a more palatable decibel.

"Val?"

I cradled the phone back against my ear as I opened the car
door. Valerie was sobbing, and there was only one good reason
I could think of for that sobbing, and that reason was passed
out in the backseat.

It seemed like a betrayal to Valerie and Joel to stay where
I was, in the presence of them both, whether that presence be
auditory or physical. I hopped out of the car and gave the door a
firm slam, hoping it would wake Joel up. I wanted him to suffer,
at least a little. I'd warned him about dating one of my friends.

But I'd warned Val, too.

"Val, are you still there?"

I knew Val was still there, because she was choking out indiscernible, snot-coated words. I had to say something, and "calm down" or "what's wrong?" weren't available options. A few months back, Val and I had made a pact to not diminish each other's emotional validity by telling each other to calm down, which is harder than it sounds. And of course, there was no point in asking Val what was wrong, because I knew perfectly well what was wrong: Joel was a serial dater.

It took another excruciating half minute, but Valerie finally hitched in enough breath to form understandable speech.

"I thought it would be different with me. You know? I thought he was through being an asshole."

"Yeah," I said.

"'Yeah'? What does 'yeah' mean? Is that your way of saying 'I told you so'?"

"No, Val. It's my way of saying 'yeah.'"

"I can't give you a ride tonight. The chance of seeing him at the house is too mortifying."

I was reminded, suddenly and vividly, of Mom's favorite soap opera, the one she watched when Joel and I were doing afternoon homework. Val sounded exactly like one of those insipid nurses with breast implants, an evil doppelgänger, and a hankering for a married doctor.

"Don't be melodramatic," I warned.

"Excuse me? Don't be *melodramatic*? That's as good as telling me to 'calm down'!"

I swore low, away from the receiver.

At least, I thought it was away from the receiver.

"Are you cussing me out now? It's not my fault you're related to a total douchebag!"

"Look," I said, "I'm really sorry about what happened. But you're my only ride to the rally. Mom and Dad are going to a concert, and I'm not about to ask Hilary Mayhu—"

"Just ask Sanger."

"No."

"Why not? She does anything you say."

"She hates politics. Anyway, she already drove me to the mall on Wednesday, and I don't want to abuse car privileges. I promised her I wouldn't be that friend."

"Well, I'm *sooo* glad that your friendship with *Sanger* means more than your friendship with *me*."

There was nothing to say to that, really. My friendship with Sanger *did* mean more to me. Sanger was my best friend. I'd known her for way longer than Val. Also, Sanger had yet to chew me out over the phone.

By now, I'd reached Dad's rock garden out back. I walked across the low bamboo bridge, my gaze flitting between pristinely raked pebbles and the morning shade cast by a long row of dragon trees.

I decided on a different method of persuasion.

"I won't let Joel anywhere near the door or windows," I said. "It's not like he's going to want to see you, either. If we're going to stay friends, you have to get over the fact that you might bump into him."

"But it's too *fresh*. Somehow he'll still know I'm outside your house, and I don't want him to think I'm a desperate psycho stalker ex."

"Uh. If Joel even thinks of you, I'm sure it'll just be like, 'Wow! How nice. She's picking up her friend for a nonprofit event.'"

"You can be so cruel."

"What?"

"You're just like him."

Again, I thought of the big-breasted blonde on Mom's soap. What was her name? Esmeralda? Anastasia?

. . . Val?

"You're my only ride to the capitol," I said, "and I'd really appreciate it if you did the mature thing and—"

"The mature thing. The MATURE thing? THE MATURE— Why don't you talk to Joel about the MATURE THING to—"

I dropped the phone from my ear, and not just because Val was screeching at an unbearable volume, but because I saw it, across the fence, between the trunks of two dragon trees.

There was a blood-smeared body in our neighbor's backyard.

Two

The smart thing would've been to cut off the call with Val and dial nine-one-one.

That would've been smart.

But that's not what I did.

I dropped the phone, Val still on the line. I jumped off the bamboo bridge, pushed through the scraggly branches of the dragon trees, and hopped the fence into my neighbor's yard.

That sounds impressive, maybe, but the bridge was close to the ground, the fence was low, and my arms came out scratched from the effort.

The body was sprawled in the spread-eagle position, face up. It was a boy. Or a man. Something in between. He was wearing sunglasses. A mint green polo. Cargo shorts. Dockers.

It's an awful truth that my first thought was not *Rest in peace* but *What a prep*.

His hands were covered in blood, his neck, too, and there was an oval-shaped stain on his polo shirt, over his stomach. Despite that, he looked weirdly peaceful lying there in the red clay, bordered by the succulents in Mr. Palomer's garden— spiky circles of greens, pinks, and magentas.

"Oh God," I said, kneeling beside the body. "He can't see this."

I was thinking of my neighbor, Mr. Palomer. The man had retired when I was in preschool, and he spent the majority of his time in the back garden, tending to his succulents or reading brown-papered books. He was slight, stooped like a shriveled bean pod, his hair flossy and gray. He looked breakable. It was only a matter of time before he broke permanently, and I refused to let Mr. Palomer's deathblow be the discovery of a corpse in his succulent garden.

I stared at the body.

So peaceful, I thought again.

I reached out to touch the guy's arm.

I realized that my hand was shaking.

Then I realized he was breathing.

The dead guy was breathing.

It was just as I processed this game-changing fact that my index finger made contact with his elbow.

"Careful," said the body. "I'm obscenely ticklish."

I screamed. Loud. Shrill. Like a child. Then I fell back, my butt hitting the hard clay with a *whump.*

The living body propped himself up on his elbows. He cocked his head at me. He didn't remove his sunglasses. It was such a preppy thing to do on an overcast day.

"Hey," he said.

"I thought you were dead," I said.

"I'm not."

His voice was young, and I decided he couldn't be older than Joel. His jaw was peppered with half-hearted acne—the kind of pimples that don't turn into full-blown zits but calmly recede back into the skin with the aid of a dermatologist-recommended topical cream. Even with the sunglasses on, it was clear he had a good face. I didn't like that about him.

"Why'd you think I was dead?" he asked.

"Uh," I said. "Maybe because you were just lying out here, like you were dead." I pointed to the bloody stain at his stomach. "I mean, what's going on there?"

The living body grinned at me. His teeth were magnificently straight.

"Corn syrup, chocolate syrup, and red food coloring."

He held up his hand, which was smeared in the stuff, and gave it a dramatic lick.

I stared.

I said, "What the hell are you doing back here, covered in fake blood?"

"Just enjoying the view."

The guy grinned again, like he'd delivered a sidesplitting punch line. His teeth were all dazzling and perfect. *This* was the sort of person who should've been working as my dentist's receptionist.

"Maybe you should enjoy the view somewhere other than Mr. Palomer's backyard. You're trespassing, you know."

"Shit. Really?"

He grinned wider. My fingers itched with a primal urge to slap him.

"Stevie?"

I turned around. Joel was standing on the bamboo bridge, my abandoned cell phone in hand. That's when I remembered Val. I really hoped that she'd hung up by now.

"Aw, man," said Joel. "I thought you saw Lemur Dude again."

Lemur Dude was practically an institution in the city of Austin. He rode the streets on a fluorescent orange Vespa, wearing only a kimono and a straw hat. In that hat, or so the legend went, roosted a black-furred lemur. I had seen Lemur Dude in person, just once, out by the food trucks on South Congress, though he flew by too fast for me to ascertain whether there really was a lemur in his hat. Sanger had been there, but Joel hadn't. This was a grave injustice in Joel's books, and he'd vowed to not rest easy until he'd seen Lemur Dude for himself. Joel was hypervigilant about the whole thing, which led to a lot of false alarms and a near wreck in a MoPac merging lane.

"No Lemur Dude," I reported back. "I thought this guy was dead. But it's just—corn syrup."

Corn Syrup Guy gave a friendly wave.

Joel screwed up his eyes. "Uh. Yeah, well, you'd better get inside. Aunt Carrie says you've got a test to take."

I got to my feet and offered Not-Dead Guy a hand. He didn't take it.

"Fine," I said. "But you *are* trespassing, so you'd better be out of here within the next minute. I'm not afraid to call the police."

"Duly noted." He was still grinning.

Creep, I thought.

I hopped the fence and joined Joel on the bamboo bridge.

As it turned out, Val hadn't hung up, and Joel had realized there was still someone on the other line. He'd just pressed the phone to his ear when I caught up with him. Before I could stop him, he spoke.

Or could I have stopped him?

He did deserve a little more punishment.

"Hey!" he said. "Yo! Sorry, I didn't realize someone was still there. Stevie was momentarily indispooooooh *fuck.*"

Joel hurled the phone at me and took off running toward the house.

"Val?" I said, pressing the phone to my ear. "Val, I'm so—"

But in place of Val's voice, there was the cheery chime of a text message. She'd already hung up. And she'd sent a follow-up text:

WHAT THE HELL WAS THAT.

I called her back.

The phone rang once. Then twice. Then three times.

"Oh my God," I muttered.

I was not cut out to deal with this much drama before lunchtime.

At the last possible second, Val answered.

"WHAT IS WRONG WITH YOU, STEVIE HART."

"Look, Val, I'm really sorry. I had no idea Joel—"

Val cut off my attempt to answer.

"KNOW WHAT? FORGET YOU. WORST. FRIEND. EVER."

A definitive click cut off Val's final screech.

That was that. I was pretty sure Val and I had just friend-broken-up. And in that moment, I felt weirdly okay about it. Maybe I *was* the worst friend ever; I mean, I'd be the first to admit I wasn't the most sensitive person, and Val required a bunch of sensitivity. Then again, it wasn't like Val was the *best* friend ever. We weren't close enough for her to yell at me that way, for her to stretch me between her and Joel, as though I'd choose her over my own cousin.

I knew Joel had his faults, the most glaring of which was that he was practically incapable of forming habits. This was advantageous when it came to drugs, alcohol, pie, and other addictive substances, but not so much when it came to things like school, chores, and girlfriends. Until junior year, Joel had maintained a C average, a room that resembled a sewage treatment plant, and an ever-growing collection of ex-girlfriends.

"I get bored," he'd explained to me once. "It's the adrenaline that sucks you in. Then, after a few weeks, you're just going through the motions, and it's not fair to anyone to keep trying."

I didn't often attempt to put myself in Joel's head, but

when I did, I imagined that his thought process looked something like this:

Calculus! YEAH! Differential equations! Badass! But wait, this involves numbers and lack of numbers, and dude, this is taking more time than I planned, and I don't get it, and calculus, who needs it?

The Strokes! Cheap poster online! Buy it! This will look sweet over my bed. Except plaster walls are so hard to hammer through, and sticky tack means going to the store, and what the hell, it looks good crumpled on the floor, too.

Ashlee Parker! Boobs! Ass! Likes the Strokes! But reaches a pitch only dogs can hear and is texting me fifty times per night and that is the last romantic comedy she will ever drag me to, and it's not you, Ashlee, it's me.

Joel was a flake, but the strangest thing was that this quality was somehow attractive to the people around him. He was the most popular homeschooler I knew. Girlfriends and devotees were drawn to him like hipsters are drawn to truffle oil. If he hadn't been my cousin, I probably would've hated him. Or, who knows? If he hadn't been my cousin, maybe I too would've been sucked into his entrancing aura.

At the start of his junior year, Joel had summoned the strength to actually commit to something for longer than the running time of a sitcom. He shaped up academically, he joined the co-op's lacrosse team, and he lost the roll of flesh that used to spill over the waistline of his jeans.

Considering that his impressive physique and scholastic follow-through had lasted nearly eighteen months, I might've been tempted to think that Joel was a reformed man in the ways of commitment. But it just took a stroll past his room—whereupon I was immediately hit by the stench of month-old corn chips—to remind me that my cousin was still the same old Joel. All it took was a call from Val.

He had his faults, yes, but Joel was my cousin, and he meant way more to me than Valerie Borkowski. And if I had to choose, if Val was making me decide, then I chose him.

I tucked the phone in my back pocket, irritated. When I reached the patio door, I turned around and peered through the space between the dragon trees. From what I could tell, Not-Dead Guy had cleared out of Mr. Palomer's backyard.

For all the fails of the past hour, at least I had that one success to my credit.

I failed the trig test, as anticipated.

Of course, Mom wouldn't know that until Saturday, when she graded all of my turned-in homework for the week. I was safe from lecture and grounding for the next two days, and I meant to take advantage of my freedom that very night, at the state capitol. That is, if I could *get* to the capitol.

My school day ended at four. I called Sanger at four o'clock on the nose.

"Darling Nicks," Sanger drawled pleasantly upon pickup. "Some of us have lives."

"If you want me to think that, you shouldn't answer on the first ring."

"Ooh-hoo-hoo. I'll have you know I've been *muy productivo* today. Wrote a ten-page paper on Charlemagne. What a jackass."

"Translation: You finished work at noon and have been coding ever since."

"*Whaaa.*"

This was Sanger's universal confessional noise.

"You're coding right now, aren't you?"

"*Whaaa.*"

Sanger was homeschooled. She too was a Normal Type, though maybe more on the normal end of the spectrum than me. She'd been to *real* schools before, and her parents had pulled her not because they didn't like the modern state of education—as my borderline Blue-Jean Jumper parents had—but because they thought Sanger was too much of a genius for a traditional school setting. And her parents were right. I had an inkling Sanger could've been one of those kids who goes to Harvard at fourteen, if that's what she'd wanted. Instead, Sanger preferred to breeze through her schoolwork and spend the rest of her time indulging in her hobbies. Like watching old movies. Or hanging with me. Or coding.

"Is this work or play?" I asked her.

"Critters and Twitters. They're local, so the name's forgivable. Get this: They're setting up a live feed cam of the parrot cages."

"Who wants to see that?"

"Some folks enjoy watching a good molt from the convenience of their laptop. Not judging. I just code what I'm told."

"Bizarre."

"People are bizarre, Nicks."

Sanger hadn't begun calling me Nicks until eighth grade, when she discovered her moms' old Fleetwood Mac vinyls. My parents claimed they named me after a great-aunt, not after Stevie Nicks, but Sanger refused to accept that.

I flopped back on my twin bed, into a collection of throw pillows and stuffed animals that I had accumulated since birth. I was a pack rat. Not bad enough to be on that reality show about hoarders, but I got sentimental about stuff, and stuffed animals are as sentimental as stuff gets.

I caught the end of my fishtail braid and dug my index finger into one brunette chink, then another. I was weighing my words.

Sanger noticed.

"You need a ride, huh?"

I winced. "I promised I wouldn't be that friend."

"You did indeed."

"And I really *won't* be that friend after tonight."

"This is such a toxic relationship."

"Val bailed on me."

"All my other friends tell me you're bad for me. I should listen."

"I am your only friend."

"See what you're doing? Classic. You isolate me, like a wolf picking off the weakest baby seal, then taking it to a secluded spot and being all, 'You don't have any other friend but me, baby seal. Time to die.'"

"In what universe do wolves prey on seals?"

"You're just fact-checking because you have no comeback to my most excellent analogy."

"Your analogy sucks."

"Speaking of which, I've got this great joke. Ready for it? Ahem. A seal walks into a club."

". . ."

"Get it? *Get it?*"

"Not funny."

Sanger harrumphed. I could hear her clacking away at her keyboard. She was still coding. I would've been irritated, only I knew from years of experience that Sanger was a talented multitasker.

"You nature freaks. Have you ever talked to a PETA supporter? They've got less sense of humor than a nihilist."

"Nihilists are plenty funny," I argued. "It's called theater of the absurd. And I too have a sense of humor. It was just a bad joke."

"So is PETA."

"*Sanger.*"

The keyboard clacking stopped. "Yes, doll?"

"You're not going to like tonight's destination."

Another harrumph, lower and grittier than the one before.

"You don't have to stick around for it," I said, buttering my voice to a persuasive timbre. "You can hang out at Bean & Co. until it's over. You love their macaroons."

Sanger sniffed. "They do make a mean pistachio macaroon."

"If you do, I'll love you forever."

"Sometimes I lie awake at night and reflect on how beautifully unconditional our love is."

"Pretty please?"

"Shut up. You know you won, like, three whole minutes ago."

I grinned up at my ceiling, one foot raised in the air, and traced a constellation of glow-in-the-dark stars with my big toe.

"Pick me up at six?" I asked.

"Okay, but supper afterward. Torchy's."

"Urgh."

Sanger and I were embroiled in an ongoing debate about the best tacos in Austin: Torchy's versus Tacodeli. We alternated dibs on which establishment we frequented, but neither of us ever changed the other's opinion. If I were really honest, I would admit that there wasn't much difference in taco quality. The fun of the debate wasn't necessarily that either of us won. It was just nice to fight for something so vehemently and know that at the end of the day, you and your opponent were still on good terms.

"Sorry, Nicks. You cut out there. I'm reading back a transcript of what I last heard, and I quote: 'Urgh.'"

"I said, I owe you my firstborn."

"At this point, we're down to fifthborn."

"Happy coding."

"See you at six."

It was six fifteen, and Sanger still hadn't shown. This was typical. I sat on the front porch, a floppy poster board in my lap. The cloud cover from earlier today had cleared, and I was sunning myself, listening to a Top 40 workout playlist.

The plus of earbuds is that for a grand total of ten dollars at your local Target, you can obtain the power to drown out a boring world whenever, wherever.

The negative is that people can sneak up on you.

It wasn't until halfway through one of those rousing, anthemic alternative band numbers that I caught sight of Joel in my periphery. I ripped out my left earbud and gave him the stink eye.

"What?"

Joel was tapping the end of his nose. He cast me a sidelong glance, like a cat that hadn't decided whether to be friendly.

"I think you're burning," he said, pointing at one of my glue-white arms.

"I am not."

"No, really, you're pinking just a little, right—"

"If you've got something to say, you'd better be quick. Sanger's picking me up any minute."

Joel bunched his lips into a pout. It didn't suit him. Joel was one of those guys who was handsome because of his confidence. Catch him sleeping or zoning out, and you'd have a wildly unimpressive face. Everything was average: dirt-brown eyes, aquiline nose, so-so hair. It was only when Joel was fully alert, self-assuredness leaking out of every orifice, that the attraction factor kicked in.

"You're leaving me home alone," he said.

"You'll love it, Joel. You, your ice pack, and a full bottle of painkillers. You can binge-watch that zombie show and slo-mo all the gory bits."

"Valerie's pretty pissed, huh?"

I shrugged. Joel was asking the obvious.

"What did you do exactly?" I asked.

"Broke up with her."

"How?"

Joel stopped tapping his nose. He shrank away from me.

I narrowed my eyes. *"How?"*

"Text."

"Bastard."

A lemon-yellow Fiat turned into the cul-de-sac. Sanger. I got to my feet, careful to keep my poster board shielded from the April breeze.

"Just you wait," said Joel, stretching his legs down the porch steps. "Ten years from now, everyone will break up over text. They'll eat over text. Exchange marriage vows over text.

Sext three nights a week. Pay their condolences via text. To you? I'm a bastard. To future historians? Visionary. A Man of the Future."

Sanger pulled into the driveway, windows down, radio blaring. She shoved her electric-red aviators atop her head, sending her short black hair into a confused jumble of hedgehog prickles.

"Hey, girl, hey!" she called. "Got a planet to save."

I took the porch steps two at a time and handed Sanger my poster through her open window. Then I crawled through the opposite window into the passenger seat. The passenger door lock had jammed several months back, and Sanger had yet to get it fixed. She didn't lack the funds, just the motivation. After all, she wasn't the one who had to climb through the window every time we carpooled. I didn't complain about it either, not because I was a saint but because it was actually pretty damn fun to crawl through the window of a lemon-yellow Fiat.

I gave Sanger confidential instructions. She nodded, then obeyed. She stuck her head out the window and shouted at Joel, "Still makes you a bastard!"

If the message affected Joel, he made no outward display of repentance. He just stretched out his arms and tilted his head back toward the sliver of dying sun on the porch.

Sanger put the Fiat into gear, and we drove off.

On the radio, a man with a thick accent was talking about underwater sound waves.

"What *is* this?" I demanded, hand going for the volume knob.

Sanger slapped it away. "Culture."

"'NPR' and 'culture' aren't always synonymous."

"My car, my station."

I squinted out the window and realized I'd forgotten my sunglasses. I tugged down the visor, but the sun had just reached that obnoxious place in the sky where a visor did no good.

"I found a dead body today," I announced.

Sanger was the type of friend who brought out the sensationalist in me.

"No shit."

"*Yes* shit. But then he turned out to be alive."

"God, I hate it when that happens."

Sanger was forced to turn down the radio to better hear me. I grinned in quiet triumph and then went on with the lurid details.

"He was literally sprawled out in Mr. Palomer's succulent garden."

"But not literally dead."

"Some complete rando. And he'd covered himself in fake blood. Who *does* that? If you're going to break into someone's house, do something decent, like steal a plasma screen."

"Whoa. He broke into the house?"

"No. That's just it. He wasn't stealing anything. He was just pointlessly hanging around the backyard, looking dead. The whole time, he was, like, smiling funny at me."

"Maybe Mr. Hobo just wanted to be your friend."

"He wasn't a hobo. He was dressed like a frat boy. He looked our age."

"Then he was high."

"I guess."

"Kids these days."

The topic had taken a quick turn from sensational to blasé. I kicked my feet up on the dash and began to count traffic lights as we passed them. Sanger had hit an impressive five greens. And two yellows. And one red. We were going fifty in a thirty zone.

"Someone wants her macaroons," I said.

"I was late picking you up," Sanger replied. "Making up for lost time."

We passed under yet another yellow light. Sanger slapped a kiss to her left index and middle fingers, then tapped her sun visor. It was a reverently observed ritual, the yellow-light slap-kiss, though I'd never asked Sanger about the significance. I didn't because every time Sanger did it, she got momentarily twitchy, like she *wanted* me to ask about its significance. It was fun, every so often, to withhold satisfaction.

"I'm meeting up with a bunch of hippies," I said. "They won't care if I'm late."

"You're being otherist."

"What? How?"

"Lumping all hippies together that way. Just because the media portrays them as lazy-ass bums doesn't mean some hippies don't value punctuality."

"Even if the media still portrayed hippies, which I'm pretty sure it hasn't since, like, 1973, the hippies wouldn't care. They're chill by nature."

"Oh my God, there's so much otherism in that statement I don't even know where to begin."

Sanger had gotten on this kick recently where she called everyone an "otherist." She thought it was ingenious, and I'll admit, it did serve a purpose. Sanger had a sharp eye for anyone who went around flinging out stereotypes like they were universal truths, *and* she had the steely guts to actually call them on it.

We crossed over Lady Bird Lake, and I pressed my forehead to the window, watching a half-dozen kayakers glide by in the rose light of sunset. We were crossing over into downtown territory. The Frost Bank Tower jutted ahead of us, a glacial palace dedicated to all things capitalistic. We'd be at our destination soon. I double-checked my messenger bag to be sure the vitals were there: water bottle, cell phone, chewing gum, glucose tablets, insulin pen.

"Look! Look!" Sanger suddenly screeched. *"The capitol dooome."*

The capitol was officially in our sights. Ever since I was a kid, I'd thought the capitol looked like a giant sandcastle, each column and window and ledge carefully sculpted from fine brown sand. The capitol was overlarge and overwhelming, just like Texas. And yet, I had this feeling that if even the puniest kid punched hard enough at one of the walls, that wall would crumble, just like it *had* been made of sand, and the entire building would collapse in on itself. I didn't *really* believe that, of course. It was just one of those backroom ideas in my brain, like the thought that ghosts visit your bedside at exactly 3:00 a.m., or that if you eat Mentos and drink a soda at the same time, you will explode.

Sanger pulled into the circular drive off Congress and shifted the car into park. I was a little less okay with climbing through the passenger window this time around, in public, but it had to be done. Sanger handed me my poster through the window.

"You caught that quote, right?" she said. "The quote about the dome?"

I gave her a blank stare. "You weren't just being stupid?"

"No! What! Jimmy Stewart! *Mr. Smith Goes to Washington*! Tomorrow. We'll rectify the situation tomorrow."

When Sanger said stuff like that, she meant it. Then and there, my Friday night was booked. It wasn't like I'd end up making plans with anyone other than Sanger anyway. Sometimes, Val and I went to the dollar theater to see a chick flick, but now it seemed Val was an ex-friend, and I would have to start dealing accordingly.

Sanger pointed at the poster. "What's it say?"

I turned it around for her to see. In black block letters, I'd written: SAVE BARTON SPRINGS.

Sanger scratched her chin. "You took the classic approach, I see. No wordplay or innuendo. You didn't even *tap into* the enormous wealth of water-related humor."

"It's important to keep our message clear and concise," I told her.

"Hmm. I guess humor would dilute the message."

"Sanger, go eat your macaroons."

"'Kay. Give those corporate bastards hell. Stick 'em in hot water, as it were."

"Bye."

"Any insults the naysayers throw your way, let 'em roll off you like water off a duck's back!"

I shot Sanger the bird.

Three

New Systematic Solutions was the enemy.

It was a soulless corporation engaged in the profitable business of something having to do with computer parts. Though the business was based in California, the head honchos were widening their market and had decided to build a secondary base in Austin.

That base encroached on the Barton Springs watershed.

Barton Springs was a community treasure. Its waters had been lovingly directed into an unfathomably large swimming pool, bordered by a grassy knoll on which locals sunned and laughed and kissed. It was a magical place, the kind of place that a pointillist painter would choose for the setting of a masterpiece.

New Systematic Solutions was going to change all that.

"Runoff." "Pollutants." "Fragile ecosystem." These were the words I'd heard on a summer day the year before, when Joel and I had been playing a round of suicide-dive-relay in the pool. Two representatives of Springs for Tomorrow Alliance came by to inform us that the water we were so blithely enjoying was in danger. That day, I'd taken home a water-stained pamphlet typed in boldfaced Futura. That day, I'd decided to do something about corporate intrusion on the local environment.

Joel was a cynic. He claimed that watersheds had been destroyed for centuries and the world hadn't imploded yet. He also said my decision to join the cause was based solely on the fact that those poolside alliance representatives had been two hot, shirtless college guys.

One can become an activist for various, complex reasons.

Sure, the college guys were attractive, but I really did care about the future of Barton Springs. This wasn't some abstract desire to do Good and be Active. Barton Springs was as much a part of my childhood as my stuffed bear Wuzzle Woo and the files of my preschool artwork Mom kept in the attic. It was as much a part of my present as my cell phone data plan and my birthday wish list. I'd learned to swim at Barton Springs, and I'd spent every summer of my life on its banks, burning my tender skin into oblivion, bringing out an army of freckles. No disgusting West Coast money-grubbers were going to dump *their* sludge into *my* Barton Springs.

I want to be clear about something here. The activism thing does not make me a Granola. Maybe I have a Granola *trait*, but overall I'm Normal. Like, I'm the most normal person in Springs for Tomorrow Alliance. Of course, you don't have to try too hard to be normal in that group.

"Stevie! Darling, over here!"

Maribel Lopez, a woman old enough to be my mother, waved at me from over by the Texas Rangers Memorial. The shadow of a bronze rifle crossed her face, cutting it across the nose into two parts.

The first time I met Maribel, she surprised me with a bear hug. It was a shock. My family wasn't big on physical affection. We didn't hug much, and we never kissed, not even on the cheek. But Maribel had wrapped me deep into her silk maxi dress and pressed a loud, wet kiss on my forehead. At first, I'd been para-lyzed by instinctual resistance. But then I'd breathed in. I'd smelled cedar and oranges. It was warm in Maribel's arms. After that, I anticipated her hugs, and I always opened my arms first.

In this particular instance, I opened only one arm for a side hug, careful to hold my poster out so it wouldn't get bent. Either Maribel didn't notice or she didn't care. She wrangled me into a full hug anyway. Citrus and cedar—the smell was always the same. I grinned against her shoulder, and when I pulled away I didn't even mind that she'd creased the top edge of the poster. The message was still clear.

A dozen STA members had already gathered. Sanger and I joked about it, but Springs for Tomorrow Alliance really was heavily composed of those of the hippie persuasion. There were a handful of concerned college and high school students, like me. The rest were either middle-aged or retired—some good-hearted yuppies, some average concerned citizens, and many with an affinity for beards and braids. Most of them didn't smell anywhere near as nice as Maribel. The founder of STA, Leslie Cobb, once informed me that she'd given up deodorant and shampoo more than twenty years ago.

"We're feeding ourselves chemicals daily," she warned me. "*Daily*. Nothing compares to one's natural oils. Let the body do her job."

I really appreciated what Leslie was doing for the cause and all, but after that conversation, I kept a friendly distance.

"So, what's up?" I asked Maribel.

The plan was to congregate outside the capitol, since that day the state senate was due to introduce an environmental bill that directly affected our cause. I didn't know all the details exactly, just that the bill had already been passed by the House by a small margin and was apparently going to run into a lot more resistance in the Senate. I'd tried to read the PDF proposal Leslie had e-mailed the group, but I hadn't made it past page two of the winding, inverted jargon.

"There's good news," said Maribel, "and there's bad news."

"Bad first."

"The bill's introduction has been postponed. The Senate won't get to it until at least next week. Of course, that doesn't mean our presence here isn't worth something. Leslie says we'll take it close to the street once everyone's arrived. Awareness is awareness, no matter what."

"Huh," I said.

Awareness *was* awareness, but I now kind of wished I hadn't put Sanger through all the trouble of driving me out here.

"We can still get plenty of new names on that petition,"

said Maribel. "Every name is vital. How're you coming on your fifty, Stevie?"

Maribel was referring to the "Petition Challenge" Leslie had given all members of STA two weeks back. We were each supposed to collect the signatures of fifty Austinites who, like us, wanted to protect Barton Springs and its source, the Edwards Aquifer. The good news was that most Austinites cared a ton about Barton Springs. The bad news was that New Systematic Solutions wasn't exactly being blatantly evil. Like, I'm sure if some dude who looked like a Marvel supervillain stood by the water's edge and tipped over a giant barrel marked with a skull and crossbones, the whole city would be in an uproar. But, wicked corporation that they were, New Systematic Solutions carried out their dastardly deeds in a subtler manner. They were polluting the water in small increments, and because their presence in Austin was such a boon for techies and business folk, the pollution wasn't getting the best coverage in the media. That's where STA and our petition came in.

So far, I'd only managed to collect thirteen signatures, two of which belonged to my parents. It wasn't that I didn't care about the cause; it was just that I was pretty awful at talking to strangers. I was ashamed, because fear of strangers is a total Blue-Jean Jumper trait. Not to mention, I was beginning to feel some major pressure from the rest of the group. Some had already turned in their completed list of fifty. Maribel had turned in hers three times over. I sucked.

"The signatures are . . . coming," I said, which wasn't a lie.

"You haven't asked for the good news, by the way."

I smiled. "Don't make me beg."

Maribel's dress swished pleasantly as she turned to collect something. When she faced me again, she was holding a giant blue Tupperware container.

"I made empanadas."

Maribel worked at a bakery downtown that was particularly well known for its cake pops and empanadas. Maribel also acted. She was part of a Shakespearean group that performed during the summer. Last year, I'd seen her play Queen Margaret in *Richard III*, and she was *good*. But what Maribel was even better at was baking healthy stuff that didn't taste healthy. Maribel's non-egg, gluten-free, completely organic, cherry-filled empanadas were almost enough to make me go vegan. Almost. I still liked blue cheese crumbles a little too much for that.

"Maribel, you're a saint," said Trevor, a college kid with sideburns and thick-framed glasses.

"Careful, my dear," said Maribel, peeling the lid from the container. "Flattery will get you everywhere."

I set my poster down, next to Maribel's sign (GET YOUR HANDS OFF MY WATER), and took an empanada. While chewing, I decided to take a little walk around the capitol grounds. Just as I'd told Sanger, the members of STA weren't particularly punctual, and Leslie was giving the absent members another fifteen-minute grace period before we moved streetside.

I walked, and I looked up. The sky was dimming. It was stuck in the peach haze that only happens near dusk, and that was a color worth craning my neck for. I ambled over to the Confederate Monument, where I proceeded to look up some more. I felt a light pressure on my shoulder. Thinking it was a bug, I swatted at it.

It wasn't a bug.

"Ow! Oh. *Oh.* So sorry! Sorry."

It was Jessica Parrish. Jessica attended my homeschool co-op. We had chem lab and art class together. She seemed nice, but she was of the Blue-Jean Jumper variety, and I was under the impression that she thought I was a heathen because I had a cartilage piercing and wore shorts.

"Hey, Jessica," I said.

Jessica nodded. She was shorter than me, and thinner, too. Her dirty-blond hair was pulled back in a thick, floral-patterned scrunchie. There was a picnic basket embroidered on her ribbed shirt. She was carrying a sign under one arm.

"Protesting too?" I asked, pointing at the sign.

Jessica's eyes widened. "Oh. I wouldn't call it *protesting*. But yes, I'm here with my family. Well, my church. And we're—"

In place of words, she waved her hand over at a group of people gathered several yards off. One of them held a yellow board over his head. I squinted to make out the words.

Word. It was a single word: DARWIN. The name was crossed out in red marker.

Inwardly, in a place that Jessica couldn't see, I cringed.

It was homeschoolers like this who gave the rest of us a bad name.

"I thought maybe you were here to join us," said Jessica. "You looked lost."

I laughed, realizing that I really must've appeared lost. Jessica looked confused by the laugh. She took a step backward.

"I'm with Springs for Tomorrow Alliance," I said. "We're, uh, saving Barton Springs from pollutants and stuff."

That was *not* the pitch Leslie Cobb had trained us to give passersby.

"Oh." Jessica frowned.

This was about the time where a socially adept individual would say good-bye and back off. But Jessica just said "oh" and went right on standing there.

"I guess I'll see you at co-op, then," I said, giving her a perfect segue to an exit.

"Oh. Yes."

She kept standing there. It looked like I would have to be the one to move.

"Bye, Jessica," I said, and I cleared out of there, heading back to the Texas Rangers Memorial.

It wasn't until I had joined up with the others that I cast a glance back at Jessica and her people. They were still congregating, talking among themselves, laughing—a great big mix of ankle socks and long skirts and longer hair. I recognized several of them from homeschool co-op. It was impossible, really, to be a part of any local homeschool group that didn't have its own Blue-Jean Jumper contingent.

"What's up with them?" Trevor asked me, empanada crumbs flying out of the corner of his cherry-stained mouth.

Maribel beat me to a reply. "*That,*" she said, "is why our cause is behind schedule. The Senate's still tied up over that education bill."

"What education bill? Oops. Sorry, Stephanie."

A spit-soaked crumb had landed on my cheek, courtesy of Trevor's incompetent eating. I wiped it away, too grossed out to bother correcting him about my name. It hadn't taken me too many STA meetings to figure out that hot college guys weren't all they were cracked up to be.

"Oooh, some proposal about 'intelligent design'"—here Maribel used dramatic, flourishing air quotes—"and school curriculum. Poppycock."

I grinned. I liked that Maribel used words like "poppycock."

"Were they trying to convert you?" Maribel asked me.

"Nope," I said.

I didn't mention that I knew half the people in the group.

A loud, electronic *bloop!* from a megaphone sounded nearby. Leslie Cobb was waving her hands in our direction, signaling us to gather closer.

"Well, friends," said Maribel, "once more unto the breach."

• • •

After the rally, Sanger drove us to Torchy's. There, she paid for my tacos by stealth. She ordered first, and she told the cashier she was ordering for me, and there was nothing I could do about it afterward, even though I was the one who owed her for the car ride.

Sanger stealthily paid for a lot of things.

The Sadler-Hamasakis were loaded. Dr. Sadler was an anesthesiologist, and Dr. Hamasaki was a chemical engineer. Sanger was their only child. They lived in a McMansion in the Hill Country. They also owned a condo at the W Hotel, which they rented out and which Sanger had nicknamed "Room 237."

I lived in a ranch starter home just off South First Street, which my parents had bought when they were twenty-one and newly married. It's not that my parents didn't do what they were supposed to do after starting up. (Which is what, exactly? *Proceed?*) My parents both worked hard, but neither of them held doctoral degrees like the Sadler-Hamasakis. Dad was a landscaper, and Mom had the unenviable task of educating Joel and me. So we never moved out of that starter house.

The money got tighter when we took in Joel. At home, no one ever mentioned the financial strains. Of course not. No one ever said, "Joel, we have to keep our house at an uncomfortably tepid temperature this summer because you're eating into the electricity bill." But Joel knew it, I think. If I heard Mom and Dad arguing about money after midnight, then Joel must've too. It was a small house, and the walls were thin as honeycomb.

On the car ride from Torchy's, I balanced my one remaining foil-wrapped fried avocado taco on my knees. I made a game of whether or not it would fall to the floorboard every time Sanger made a sudden stop. It only fell three times, the last of which was when Sanger screeched to a stop in the Barton Springs Pool parking lot.

Sanger and I went to Barton Springs at least once a week during the spring and summer months. The pool was a treasure to the community, yes, but more than anything it was *our* treasure—the place where I had taught Sanger to dive and she had taught me how to burp voluntarily and where we'd shared uncountable secrets. Since Sanger had gotten her Fiat a year back, we'd made a habit of going out to Barton Springs after sunset, when the pool was still open but the lifeguards and crowds were gone, and a laminated sign on the front entrance read: SWIM AT OWN RISK. That night, Sanger and I sat at the pool edge, feet dipped in up to the shins, while we finished off our last tacos, all at our own risk.

It was unseasonably chilly, and the pool was empty, save for a dark-haired man swimming laps across the deep end. High up on the poolside's grassy bank, a circle of silhouettes was cackling and playing house music, which came out tinny and distorted through phone speakers. Every so often, the wind dragged down a pungent whiff of pot.

My phone pinged with a text message, and as I unlocked the phone I saw that I'd already missed two before it. They were all from my mom.

The first had been, *Have you met new neighbor boy? Your age and very nice. Should introduce yourself sometime.*

Then, *Louie Wilson gets better with age!!*

Then, *I love you SO much, sweet pea. <3 <3 <3*

"What's up?" Sanger asked, noticing my concentrated silence.

I pocketed the phone. "Mom's drunk-texting."

"Ahhh, it's a Louie Wilson night."

I nodded.

One of Dad's high school friends, a guy by the name of Louie Wilson, had made a big name for himself in Austin as a local folk icon. That's saying something, because Austin is jammed full of local folk icon wannabes. My parents were always in an excellent mood after Louie's concerts, courtesy of good music, nostalgia, and a healthy dose of alcohol. The twenty-four-hour period after a Louie Wilson concert was the best time to ask for either a favor or forgiveness. Joel and I had dubbed it the Louie Wilson Afterglow.

"Ask her if you can have a red panda!"

"*You* want a red panda, Sanger."

A red panda was one of the few things Sanger's moms refused to buy for her, because Dr. Sadler was allergic to pet dander. Also because it's illegal to own a red panda.

"I'm just saying," said Sanger, "you should take advantage of this golden window of opp— Hey, is that guy okay?"

I followed Sanger's sight line to the middle of the pool,

where a head was bobbing in the water. It was the dark-haired man from before, only his figure was now smaller, more distant. His swimming had turned into erratic head bobs, which were fast turning into the more sinister kind—slow dunks, with only brief appearances at the water's surface.

"Is he drowning?" Sanger asked, but I was already peeling off my sneakers. "Wait, what are you *doing*? He looks like a full-grown dude. He'll drag you down."

"I know what to do," I said, and that was mostly true.

Sanger and I had both spent a significant amount of our lives at Barton Springs, but while Sanger preferred floating and sunbathing, I preferred diving lessons and the annual rescue and emergency course provided by Parks and Rec.

I knew what to do in this situation, even though it wasn't ideal. The guy was too far from all edges of the wide pool; I was going to have to swim out. I sprinted to the nearby lifeguard stand and unhooked the life ring hanging from one of its legs. Then I made a running jump into the pool.

Aprils in Austin were usually warm—steady 70s and sun—but Barton Springs remained chilly year-round, and the sudden plunge punched the breath out of me and fast leached away the heat from my skin. I pushed through the shock and began to swim, clutching the life ring in front of me. I paddled forward to the dimly decipherable blotch that was the drowner's head. I watched as it slipped below the surface again, and my body burned with panicked adrenaline.

"Come *on*," I said aloud. "Just hang on a little longer."

I paddled harder. I heard Sanger shouting behind me, though I couldn't make out her words. Then, a sudden spray of water broke across my path, and a face appeared before me. It took me three stunned seconds to realize that the drowning man had been swimming toward *me*. He hadn't been drowning at all.

The guy propped his arms on the life ring and gave me a pleasant, unperturbed smile. I recognized the smile. It took me another three seconds to place it.

And then the Living Body from this morning spoke to me.

He said, "Your mom said you liked to come here."

"What?" I said dumbly. Water trickled down my nose.

"Mrs. Hart," he said. "Your mom. She said you come out here a lot."

It took me three more seconds to solve the final mystery.

This was the new neighbor boy Mom had texted me about.

"You're—you're not drowning?" I spluttered.

"I'm fine," he said. "Though I appreciate you trying to save my life again. Shows you really care."

I shoved the life ring at him, releasing my hold entirely.

"Then you can paddle yourself back," I said.

I wasn't sure if I was angry, but I was definitely too shocked from cold water and new developments to stay out there making small talk. I swam freestyle back to shore, where Sanger was crouched, hand extended to help me out of the water.

"What was that about?" she asked, once I was back on solid ground.

She was still looking out to the water. The Living Body was paddling toward us, one arm linked around the life ring.

"That's him," I hissed. "That's the stoned frat boy. The one from Mr. Palomer's garden. It's *him.*"

"No way," Sanger said, excitement lighting her eyes. "Seriously?"

I nodded, then set to work squeezing out my sopped T-shirt. I knew now, I was absolutely angry. I watched with narrowed eyes as my apparent neighbor came to a floating stop at the pool edge.

"Hey," he called up to Sanger.

"Hey yourself," she replied. She crossed her arms. "Were you intentionally trying to freak us out?"

"Um," he said. Water was streaming from his dark hair and over the edges of his cheekbones. His face was nicer than I remembered from earlier that day, though that may have been because it was a Person Face now, and not a Corpse Face.

"So were you drowning, or what?" Sanger pressed. "You shouldn't fool around like that, you little shit."

"Yeah, okay," he said, resting his chin on his pruny knuckles. "I'm Max Garza, by the way. In case you didn't know."

Up until this point, I'd been making hard work of wringing out my soaked clothes. I now looked down at this Max Garza, teeth chattering, my expression inhospitable.

"Why didn't you tell me who you were this morning, when I was yelling at you?"

Max shrugged. "I don't know. It was fun, you thinking I was some nutcase."

"It was fun," I repeated, unenlightened.

"I would've told you eventually."

In a flurry of movement, Max tossed the life ring up on the pool's edge and pulled himself out after it. Water sloshed down the whole of his deep-tanned body, and as he straightened I noted that we were the same height. That is to say, Max was short. His swim trunks, like his Bermuda shorts from earlier, were patterned in pastel plaid. Just below the hem on his right thigh, a jagged scar ran along his skin, curved downward in the shape of a toenail clipping.

"Your name's Stevie, right?" he asked. "Stevie Hart."

He offered me his hand to shake. Out of instinct, I shook it. The handshake wasn't just wet; it was—*off* somehow. I looked down.

Max said, "I have three fingers on that hand."

He let go and raised his right hand to eye level. In place of a ring finger and a pinkie was nothing but puckered skin, sealed up just above the knuckles.

I said, "Oh."

"I like to be upfront about it," he said.

"Uh, yeah. Honesty's the best policy."

I realized too late that the adage I'd just used didn't really have anything to do with this situation.

Max didn't seem to mind. "Sorry I creeped you out," he said.

"Are you really?" I asked.

"I don't know," said Max. "Am I really?"

I wasn't in the mood to play games, especially with a guy who'd made a fool of me twice in one day. First I'd thought Max Garza was a dead body. Then I'd thought he was a drowning man. I wasn't sure which assumption was worse, but they were both equally stupid, and I was so *stupid*, I told myself as I stared at Max and he grinned back.

"Hang on," he said.

He skirted Sanger and me, and we both watched as he dripped over to the grassy bank. There, he knelt and rummaged through a canvas messenger bag.

I cast Sanger a wary look. She spun her index finger toward her head and whistled low.

"Maybe we should just make a run for it," I suggested.

"Aw," she said. "We can take on a psycho. There's two of us. Anyway, I'm intrigued, aren't you?"

I *was* a little intrigued, but my self-preservation instincts were still whirring warningly. Even if Max was my neighbor, and even if Mom thought he was a nice enough kid to warrant a drunk text, that didn't mean he wasn't a psychopath or a pervert. I glanced up the bank, figuring out the quickest, least steep route of escape to take, should Max try anything funny.

Max found whatever he was looking for in the messenger bag and returned to us. First he tossed me a towel.

I caught it but gave it a grimace.

"You're practically convulsing," Max said.

"Yeah, well, you've got to be cold too," I said, waving the towel back at him.

Max shook his head. "I'm from the North. I've got thick skin."

I didn't want to give this guy the satisfaction, but I *was* really cold. I wrapped the soft terry cloth towel around my shoulders. Then I noticed Max holding something thin and yellow in his three-fingered hand. It was a sheet of legal pad paper, folded hamburger style.

"There's sensitive information in here," he said. "I haven't shared it with anyone until now. But I think"—he took a deep breath—"this is a sign."

"What's a sign?" I asked, not bothering to hide my irritation. Whatever was written on that paper couldn't possibly justify the melodramatic presentation.

"You and me," said Max, pointing between the two of us. "We've run into each other twice in one day. You've tried to save my life *twice in one day*. I mean, that's a crazy coincidence, isn't it?"

"Not rea—"

"Oh, for the love of God, Stevie," Sanger cut in. "Tell him it's a sign."

"I don't believe in signs," I said obstinately.

"All right," said Max. "But it has to *mean* something at least, doesn't it?"

Sanger hopped into my periphery, thumbs-upping me like a maniac.

"Fine," I said. "It means something."

It means you're unhinged. It means I should mind my own business from now on.

Max nodded slowly. Then he handed me the piece of legal pad paper.

I opened it.

At the top, in black marker, this is what was written:

23 WAYS TO FAKE MY DEATH WITHOUT DYING

I lowered the sheet of paper, and Sanger scooted in to take a look.

"What is this?" I asked.

"That's what you interrupted," Max said. "I'm going to do them all. I'm going to fake my death in twenty-three different ways. And I'm going to do it before summer starts."

I looked at the paper again.

1. *Choke on a hamburger*

2. *Drown in a public pool*

3. *Hit by a car*

4. *Cardiac arrest*

5. *Bitten by a brown recluse*

"That's really messed up," I said.

"You didn't even read the whole thing."

"Well, *I* want to," said Sanger, snatching the paper from me. As she read the list, a smile climbed her face. She snickered, once. Then she folded the paper back up and politely handed it over to Max.

"That's great, man," she said. "Nicks, don't you think it's hysterical?"

"Not particularly." I turned back to Max. "Why do you want to fake-die?"

"That," he said, "requires a lengthy explanation."

"My favorites!" chirped Sanger.

She grinned over at me, noted my lack of amusement, then checked herself. Some people say that when friends get really close, they can engage in a special type of telepathy. For example, at this point, Sanger would've been able to give me a look that asked, "Don't we like this guy?" And I would have given her a look back that said, "Unequivocally, no."

But Sanger wasn't one for silent looks. She had the guts to just ask me out loud, "Don't we like this guy?" And I didn't have the guts to say, "Unequivocally, no." Which meant we ended up sitting on the bank of Barton Springs Pool, listening to Max Garza's explanation.

Four

He introduced himself game-show style.

"I'm Max Garza," he said, "and I moved here from Dallas. Mr. Palomer's my grandfather. I'm seventeen and a rising senior. My interests include yoga and long walks on the beach."

I looked at Max Garza like he was being stupid, which he was. He caught on.

"I was just kidding about the yoga," he said.

"What?" Sanger asked. "Was that a joke because you think it's a girl thing? Because that's sexist."

"No," he said. "I'm just more of a Pilates man myself."

Sanger laughed as though Max had cracked the funniest joke in a comedy sketch. I still looked at him like he was stupid, which he still was.

"It's April," I said. "Why are you moving to Austin mid-season?"

Max raised his three-fingered hand in the shape of a peace sign.

"That's why," he said.

"You're a pacifist?" asked Sanger.

Max suddenly looked very serious.

He said, "There was an accident."

Sanger and I stared at him for one long moment.

"Care to elaborate?" I said.

"So, I was in shop. We were doing this boat project. Tiny boats, like the kind you can only fit Lego men inside. We were going to determine which one was fastest and most buoyant, and, well, that's not important to the story." Max looked lost for just a second, like he'd walked into a room and forgotten why. Then he shook his head, purpose back in his eyes. "Right. I was in shop. There's some dangerous equipment in shop. So Caleb Fawcett was circular sawing, and Dylan McCavish and I were, um—'roughhousing,' I believe, is the term the adults use. Playful blows were exchanged. Caleb got distracted. Fingers were detached. I fell. Then a piece of scrap metal sliced open my right leg. They rushed me to the hospital. I could've died. I almost did."

"Oh my God," said Sanger.

"Are you making this up?" I asked.

I knew it wasn't the right thing to say, but it was the only thought in my head.

"No. All the facts are verifiable. Though I *am* making it sound dramatic."

"Yeah, you are," said Sanger, snorting. "You're a real ham, you know that?"

"Debate club."

"At least your talents have not been wasted."

"Anyway," said Max, "after all that excitement, my parents

were pretty pissed at the school. They were like, if we're going to shell out a shitload of private tuition money just for our precious boy to get his appendages hacked off, no thanks. So they pulled me out of St. Michael's and shipped me down here to go to this nontraditional school for gifted students. It's all Montessori method or something. Until that starts up in June, I've got a free pass. I'm supposed to be recuperating with my gramps, making new friends, et cetera."

"That's rough, man," said Sanger.

She rested a clover chain she'd been making on my damp shin. Then she tilted her head at Max, who sat cross-legged across from the two of us, but she said nothing else.

"Could they not reattach your fingers?" I asked weakly.

"Uh," Max said. "So after the accident, everything was pretty chaotic, and they were mainly focused on calling an ambulance and getting me to the hospital. So when Mr. Holt finally thought to get the fingers, they couldn't find them any-where. Like, they searched *everywhere*. The rumor is that Zach Brandt stole them and whittled the bones into nose rings, but no one can prove that."

I felt queasy. I stared hard at Max.

"This is a prank," I said slowly. "You told all your friends back in Dallas you could convince some unsuspecting Austinites with your elaborate story."

Max raised his three-fingered hand. "I swear to God. I *swear* it. Look it up on your phone if you want. Right now."

Sanger was the one with the smartphone. She dug it from her purse, opened the Internet browser, and searched the words "Max Garza Dallas school accident." The first link was to an article published by the *Dallas Observer.* It was dated nearly a month back. Sanger clicked on the link. We both read. When I was through, I looked back at Max.

I felt even queasier. I tried straightening up and breathing through my mouth. My stomach felt like it was slowly ballooning up into my esophagus. I kept picturing a sinisterly whirring circular saw, a gruesome geyser of blood. Part of me wanted to ask exactly how it happened, but the other part was fairly certain that if Max told me one iota of more detail I would puke on the spot. I asked him something else instead, something I'd seen in the article.

"Your name is Maximilian?"

Max looked grim. "Yeah."

"It's not a bad name," I said quickly. I now felt massively guilty for doubting his story.

"Yes, it is," said Sanger, stowing her phone away. "It's ridiculous. No offense."

"It's a family name," said Max. "You know, after my great-grandfather, the Holy Roman emperor."

Sanger sniggered. I wasn't in a particularly laughing mood.

"I'm really sorry," I said. "About the whole thing."

"It was surreal," Max said. "I know this makes me sound like a total hoke, but it was life-changing."

"I bet," said Sanger.

"No, but really. I was lying in that hospital, not sure if I would make it, and I was thinking about what a stupid way it was to die: leg sliced open by scrap metal, fingers chopped off in shop."

"There are worse ways to go," said Sanger.

"Name one."

"Choking on a Twinkie," she suggested.

Max weighed the argument. "Debatable," he finally concluded. "So a few days later, I was online, scrolling down my wall, and there were all these people from school who'd written these get-well messages, you know? 'Stay strong, buddy. Hang in there.' Shit like that. And *then* I realized that some of these people? They thought I had died. Legit *died*. They'd written stuff like 'I miss your laugh, dude. Losing you like this was unfair.' They thought I was *dead*."

"Are you sure *that* wasn't just a prank?" I asked.

"My aunt Ellie sent my parents a bouquet. She called to ask when visitation was. Apparently, the first news report to go out said it was a *fatal* accident at St. Michael's Prep. It was like, in a way, I really had died."

"Whoa," said Sanger.

"The paper printed a retraction, or whatever it is they have to do to keep from getting sued. But here's the thing. Afterward? No one came to visit me. I didn't even get a text that was like, 'Haha, man. Thought you were dead.' No one cared that I was still alive. It was so fucking depressing."

"I'm sure someone cared," I said.

"Well, my parents, I think, but that doesn't count. Where was I?"

"Depressed," said Sanger.

"Right. So I got into this funk. It was my dark night of the soul or whatever. But then. *Then.* Then I had a revelation. I had it while I was lying flat on my back."

"You decided you were going to fake your death for real and attend the funeral, like in *Huckleberry Finn*," I suggested.

"Uhh. *Tom Sawyer.*"

"What?"

"It's Tom, not Huck. God. You're a homeschooler. You're supposed to know this stuff. We're getting off track. I was just about to get to the life-changing part."

"All right."

"So, in the dark funk, I realized something. That thing people say about dying alone? I *got* it. I was like, yeah, if I'd died back there in that workshop, I would've died all alone, and people would've been bummed enough to write condolences on my wall, and then they'd just move on. It freaked me out. And that's when I made it. The list."

"Uh-huh," Sanger said slowly. "I'm not sure I'm following your train of thought."

"Think of it this way," Max said. "What's the thing people fear the most?"

"Public speaking," said Sanger.

"What?"

"They did this poll," she said. "People fear public speaking more than death. Like, people are more afraid to give a eulogy at a funeral than be inside the coffin."

"Well, forget about that. I'm an excellent public speaker. I'm afraid of *death*. That's what I figured out when I was lying there. I am fucking terrified of death."

"Isn't everyone?" I said.

"No, but I don't mean 'death.' I mean '*Death*,' with a capital *D*. Death has it out for me. He's tried to kill me twice now. He's messed around with me, and now I'm going to mess around with him."

"You think Death is a sentient being?" I asked.

"I don't know what Death is. I just know he's screwed me over one time too many."

I kept staring at Max. I was trying to take him seriously. I really was. And I felt awful about what had happened to him. I really did. But this was too much.

"You think I'm crazy," Max guessed.

"You don't think trying to almost kill yourself twenty-three times isn't crazy?" I asked.

"Well."

"And another thing. How has Death screwed you over? Isn't the very definition of Death screwing someone over, I don't know, *killing* them?"

"Well."

"Your logic has some holes. Like, big ones."

Max looked genuinely upset.

"You've *ruined* it," he said.

"Ruined what?"

"It was a sign. It *meant* something, you trying to save me today. I wouldn't have told you all this personal stuff if I didn't think it meant something."

"What could it possibly mean?"

"That you're someone who would understand, who would *get it*. And I need that. I need an accomplice."

"An accomplice."

"An accomplice."

"What, you mean us?" said Sanger. She pinched my side. "He means *us*."

"I decided it this morning," said Max, "when I was doing number thirteen, killed in battle, in Gramps' backyard. It happened when you"—he pointed to me—"saw me. I realized how much better the experience was with an audience. And for some of these deaths"—he pointed at the water-stained piece of paper—"I'm going to need help, to be sure things turn out okay."

"You mean," I said, "so you don't end up actually killing yourself."

"Something like that."

"But you don't even know us."

"Yeah, but the *sign*. You already helped me twice, without even knowing who I was. Plus, we're neighbors, so it's convenient. Plus, you're—well, you know."

"I'm what?"

"Your mom said you're homeschooled. I thought you'd be hard up for entertainment."

"Max," I said, "what do you think homeschoolers do?"

"I don't know. Read the Bible. Watch PBS. Knit."

He was wearing the judgy face.

I folded my arms. "I'm not hard up for entertainment. Also, your plan sucks."

"Sooo. You won't be my accomplice?"

"No. Sorry."

I added the "sorry" because Max *had* gotten his fingers sawed off a month ago.

Max let out a long, hoarse groan. He stared at me in the greenish glare of the pool's overhead lights.

"Did I spin it the wrong way?" he asked.

"I don't think there's a right way to spin it."

"Well, I think it was excellently spun," Sanger piped up. "I think it's genius."

Max grinned approvingly at Sanger but snapped his attention back to me.

"See? Your friend thinks it's genius."

"Yeah, well, Sanger can do whatever she wants," I said, getting to my feet and wiping wet grass from my legs. "Personally, I've had my fill of witnessing your almost deaths."

"Nicks, he said he was sorry. Don't hold a grudge."

"I'm not holding a grudge," I told Sanger. "I just think the whole thing is ridiculous."

"But it could be *fun*," Sanger insisted. "And Max is so . . ."

I frowned at her. Max was so what? Nice to look at? Yes. Strangely entertaining? Sure. But she was right: I was still holding a grudge. Twice today, Max had sent my heart racing. Twice, he'd made me feel like an idiot. I didn't want to stick around to see how many more times he'd make that happen.

Sanger didn't finish her sentence. She sighed and got to her feet.

"Fine," she said. "Nicks knows what Nicks wants. But I'm on board."

"Awesome," said Max, his voice muffled by the dry T-shirt he was fitting over his head.

"We should be going," I said.

The night chill was getting stronger, and my nose and toes had gone cold. I knew I'd have to give Max back his towel, but I kept clinging to it.

"Yeah, me too," said Max.

He got to his feet, slinging his messenger bag across his shoulder.

"You drove here?" Sanger asked him, but she was looking at me with sinister intent. My lips parted as I realized exactly what Sanger was trying to do.

"Yeah," said Max. "Oh! Hey, I could drive you home, Stevie. You know, I'm just next door."

Sanger had made it that easy. She cut me off before I could reply.

"Oh, *would* you, Max? I live all the way out in the Hill Country, and it's an absolute pain to take Stevie home."

She was grinning maniacally now, and even though I knew Sanger didn't really consider it a pain to drive me home, I was mad. Max noticed the homicidal glare I was directing at Sanger.

"Uhhh," he said. "You know, only if you want to."

But I couldn't say no, of course. Sanger knew it, and Max knew it too.

"It's whatever," I said. "As long as you don't mind me getting the seat wet."

Max motioned to his own damp body. "Do I look like I care?"

And as if that settled everything, he set off up the steep bank, toward the parking lot. Sanger and I followed, in step with each other. I socked Sanger hard in the side. She took it with grace, then leaned in close and whispered, "You're welcome."

"I don't like him," I whispered back, praying that the night would hide my blush. "He's insane."

"Mkay," Sanger said.

When we reached the parking lot, Sanger pranced ahead of me and pulled Max aside. She said something in a low voice that I couldn't pick up. He said something back. Then Sanger loped off, blowing a kiss in my direction.

"Tomorrow night, doll!" she cried, before throwing herself into the Fiat and careening out of the lot, lights ablaze.

Max led the way to his car. It was a BMW.

Of course it was a BMW.

When we got inside, he opened the moon roof.

Of course he had a moon roof.

"Sorry," he said, cranking the key in the ignition. "The leather's still kind of overheated. Takes it a while to cool down."

Of course he had leather seats.

When Max pulled out of the lot, he actually stopped at the stop sign. He even used his turn signal. I was impressed. One thing I hadn't expected was for him to be a good driver.

"So, I *think* I know how to get back," he said, "but I may need some navigational help."

"Just stay on Barton Springs Road. I'll tell you when to turn."

I looked at him. I looked at his hands on the steering wheel. I wondered how many fingers had to be missing before they revoked your driver's license. Then I immediately hated myself for wondering. Sanger would have probably slapped her favorite word, "otherist," on that.

"So," I said, trying to distract myself from my non-PC thoughts. "Dallas."

"I'm not *from* Dallas." Max spat out "Dallas" as though it were a vulgarity. "I grew up in Montreal."

"Really? My uncle lives in Montreal."

"The people of Montreal are a fine breed."

"Yeah, my uncle is kind of a bastard."

That hadn't been smart, I reflected. I shouldn't have brought up my uncle.

"The people of Montreal are a fine breed, *generally speaking*."

"Turn right here."

Max turned right there.

"So, what makes your uncle a bastard?"

I really shouldn't have brought up my uncle.

"You met Joel," I said.

"Yeah."

"He's Joel's dad."

"I thought Joel was your brother."

"Cousin."

"Okay. Go on."

"So my uncle left my aunt Lynn when Joel was four. It turned out he had this whole other family in Canada he visited on the weekends, while he was on 'business trips.'"

"*What?* No way. I thought that kind of thing just happened on the Oprah Channel. Like, you know, telepathic twins and getting switched at birth."

"You watch the Oprah Channel?"

"You're not done talking about the bastard uncle."

I shrugged. "That's pretty much it. Aunt Lynn got full custody. None of us talked to Uncle Greg until Aunt Lynn died a few years ago. He showed up at the funeral. It got really nasty. He was threatening to take Joel away, but Aunt Lynn left sole guardianship to my parents, so he really couldn't touch us. He was just an asshole about it. And then he ran back off to Canada, and we haven't heard from him since."

"Dude."

I really, *really* shouldn't have brought up my uncle. Maybe Max being so ridiculously open about his history had activated my urge to do the same—like, you lower your shields, I'll lower mine. But Joel would've killed me if he knew I was telling the new neighbor about his familial difficulties. Not to mention, the whole thing had put a damper on the conversation.

"That was heavy," I apologized.

"No, it's cool. Maybe I can redeem the *Montréalais* in your eyes."

I perked up. "Do you speak French?"

"Just the pretentious kind. You know, like *à la carte*, *encore*, *coup de grâce*. Why? Do you think that's hot?"

"Not anymore."

"Damn."

"Another right here."

"Are you taking me in a circle?"

"Maybe."

"You're never going to let me live down today, are you?"

"Well. You really messed with me."

For a small second, Max let his eyes slide from the road onto me. I made a careful study of the AC slats.

"Sanger said she'd be your accomplice," I reminded him.

"Yeah, but full disclosure: I'm not just in the market for an accomplice. I'm looking for friends. I have no friends."

I laughed.

"No, no," he said. "That wasn't a joke."

"Oh. Sorry?"

I guessed that counted as both a "sorry I laughed" and a "sorry you have no friends."

Max slowed to a stop at a red light. He looked over at me, and this time I looked back. He seemed so serious.

He said, "Be my friend."

I laughed again.

"What? *What?*"

I shook my head, still laughing. Who *was* this guy?

"What?" he asked again. "What am I doing wrong?"

"I'm homeschooled," I said, "and even I can tell that you're socially impaired."

The light turned, and Max slowly rolled through the inter-section.

"If you actually thought that," he said, "you wouldn't say it. That'd be cruel."

"I can be pretty cruel."

"Really?" He cast me another sidelong glance, apparently assessing my character in the process. "You don't look cruel."

"Freshman year I took an empathy test. I got a sixty-two."

"Out of?"

"The usual hundred."

"Yikes. So, if I got mugged and was, like, bleeding out on the street, you wouldn't help? You'd be all, 'Meh, think I'll pass'?"

"I don't know," I said. "I think I'd have to score a thirty to be *that* heartless."

"This is good to know. Friends know this kind of thing."

I shook my head in disbelief. I thought about what Sanger had told me earlier today: *People are bizarre, Nicks.*

Max was bizarre. He was good-looking and well-if-preppily dressed and super self-confident, and the fact that he was asking me to be his friend was bizarre. He seemed like the type of guy who had plenty of friends. So I told him as much.

"I just moved," he reminded me.

"Oh, right."

I hadn't moved in my entire life. I'd never given much thought to the ramifications of moving, like leaving all your old friends behind and starting from scratch.

Max was able to navigate the rest of the trip home. He eased the car into Mr. Palomer's driveway and clicked off the headlights.

"Look," he said. "If you don't want to hang out or whatever, that's fine. For all I know, your parents could be trying to set us up."

"Excuse me?"

"That's how homeschoolers do it, right? The parents whisper to each other in the back pew at church and decide that little Zeke and Martha ought to court, but only so long as they're accompanied by a chaperone and don't look into each other's eyes for more than thirty seconds at a time, because as we all know, a full minute of eye sex could lead to eye pregnancy."

"We're not those kind of homeschoolers."

I said it like I was angry, because I was. Then I opened the passenger door.

"Hey!"

Max reached over the console, but didn't quite touch me.

"You *were* supposed to laugh at that," he said. "I'm just trying to break the ice here."

"Because you need new friends."

Max nodded fervently. "I've got weeks of dead time until summer school starts up, and if I don't start hanging around human beings other than Gramps, I will cry."

"You will *cry*?" Was that the best he had?

"I already feel a little bit weepy, and I've only been here two days."

"Well, that's your problem. You haven't given it enough time. Have a little patience."

"Tell me something you want," he said. "Something I can do."

Despite everything, I smiled. "Are you trying to buy my friendship?"

"*What?*" Max looked disgusted. "I would never do anything so base. I'm just trying to, you know, make things right."

"You really care that much about what people think?"

Max said nothing, but it wasn't a question that really needed answering.

I dragged the sole of my sneaker across the floorboard, considering. I'd realized I wasn't going to shake Max until I gave him something, anything that he thought would redeem him in my eyes. I just wanted to get in my house. The queasiness from earlier, when Max told the story about losing his fingers, had returned—this time far stronger and more uncomfortable than before.

"Okay," I said. "There's one thing."

Max opened his arms wide. For a panicked second I thought he was going to try to hug me. But he didn't. He just flapped his arms like a bird taking off.

"Please," he said. "I'm *offering* myself to you."

I said, "Fifty signatures."

"Come again?"

"I've got this petition, and I need fifty signatures. If you're really serious, you can get them for me."

"Fifty signatures," Max said, musing. "This isn't for anything shady, is it? Like the disenfranchisement of high schoolers?"

"High schoolers aren't franchised to begin with."

"*What.*"

"It's to save Barton Springs."

"What's Barton Springs?"

"The pool you were just fake-drowning in, Max."

"Oooh."

"It's about pollutants and stuff," I said. "Nothing too interesting."

For some reason, I felt my skin heating up. Why was I embarrassed to be telling Max this? I cared about STA, really cared. It *was* interesting. It was worth talking about, not sweeping aside like a stupid hobby. I cleared my throat and met Max's eyes.

"You'd really be helping me out," I said.

"Okay," said Max.

"Okay?"

"Yeah, just get me that petition. It's done."

I didn't know if I believed Max, but something in his even tone made me *want* to believe him.

"Thanks," I said.

"Don't thank me," said Max. "This is a transaction. It means you and I are friends now, remember?"

I gawked. "You said—"

Max just raised his eyebrows.

I swatted his shoulder. It wasn't until the action was complete that I realized what an intimate gesture it had been. It was something I would do to Sanger, not to Max, the new neighbor I barely knew.

"Our first fight!" said Max. "I'm journaling about this tonight."

"I've changed my mind."

"Too late. You made a deal. Fifty signatures. The shake made it official."

"We didn't shake on it," I said.

"We didn't? Well."

Max stuck out his three-fingered hand.

It felt rude not to shake it, if for no other reason than that it was a three-fingered hand. So we shook on it. It was a little thrilling, striking a deal like that. I felt powerful. I also still felt sick to my stomach.

Apparently, I was beginning to look as ill as I felt, because Max asked, "Are you okay?"

"Yeah," I said. "Fine."

Then I puked into his lap.

Five

Everything I did that night, post-vomit, was done in shame. I apologized profusely to Max in shame. In shame, I watched him wipe off his trunks and leather seat as best he could before I was sick again, this time on the driveway. In shame, I let Max lead me up the steps to my front porch. In shame, I mumbled good-bye. Then I went inside.

A guttural howl and the clatter of gunfire echoed down the hallway. Joel was in the den, watching his zombie show. He paused it when he saw me standing on the threshold.

"Shiza, Stevie. You look goddamn awful."

I started to cry.

"Whoa," said Joel. "Whoooa."

The television clicked off. The den lights turned on. Joel was at my side. He led me to the couch as I gargled out non-sensical words and snivels.

"How's your sugar?" was the first question he asked that I was capable of answering.

"It isn't my sugar," I choked out, even though I was sure my blood sugar couldn't be in good shape after so much puking; I'd need to hydrate on some juice, and soon.

"Okay. Okay, well, if you're menstruating, just say so. I'll get out of your hair."

"It's not that," I said. "It just *happened*. All over him."

Then I sobbed some more.

Over the next few minutes, Joel extracted the necessary information from me: that what "just happened" was that I'd puked, and that "him" was Max Garza, the new neighbor Joel had met that morning as Corn Syrup Guy. Joel rubbed my back, and he told me I'd be okay, that I just needed to clean out my mouth and take a shower and that everything would look better in the morning.

Which would've been more comforting if I hadn't seen Joel's shoulders shaking with laughter. I told him this wasn't funny, and he told me it was a *little* funny, and then he smiled in a way that made me laugh, despite my best efforts to remain a slobbering mess.

Eventually, I made it into the shower, then bed, where I downed a tall glass of cranapple juice. To distract myself from the ramifications of puking on my hot, eight-fingered next-door neighbor, I started a *Gilmore Girls* marathon. I put in a season six disc, because season six is when Rory, the protagonist, goes absolutely apeshit and makes one bad life decision after another. I was trying to put things into perspective.

Thirty minutes into the marathoning and just as I was checking my sugar, Joel poked his head in.

"Checkup," he said.

"Better," I reported. "Not in a coma, anyway."

"So, I don't need to call Aunt Carrie?"

I shook my head. The last thing I wanted was Joel interrupting Mom and Dad's concert to inform them I'd hurled up tacos in Mr. Palomer's driveway.

"If you tell them anything," I said, "I will kill you."

"Right."

Joel leaned against the door in a familiar way, rocking up and down on the balls of his feet, causing the door hinges to screech.

"Sooo," he said. "So, *Valerie*. Has she said anything to you?"

I narrowed my eyes. "We're not on speaking terms, thanks to you. Why? You're not trying to get her back, are you?"

"No!" Joel let go of the door, flinging it fully open in a gigantic screech. "No, of course not. I was just wondering if she, you know, said anything to you. It's cool. It's whatever. I was just wondering."

"We're not talking."

"Okay. Cool. But, like, this morning? On the phone? She didn't say anything about me?"

"Only that you're an asshole."

"Mhm. Cool, cool."

"Yeah. Cool. Is that it?"

I didn't necessarily want to get back to *Gilmore Girls*. I was just getting weird vibes from Joel. It was like he was expecting something. Like it was his birthday and I'd forgotten to get him a present.

"I guess so," Joel said, tapping at the door. "So, you really hurled all over that guy?"

"Bye, Joel."

Joel grinned a wide grin. He seemed to have forgotten about the mortal agony his face had been in just that morning.

"Byyyye," he said, creaking the door shut slowly.

I didn't unpause the television. Up until that moment, I'd been doing a decent job of suppressing the events of that evening. I'd distracted myself with sobbing and showering and fictional domestic drama. Now, thanks to Joel, my mind had whirred back into action, and I was reminded of just how embarrassed I ought to feel.

It had been a *bad* puke—three tacos' worth, plus a little of the tuna salad I'd eaten for lunch.

I hoped that Max Garza would do me a favor and pretend I didn't exist. If we ever crossed paths again, I prayed he would act like I was nothing more than a heat shimmer on a desert highway. I wouldn't be offended; I'd be grateful.

I remembered that I'd gurgled out some form of apology on the way up the porch steps, so I figured that had wrapped up any loose ends between the two of us. I also remembered that Max had said some things as he'd helped me to my feet in the driveway and pushed back sick-stained strands of hair from my face. I couldn't remember now what those things had been. When you're sick, all you can really think about is getting better, not your dignity or temporarily unimportant factors like people's words or good opinion of you. It's afterward that you realize the full extent of your humiliation. The only thing worse than getting sick in public is the sick fallout.

Now that I wasn't busy being violently ill, I had time to really think about things.

Twenty-three fake deaths.

I wondered why it was twenty-three. I also wondered how a prep could be so morbid. If Max had blue hair and a lip piercing and wore black skinny jeans, then I wouldn't have been surprised. Maybe it was the fact that the morbidity was so unexpected that made it so unacceptable.

I didn't feel bad about saying no to Max's proposition, even though I wasn't even entirely sure what that proposition entailed. *An accomplice.* He wanted me and Sanger to help him almost die but make sure he didn't go too far. And what else? Take photographs, maybe? Upload them to the Internet? Whatever he wanted, it was weird, all around.

No thanks, I said to the memory of Max in my head. *No thanks.*

My phone lit up. A text. Sanger.

You alive?

No thanks to you, I texted back.

I decided not to tell her about the puking. It wasn't that I didn't trust Sanger with the information. It was just that even the thought of admitting what happened over text made me feel really pathetic.

Apparently, Sanger decided that this brief text exchange was proper closure to the events of that night, because she launched into an entirely new topic.

MOVIE NIGHT, BIOTCH. >:] THE PLAN:

Thirty seconds passed. I hated that about Sanger's texts. She sent them in short, small bursts with long intervals in between. Sanger was a slow texter, which was odd, because she was really fast at just about everything else. The thing was, she insisted on texting with one thumb. I'd told her plenty of times that it was an inefficient method, but she never listened.

"It's too late," she'd say. "I learned it this way. It's forever concreted in my muscle memory. You might as well try teaching me how to write with my left hand."

Finally, I received the Plan, piecemeal.

Pick up @ 6.

Time passed.

Meal: CHILI, courtesy of Alma. Movie: J STEW.

Time passed.

make it a sleepover?

At this point, I thought it safe to respond.

Me: *Cool. Can you pick up @ 5:30*

Sanger: *K, but you sound deal.*

Sanger: *dead*

Sanger: *FU, AUTOCORRECT*

Sanger: *desperate!!!*

Me: *poor baby*

Sanger: *I'm your ride; be nice.*

Sanger was the only person I knew who used semicolons in her texts. I theorized they were her attempt to make up for her pitiful slowness. I joked that if she'd gone to a normal public school and had a normal amount of friends, she wouldn't be so textually stunted. She joked that if I'd gone to a public school and had a normal amount of friends, I'd have gone on an actual date by my sixteenth birthday.

But Sanger and I didn't go to public school, and we mainly just had each other. Even though we joked about our deficiencies, we didn't mind them. There weren't a lot of public schoolers around to rub in our face what we could or couldn't do or what we had or hadn't experienced. All in all, we considered ourselves pretty lucky.

Friday started off like a normal weekday. I answered fifteen chemistry questions and self-graded. I read about the judiciary system from my American Government textbook and watched a curriculum DVD on Justice John Jay. I ate lunch in the kitchen, but not with Joel, who had a strong aversion to eating noises and refused to dine with other human beings whenever possible.

After lunch, I reviewed forty vocab cards for the ACT. I hated those cards. I hated the fact that the Older Generation forced my Younger Generation to memorize words like "antediluvian"—words that we had never used and would never use in an actual sentence pertaining to actual life. Except that Friday afternoon, when I had to write the word in a complete sentence:

The word antediluvian is itself antediluvian.

During my two o'clock break, I checked my e-mails. I'd received one from Leslie Cobb, leader of Springs for Tomorrow Alliance. It was a group e-mail, and it was flagged as urgent with three red exclamations marks, like all of Leslie's correspondence.

Subject: New Developments!!!

Greetings, World Changers!

As you all know, Thursday's rally turned out to be anticlimactic due to the Senate taking longer than usual to pass an education bill. Not only did this upset the timeliness of our rally, but it also gives New Systematic Solutions more time to continue its environmentally reckless practices, unchecked. Until we pass this new bill into law, the degradation of our priceless watershed will be completely LEGAL.

As citizens, our hands are tied on certain points. But here's one thing we can do: GET MORE OF THOSE SIGNATURES. Think of this delay as a perfect opportunity for us to gather more names

on our petition and halt New Systematic Solutions in its tracks.
I've attached a PDF of the petition in case any of you need a fresh
copy.

Remember, the goal of the Petition Challenge is for each of you to
gather FIFTY (or more!) signatures by our next rally on April 17. I
know it sounds like a lot, but I have full confidence in this group.
We've accomplished so much already. Let's not give up the fight
now.

Leslie Cobb

Founder, Springs for Tomorrow Alliance

"In a gentle way, you can shake the world." —Mahatma Gandhi

The e-mail served as a good reminder. I took my creased
copy of the STA petition out of my top desk drawer and looked it
over. Thirteen signatures. Unwillingly, I thought back to the night
before, to that stupid promise of fifty signatures I'd extracted
from Max. Obviously, the vomit had made that deal void.

I stuffed the petition into my overnight duffel. I'd yet to
get signatures from Sanger's moms, who I knew would be on
board. I also figured Sanger and I could take some time Saturday
morning to make rounds in her neighborhood. Sanger didn't
like politics, but she liked talking loudly to strangers.

When it came to schoolwork, I saved the best for last. Once all other subjects were out of the way, I indulged myself in at least two straight hours of "scholastic reading." New Horizons, the curriculum we used, was based on a holistic philosophy. The idea was that students learn best when their subjects overlap and complement each other. That meant that my reading materials corresponded to my history materials.

This week's read was *North and South* by Elizabeth Gaskell. It was a story about an English girl named Margaret who has to travel north to a dingy mill town, where this guy named Mr. Thornton treats everyone like shit but apparently has a heart of gold. I hadn't gotten to the heart-of-gold part yet. I thought Margaret was boring and needed to stop blushing so much and saying whiny stuff like, "Oh! I should not have left her— wicked daughter that I am!" I also thought that she should stop starting every other sentence with "Oh!"

I read past five thirty. Sanger was always late, but every time she acted as though her lateness was a novelty. And every time, she apologized or tried to make up for it, like it was a one-time thing only, which I guessed was better than Sanger not caring about her tardiness at all.

At 5:40, I ticked up one of the front room blinds to check the driveway. Miracle of miracles, Sanger was there. Someone was talking to her through her open window. Cold horror bloomed in my chest. I ticked the blind open wider, as though doing so would change the entity of the person talking to Sanger.

It was Max Garza.

I decided I should pretend I was running late and hide out in the house until Max disappeared. Then I reconsidered. It was possible, I realized, that Max was just hanging around Sanger's car *until* I showed up, in which case the best thing to do would be to suck it up and get it over with.

I released a moan, slung my duffel over my shoulder, and tromped into the den to tell Mom good-bye. I found her at the computer, where she was working on an Excel spreadsheet. Mom had gotten her associate degree in accounting, and she took care of the financial side of Dad's landscaping business.

"Everything all right, soldier?" she asked, eyes fixed on a screen full of numbers.

"Great," I assured her. "How was the concert?"

"Louie is a musical genius."

"So I've heard."

"How was the rally?"

"Oh, you know."

"Hmm."

"Sanger says that Alma baked those ginger cookies again. I'll bring some back for you and Dad."

I would've brought back cookies anyway, but I was anticipating the fact that by the time I got home Saturday afternoon, Mom would have graded my trig test.

Mom patted my arm. Her cold brass bangles jangled against my skin.

"Angel, sweet angel," she said.

I pecked her on the cheek and said good-bye.

There was no more delaying the inevitable after that, save a brief detour to kitchen, where I gave myself an insulin injection and then tucked away the pen and a few cartridges into my duffel. Then I went outside.

"Nicks!" Sanger cried.

Max turned around. I turned red.

He smiled at me.

I wanted to die and decompose into fertilizer, right there in Mom's front garden. Instead, I gave Max a half wave and said a "hey" that wasn't audible to anyone outside a one-inch radius.

"The stories this man tells!" Sanger squawked. "Can we keep him? Can we teach him tricks?"

I'd known Sanger since third grade, but I still marveled at the way she got so familiar with people so fast. I could only hope she would realize, upon closer inspection of Max, that he was a total whack job. For the time being, I observed the spectacle of two risk-taking extroverts in action—Sanger charming Max and Max charming Sanger. It was like something you'd see on Animal Planet.

"He let me take a good look at the war wound on his leg," Sanger said. "The one he almost bled out from."

"Yeah, I bet he shows that to all the girls," I said.

Max gave me a funny look. I focused intently on my duffel zipper, pretending it had gone off its track.

"It's such an insane story," said Sanger. "Have you thought about writing a memoir?"

"Oh!" Max said, doing that thing where he spread his arms wide, like a bird taking wing. "It is in the *works*. I've penned the first chapter already. It starts with a premonitory nightmare I had as a three-year-old."

"I don't even know if you're joking, Max," said Sanger, "and that is what I love about you."

It was familiar stuff like *that*. Sanger used "love" in direct reference to Max's person and she'd only known him for a day.

Then Sanger said something even more familiar, and I was so pissed at her for it.

"So, Max, why don't you join us tonight? You have to, actually, because I just texted our cook to set out an extra bowl of chili."

I felt Max look at me again. I didn't look back again.

"Uh," he said, "would that be all right? I don't want to interrupt your girl plans."

"It's fine, dude!" Sanger said. "We're just going to gorge ourselves on comfort food and watch an old movie."

"Living on the wild side," said Max.

"Come on. You're new here. I bet you have zero plans."

"Uhhh, yeeeah, how do *you* feel about it?"

Max was addressing me. It would've been rude not to respond.

"Sure," I said. "That's fine."

I couldn't say anything else. Even if I said no, like I wanted to, the whole night would still be ruined because Sanger would be mad about it.

"Really?" Max pressed. "I don't want to intrude or anything."

"No, no," I said. "You should come. Sanger lives in a palace, so if nothing else, you should come to see the chandeliers."

Max nodded. "Sweet. Let's go."

He galloped around the car and yanked at the passenger door handle. Of course, it didn't open.

"Window," I said.

"Awesome," said Max.

He grabbed the roof of the car and fit himself inside, feet first. In the thick of it, as he was crawling into the backseat, he kicked Sanger in the shoulder. He didn't notice, and she didn't say anything.

"You should've offered our guest shotgun," Sanger chided once my duffel and body were safely inside the Fiat.

"I'm taller than him," I said, "so I need the extra leg room."

This wasn't true; Max and I were the same height. It was a bitchy thing to say, but I was still flustered after having to maneuver through the window with Max in close quarters, watching.

Sanger didn't make any more reprimands. She shifted the car into reverse and cranked up the radio.

"GRIEG," she roared over a ruckus of sundry brass instruments. "MY FAVE."

She coasted through a four-way stop, then tugged on my sleeve. In a conspiratorial whisper she said, "Ask Max who his favorite composer is."

"Ask him yourself."

"JOHN WILLIAMS," Max shouted, pushing his face toward the console.

I watched Sanger's reaction. I could see it in her eyes: Her respect for Max was plummeting. He caught on to Sanger's less-than-impressed face.

"WHAT? STAR WARS. INDIANA JONES. HARRY POTTER."

"HUSH NOW," Sanger said, waving him back. She cranked the volume louder.

The driver had spoken. We listened to Grieg the whole way out to the Hill Country. In between pieces, a man with a molasses-smooth voice informed us that we had just listened to *Peer Gynt*, and were now embarking upon a musical journey through *Lyric Pieces* for piano. Sanger went seventy-five miles per hour on the highway, but neither she nor I rolled up the windows. The music was deafening, and so was the wind, which shot in prickly hands and tied my long hair into knots. The sky was cloudless and blue and yellow and more yellow, and I breathed it in, and I exhaled it, and then I breathed deeper than before. I forgot about the fact that Max was in the backseat. I forgot about the trig test and the petition and Valerie Borkowski. I raised my palm to the open window and placed it against an invisible glass of pressure.

Sanger turned off Highway 71 and onto a two-way street. The road was bordered by short grass and tan dust, an open field hurtling in every direction toward opposite horizons. We were going slow enough now that I could shove my head out the window and yell. Not words, just a yell. Sanger called it the "barbaric yawp," which was something she'd taken from a poem she liked by either William Wordsworth or Walt Whitman—I could never remember which.

Sanger turned off the radio entirely, plunging us into an abruptly music-less vacuum. That was the way Sanger did things: very loud, or not at all. She leaned her own head out the window, and she closed her eyes, and she screamed. It would've been such an awkward scream anywhere else, outside of that car and outside of that moment. The car swerved.

"Hey," I heard from the backseat. "Hey, not a good idea."

I glanced back. Max looked nervous, which was weird. The day before, he'd seemed like the kind of guy who didn't get nervous about anything.

I tugged on Sanger's sleeve. She plopped back into her seat, grinning.

"What?" she demanded. "I had both hands on the wheel the whole time. Is my man Max babying out back there?"

She shifted the rearview mirror to get a better look at Max and said, "I'll have you know I am accident free."

"'Cause you've been driving for, what, one year?"

Sanger sniffed loudly. She punched Grieg back to blaring.

We drove on. Every so often, we passed a clump of trees and a private drive that led off to one of the many McMansions in the area. Then, suddenly, there was a shock of purple in the passing grass.

Bluebonnets. They were the first of the season. I loved bluebonnets. I didn't care how kitschy or Texan they were. I loved them in a simple, unwavering way, the same way I liked ice water after a run. They were sure and constant and they never got old, not in my books.

"Bluebonnets," Sanger said, her voice tinged with disdain.

Sanger didn't feel the same way as I did. She hated blue-bonnets in a simple, unwavering way, the same way she hated black olives. There wasn't a reason, only taste.

After a while longer, Sanger turned right, onto one of the private drives. Gravel clunked and tittered against the Fiat as she followed the cedar-lined path up to Hamasaki House. Most of the houses out here were done in the southwestern style—stucco, adobe, red roofs and tan walls, wide windows made of whole panes of glass. Hamasaki House was totally different. It looked like a majestic manor straight out of a BBC period drama, the kind of place inhabited by a jilted old woman or a conniving businessman responsible for a Ponzi scheme.

Sanger and I were in love with that house. It was impossible not to be. It was a two-story behemoth of gray stone and wood lattices, swallowed in crawling ivy. The windows were made up of tiny panes, each one a little warped. There were eight bedrooms and two kitchens and winding stairs and an echoing atrium, and the whole place was done up in a way that looked very old but smelled new.

It was the backyard I liked the most. Sanger's mothers had hired my dad to do the work. The garden path was made of smooth, white pebbles and wound around several little ponds. In the biggest pond swam a half-dozen carp. Overlooking the pond was a blue-and-white pagoda. Inside the pagoda were bonsai trees that my dad checked on once a week. My dad loved his work at the Sadler-Hamasakis'. He'd told me at least five separate times that they were his favorite clients, which suited me just fine, because Sanger was my favorite person.

I'd first visited Hamasaki House when I was eight. I'd had several long summers to get used to the grandeur. Max had not.

"Holy shit," he said as we got out of the car. "This is an establishment."

We entered through the kitchen door, and I made a pit stop to store my insulin in the fridge. Alma, the Sadler-Hamasakis' cook, had left out a serving tray on the granite island. It was loaded up with three bowls of chili and a long plate of corn bread. The tray looked comically large in Sanger's small hands, and it shook as she hoisted it up and led us upstairs to her room. I didn't offer to help. I knew Sanger would get offended and say no. Max did offer to help. Sanger got offended and said no. By the time we reached the second-story landing, a decent amount of everyone's chili had sloshed out on the tray, but Sanger's pride remained intact.

Sanger's room was painted in the same obscenely yellow shade as her Fiat. She had two walk-in closets and a flat-screen television and a brand-new Mac desktop. Whenever I felt myself getting unreasonably jealous of Sanger's living situation, I reminded myself that I would probably go blind from the yellow walls within a month's time.

"Stevie and I always watch our movies here, Max," Sanger said, hopping onto her bed and turning on the television. "Hope that's not awkward."

Max smiled generously. "I will never complain about being on a bed with two hot girls."

I snuck a look at Sanger. I was biting down a grin, though I wasn't sure why. I was still kind of pissed at Sanger for this whole setup. I'd been planning on girl time, not sitting cautiously on Sanger's bed with my back propped against the pillows, self-conscious about how far my shirt was riding up and if my eyeliner had smeared.

Max was making me less comfortable. And I hated that I felt the need to be less comfortable, because it meant I cared about Max's opinion, and I cared that he'd called me "hot," even though he'd probably only thrown the word out the way he would any overused adjective, like "awesome."

Sanger didn't return my smile. She was intently focused on the remote control.

"I downloaded it this morning. It should be in—oh, there. They filed it under 'Stewart' instead of 'Capra.' Idiots."

Max had discovered a pink ballpoint pen on Sanger's nightstand. He was clicking it with the thumb of his three-fingered hand.

"Stop that," Sanger said, smacking his hand hard. The pen clattered to the floor. "God, that was so annoying."

Max looked startled at first. He looked at Sanger the same way I'd looked at her in third grade, when she'd come up to me in co-op art class and painted a big blue streak straight through my picture of a windmill.

"It's cooler that way," she'd said with utter certainty.

And instead of getting angry with her, I'd laughed the same way Max was laughing now.

The movie started. White text on a black screen informed us that this film had been restored by the Library of Congress.

"*That,*" said Sanger. "That right there. That's how you know it's a good movie. The effing Library of Congress. Oh. Oh! Hang on. I forgot. . . ."

She hopped off the bed and ran from the room without further explanation. She'd been sitting between Max and me, and now, with her gone, I felt uncomfortably closer to Max than I had before. I could see the wrinkles in the sleeve of his polo shirt.

I pretended to be watching the movie, but I could feel Max's eyes on me.

"You feeling okay?" he asked.

"Yep," I said.

"You didn't want me to come."

I shrugged, even though I knew it wasn't fair to be so nasty to Max. I was the one who had puked on him.

Max grabbed the remote. He paused the movie.

"It wasn't a big deal, what happened last night," he said. "I was just worried your parents would think I'd gotten you high or drunk or something."

"They didn't."

"So, what, do you just not like me? Or are you, like, mad I said that stuff about you being homeschooled?"

"No, I'm fine," I said. "I just . . ."

I couldn't finish that sentence. What was I supposed to say? "I care what you think"?

"I got five signatures today."

I blinked at Max in surprise. "W-what?"

"Five," he said, holding up his right hand to emphasize the number and then stopping abruptly, as though he had only just realized he was two fingers short. "Oh wait. Um." He held up his left hand instead, grinning.

I shook my head. "I thought after what happened last night, you wouldn't be game anymore."

"What? After just a little spewing?" Max scoffed. "Once

again, you severely underestimate how badly I need friends."

"But you don't have a copy of the—"

"Yeah, I did some searching online. Found the website for Springs Forever and Ever, or whatever. Pretty sleek setup for a nonprofit."

"Sanger made it," I said. "She has this website business."

I didn't add that I'd begged Sanger for weeks to make a website for a political purpose, which was strictly against her code of ethics.

"Anyway," said Max, "I downloaded the petition. You were right: It *is* boring."

I smiled at him. Really smiled.

I knew now: Max was for real. He was ridiculous and morbid and a little too desperate for friends, maybe, but he was for real.

"I was pretty bitchy about your whole death-plan thing," I said.

Max shrugged. "You had a right."

"Well, if you and Sanger do find yourselves hard up for another *accomplice*, or whatever, you, um, know where to find me."

Max scraped the bottom of his chili bowl and spooned the last of its contents into his mouth. He gave me a big, close-lipped smile.

"Okay," he said, once he'd swallowed.

Sanger careened back into the room.

"Okay," she said. "Okay, okay. Here."

She dropped a set of stapled papers before us. At the top of the first page, in large Arial font, she'd typed: AN IDIOT'S GUIDE TO FRANK CAPRA.

"That's all you need to know," she said, climbing back on the bed and crisscrossing her legs. She shoved a piece of corn bread in her mouth and proceeded to talk around it. "The man was a genius. You're gonna want to watch all his films after this. I guarantee it."

I was used to these guides. Sanger made them for all areas of my life she deemed culturally deficient, ranging from my knowledge of Baroque music to Baz Luhrmann films. Because of this practice, Joel thought Sanger was pretentious, and he made a point of telling me so about once a week. I could see how people would think Sanger was pretentious. Maybe she was. But it was hard to fault her for it when I found that Bach really did help me concentrate on chemistry homework and that *Strictly Ballroom* really was the perfect rainy-day movie.

Guides in hand, the three of us watched *Mr. Smith Goes to Washington*. Like nearly everything Sanger made me watch, it was good. It was all about the Little Man standing up to the Big Man, and it closed with an epic filibuster scene. The story made me think a lot about Springs for Tomorrow Alliance and the petition I'd packed in my duffel. STA was totally Jimmy Stewart, and New Systematic Solutions was the corrupt senior senator named Joseph Paine. That made me feel good about myself and the work STA was doing. Tomorrow, I vowed, I would get more signatures on that petition, even if that meant walking inch-wide blisters into my heels.

After the final scene—a celebratory uproar in the Senate chamber—the movie did us the courtesy of telling us that it was "The End." Max slow-clapped. Sanger beamed.

Solemnly, she said, "Every American should watch it."

I acknowledged that *Mr. Smith Goes to Washington* was, in fact, a fine movie and that yes, I would definitely watch more Frank Capra if afforded the opportunity. Then I excused myself to go to the bathroom. My bladder had been strained since the movie's thirty-minute mark. I also wanted a chance to check my sugar, which I could've just done on the bed if stupid Max hadn't been there.

It was when I reached into my purse that I noticed it. There, tucked into the cell phone pocket I never used, was a creased bit of pink construction paper, shaped like a heart. Its edges were lined with the remnant of a multicolored glitter border.

It was the BFF card.

Sanger and I had made the BFF card when we were ten. It was the result of having watched a cartoon spy movie called *Underground Heroes*, in which the two main characters— anthropomorphic cat spies—use a special metal disk that can sense the other's presence. Whenever one of the cats is in trouble, she just flings the disk out and it miraculously finds her partner, alerting her to the situation. I can admit now, that metal disk was a pretty stupid device. But at the time, Sanger and I thought it was ingenious. So we'd created the BFF card—a sort of metal disk with its own set of rules.

"Whenever one of us is in trouble," Sanger had explained, "or we need a favor, we hand over the BFF card. It means the other one helps out, no matter what. No questions asked."

"No questions asked," I'd agreed.

The BFF card had served us well. Over the years, we'd passed it back and forth by way of backpacks, pockets, mailboxes, and windowsills. Each time, we'd attached a single sticky note to the heart, explaining the requested favor—sometimes ridiculous, sometimes serious, but always to be performed with no questions asked.

Bring modeling clay to co-op.

Tell Mam I'm a safe driver.

Buy that shirt at Macy's, because you're fabulous.

Tell Alma I'm looking faint and probably need an extra piece of cake.

Come to my place with a box of tissues?

"Accidentally" kick Ethan in the shin under the table during Bleeding Heart Hour.

It had been several months since the BFF card had been in play. I'd been the last one to cash it in. After all my weeks of begging Sanger to create the website for STA, I'd finally resorted to the card. That was definitely the biggest favor either of us had asked to date, and I knew Sanger was not one to be outdone. Whatever she came up with was going to be epic and probably embarrassing, and the fear of what was coming had occasionally kept me up at night. Now the waiting was over. I tugged the glittered heart out of my purse, unfolded it, and read the creased sticky note inside:

Help Max with his death list.

When I returned to the bedroom, Sanger was rolled on her side in the fetal position, snorting with laughter at something Max had said. She hushed up when she saw the pink heart in my hand. She smiled. I could never figure out how Sanger managed a smile like that—simultaneously guilty and unashamed.

"So, Nicks," she said. "Max said you might be interested in joining us after all."

I don't know how I hadn't seen it coming. Of course this was how Sanger would play it. This was the sort of situation the BFF card was made for. I felt coerced. I felt tricked. I also felt excited. In a way, this seemed like an inevitability. And it was no questions asked.

"Yeah," I said. "Yeah, I am."

Sanger's face was aglow. "Tonight," she said. "It begins tonight."

Six

Sometimes three otherwise competent human beings can collectively overlook one massively important detail. That night, I had planned to sleep over at Sanger's. Max clearly hadn't. Yet on the entire car ride out to the Hill Country, no one had paid attention to the fact that Max didn't have a ride home.

It wasn't until the Drs. Sadler-Hamasaki came home that Sanger looked at the clock, swore, and sat straight up from where she'd been sprawled on the bed.

"Max," she said. "How are you ever going to leave this place?"

"Uh," said Max. "I thought you'd be driving back?"

"Are you kidding? I've already made the drive once today, and that's my limit. That's why I always hold Nicks hostage for a sleepover: I'm lazy. Also, the car doesn't get good mileage, and despite what you may think, I don't have *endless* gas funds."

"Uh," Max said again, and it became clear that this was his only remaining solution to the quandary.

Sanger led us downstairs. Her parents were in the main sitting room, watching the Masters Tournament. Her mom, Dr. Sadler, was drinking red wine. Her mam, Dr. Hamasaki, was drinking Guinness out of the can.

"Parental Unit," she said, stepping directly in front of the big screen.

Her mom paused the DVR.

"Sanger," she said.

"Hello, Stevie!" Dr. Hamasaki said, smiling pleasantly over at me.

Dr. Hamasaki was gorgeous. She was very petite, and her hair looked like something from a L'Oréal commercial. I got uncomfortable around her, not because she wasn't nice, but just because she was so damn beautiful.

"Who's this?" asked Dr. Hamasaki, pointing at Max.

"Max Garza," Sanger said. "He's Stevie's friend."

I laughed a little. It was a laughable introduction.

"It's a pleasure," said Dr. Sadler, though she was still looking at the paused screen.

Dr. Sadler was a plump woman with suntanned skin and curly blond hair. She wore a lot of rings on her fingers. She also dressed like a model from an Ann Taylor magazine, only the clothes never quite fit her right and, instead, tended to bunch around her waist. She was harder to get to know than Dr. Hamasaki, but I liked her a little better because she'd told me once that I could cut it in med school. Not that I planned on going to med school. It was just the way Dr. Sadler had said it, with such emphasis, like my intelligence was obvious and uncontested.

"Anyway," said Sanger, "I was wondering if Max could stay over? But, like, in a separate bedroom. Clearly."

The Drs. Sadler-Hamasaki shared a look.

"He can take the orange room," said Dr. Sadler.

The orange bedroom was on the west side of the house. Sanger's was on the east. Both were on the second floor, but you had to cut through the downstairs kitchen, sitting room, music room, and parlor to get from one to the other. Apparently the Sadler-Hamasakis deemed this distance sufficient enough to prevent Max Garza's sperm from reaching either Sanger or me.

"Excellent," Sanger said. "Thanks, you two."

She waved Max and me back into the kitchen, then up to her bedroom.

"All settled," she said, closing the bedroom door. "That's a load off everyone's shoulders. Now we can focus on the task at hand, and that is *the list*."

The list may have been Max's brainchild, but Sanger had cast a spell over Max as much as she had over me when I was eight years old. I saw it in the way he looked at her that night: eyes wide, lips parted, as though to say, *Whoa, she isn't kidding. She really just said that, and she really did mean it.*

Max had told us he wanted accomplices. What he got in Sanger was a ringmaster, a war strategist, a mad genius. When Sanger got sold on a project—whether it was her website business or being my best friend—she slammed herself into it at maximum speed, and she didn't let up. Max's list was no exception.

It started with a neon-green poster board and a box of Magic Markers. Sanger owned an endless supply of neon poster boards. She used them primarily for homework presentations. The Drs. Sadler-Hamasaki sent Sanger to co-op with me on Mondays and hired a tutor for her on Wednesdays and Fridays. Sanger did all the schoolwork in between. At the end of each month, she gave her parents a seminar on what she'd learned, devoting one neon poster board to each school subject. It was very different from how I homeschooled, but it seemed to work. Sanger's test scores were always good, and she had won first place at the 4-H state public speaking tournament two years in a row, which had to count for something.

That night, Sanger used her poster board for less educational purposes. Across the top, in purple bubble letters, she wrote:

THE PLAN
Complete all 23 by June 1

THE PLAYERS
Max—Official Faker
Sanger—Research
Stevie—Documentation

"What do you mean, documentation?" I asked. "Like, photos and stuff?"

"Indeed," said Sanger. "You're responsible for making sure each of Max's fake deaths lives in infamy. You will use *this* and *this*."

Sanger handed me a digital camera and a blue velvet notebook that had the words "DREAM JOURNAL" embroidered on the front. I flipped the journal open. It was empty.

"Better in theory than practice," she said, nodding at it. "I never remember dreams. It's because I wake up naturally from REM sleep, or something."

Sanger looked at the objects she'd placed in my lap. She shook her head, as though something was wrong. She went into her walk-in closet and rummaged around.

Max turned to me and said, "You can still change your mind."

"No," I said. "No, I want to. You got those five signatures."

That may not have made much sense said out loud, but it did in my mind. In less than a day, Max had tracked down five signatures for STA. If he'd done that, then I could play along with this game of his. And then there was the totally unrelated matter of the BFF card, which I decided I would never tell Max about. There were some parts of my friendship with Sanger I still wanted to keep private.

Sanger emerged from the closet. She was holding a Polaroid camera. I recognized it as a gift I'd given her on her tenth birthday. I'd worked chores for seven months to afford it.

"More immediate," she said. "This way, you can tape photos straight into the journal. There's not enough film in there for twenty-three, but I can order some more online."

I took the Polaroid and gave Sanger back the digital camera. I was relieved. I got nervous around superexpensive things like cameras and smartphones. I felt the same way about them as I did about babies: afraid I'd drop them or press the wrong button.

"Okay, Max," said Sanger, holding up the now infamous sheet of legal pad paper. "You've already crossed out two of these: number thirteen, killed in battle— Wait, which war?"

"Boer."

"Brave choice."

Max pointed to his stomach. "Bayonet finished me off."

"The other completed death," said Sanger, "is number fourteen, impalement. How the hell did you fake *that* one?"

"That was before I left," said Max. "In Dallas."

Which wasn't an explanation, but Sanger took it like one.

"The best strategy," she told us, "is to start with the more easily accomplished tasks and work our way up to the spectacular. Some of these will require intensive research"—here, she pointed to herself, the newly appointed Researcher—"but I see a few we could knock off tonight."

"Awesome," said Max.

He was sitting cross-legged on the floor, but somehow I got the distinct impression that he was bouncing up and down.

We set about the monumental task of copying the fake deaths from Max's list onto the poster board in order of what we deemed easiest to hardest in terms of execution, though we kept Max's original numbers attached to each death. (He insisted.) There was some contention about the in-betweens, like whether asphyxiation outranked a ruptured appendix. But we unanimously agreed on the final fake death to be performed: **17. Spontaneous combustion**.

"I don't know how we'll pull it off yet," Max admitted, "but that'll be the *pièce de résistance*."

"Damn, Max," said Sanger. "I bet your accent brings all the girls to the yard."

Once we'd ranked the deaths according to difficulty, Sanger made a separate list of all the weeks between now and June 1.

"We'll split 'em up," she said. "Three new fakes a week, more or less, depending. That'll get us through the list by the time—" Sanger hesitated. I was sure she was about to sneeze, but instead she shook her head and said, "Um, by the time Max starts up school."

She clumped the first three fake deaths together and labeled them "THIS WEEK."

The deaths we'd deemed easiest to pull off were **8. Allergic reaction**, **3. Hit by a car**, and **21. Scared to death**.

"Scared to death?" I said. "Really?"

Max said, "I was scraping the bottom of the barrel at that point."

"No, it can actually happen," said Sanger. "It's the whole fight-or-flight thing. If the body produces too much adrenaline, it's, like, toxic to your organs. Terror can literally trigger a heart attack."

"Then isn't that the same as number four?" I asked. "The cardiac arrest?"

"No," said Max. "The *causes* of the heart attack are totally different."

I made a face.

"What's wrong?" Sanger poked my shoulder with her uncapped marker. Indigo ink bled into my freckled skin, but I didn't protest. Sanger and I had given each other more marker-based tattoos than I could count.

"Nothing," I said. "It's just, it makes me feel weird about people who really *do* die that way. Isn't it irreverent to fake a death like that? Maybe all the local ghosts of the people who died of heart attacks are going to haunt us."

"Local ghosts?" Max laughed. "What, as opposed to regional ghosts?"

"I sincerely hope they do," said Sanger. "I hope they haunt Max so that we can mark number twenty-one off the list all the more easily."

"We don't want Max to *actually* die," I said.

"Meh." Sanger shrugged. "He told us, he's got thick skin."

"Where's the flash button?"

"The glory of a OneStep camera, Nicks! It'll go off automatically when you snap the photo."

It was dark out. Sanger stood in the garage, flipping her key ring around her index finger, a steady *crr-link, crr-link, crr-link.*

"But remember," she said, "video first. We'll take the picture after."

I remembered. I was just asking stupid questions now, trying to delay the inevitable. Sanger was going to fake-run-over Max with her Fiat. I was going to video-record it on Max's smartphone. A part of me was thrilled by the idea. Another part of me felt ill the way I had in Mr. Palomer's driveway. The largest part of me felt like I was about to commit a crime.

Max stood a few yards from me, in the middle of the Sadler-Hamasakis' long driveway. Even in the white glow of his cell phone, I could barely make him out.

"Hang on," he said. "I'm texting Gramps. I think I'm supposed to let him know when I'm staying out."

"Your granddad texts?" I asked.

"I taught him how when I was a kid. I consider it one of my crowning achievements."

"So," I said, "why doesn't your grandfather live in Dallas?"

"Why would he?"

"Well, he's pretty old. And sick. I just wondered why he wouldn't want to live closer to family."

"I don't know," said Max. His teeth shone in the phone glow. "Actually, I do. He doesn't like my dad. He doesn't like Dallas, either. He told my mom once that he'd rather die in Austin than live in Dallas. So."

Max finished texting and handed the phone over to me.

"Honestly?" he said. "Mom doesn't like Dallas much either. I think she was happy about what happened. I mean, not that I got sliced up, but that I moved here. You know how to work that phone?"

"I'm homeschooled, not a caveman."

"Okay, okay. Just checking."

"What's your passcode?"

"Quadruple zero."

"Wow. Unbreakable."

"Yup."

I unlocked Max's phone and went to video capture. I stepped a few more paces back from the driveway. Then I waved toward the garage.

A few seconds later, Sanger shouted, "Are you guys ready or *what*?"

"I just waved at you!"

"Ooh. 'Kay. Well, take your marks."

"Does it concern you that she can't see us?" I asked Max.

"She will once the headlights are on."

The plan of action was this: Sanger would start the car. I would start the video. Then Sanger would rev the engine a couple of times and drive the car down the driveway at a speed not to exceed thirty miles per hour. Max would stand off to the side, out of the car's path, but from the camera's perspective, on the *other* side of the driveway, it would look like Max was in harm's way. Just when the car reached Max, he'd face-plant into the grass. And so, we all theorized, we would effectively fake Max's death.

Sanger had warned her moms that she was going to show off the car to Max, just so they didn't hear noises outside and call the police.

"This is your last chance to bail," I told Max.

"It's *your* last chance to bail," he replied.

Sanger started the engine. She flicked on the headlights, shooting a sudden wash of light onto the dark lawn. I could see Max now. He stood facing the car, hands shoved in his pockets. He was still standing in the middle of the driveway.

I started the video.

Sanger revved the engine a couple of times. Then she shifted the car into drive. Max was still standing smack-dab in her path.

"Max," I hissed. "What are you doing?"

Either he didn't hear me, or he chose to ignore me. My eyes flitted down the drive. The yellow Fiat was fast approaching.

"*Max.*"

A sharp staccato of honks blared from the Fiat. I wasn't sure if Sanger was doing it for dramatic effect or if she too had realized Max wasn't where he should have been. Max remained planted where he was.

The car slowed, but Sanger still drove straight ahead.

"Max!" I shouted. "What the hell are you *doing*?"

The Fiat sped closer. Closer.

Sanger slammed on the horn, one long and shrieking blast.

And Max jumped. He hurled his body out of the way, to the right side of the driveway, where we'd planned for him to stand all along. The Fiat passed, quick and solid and terrifying. I gripped the phone hard, stopped the video, and tapped the flashlight button. Then I went running, waving the light ahead of me. Max was sprawled on his back in the grass, motionless. I got on my knees. I shoved at his shoulder.

"Max," I hissed. "Hey. *Hey.* Are you okay?"

Max didn't reply.

Had he hit his head when he jumped? Had too much adrenaline shut down his vital organs—the fight-or-flight thing Sanger had been talking about earlier? My brain flipped through every possible scenario as I shoved him harder. I was vaguely aware of the sounds of Sanger cutting the engine and slamming her car door.

"Dude!" she was shouting. "Dude, *dude.* What the *hell.* I seriously could have killed you, you little turdfa— Whoa. Is he okay?"

Sanger's sneakers crunched on the dry grass as she came to a stop beside me, breathing hard.

"I don't know," I said. "He's not responding."

Max's eyes shot open. He grinned up at us both—a sinister, toothy smile. Sanger screamed. I dropped the phone on his chest.

"What was *that*?" I demanded. "God, Max, I thought you were dead!"

"Again?" he snickered.

In that moment, I experienced the instinctual feeling that must lead some people to commit crimes of passion.

Max shone the phone's flashlight in my face. "And you said you weren't empathetic."

"I'm not," I hissed. "I am *this* close to killing you for real and feeling absolutely no remorse."

"It's not authentic if I don't actually fake the death," said Max. "Anyway, I was waiting for you to take the picture."

The Polaroid. I'd completely forgotten.

"Hang on," I said.

I got up and ran to the other side of the driveway, where I'd set down the camera. I felt around blindly in the prickling grass until my knuckles rapped into something solid. I brought the camera back, hating Max all the way.

"So," I said, peering through the viewfinder, "I just take a photo of you looking dead?"

"That's the general idea," said Max.

Sanger scurried out of the shot. I focused through the lens and hooked my finger on the shoot button.

"Okay," I said. "Play dead."

Max was already back in his sprawled position, head tilted to one side. I took the shot. The flash crackled, and the camera spit out the photograph. Sanger snatched it and eagerly began waving it around.

Max came to life again and propped himself on his elbows.

"Well?" he asked.

"Let's head back to the garage," said Sanger, nodding to the Fiat. "We'll talk logistics in my room. A job well done, team."

Sanger was getting a kick out of this. Even more than usual, she seemed to enjoy listening to her own voice.

We all piled into the Fiat, and Sanger drove us back into the three-car garage. On the way, I turned on the dome light and watched the photo fully develop in my lap. I handed it over to Max when we got out. He gave it a hard looking-over.

"It's creepy as fuck," he said approvingly.

The flash had lit his limp body in the spooky way flash always hits a nighttime shot. It was extra spooky given the subject matter. I thought again about ghosts angered by Max's mockery of death. I didn't technically believe in ghosts, but it was getting late, and the chill from outside still hung on my skin. I felt better once we'd returned to the yellow warmth of Sanger's room.

With no small degree of glee, Sanger marked out **3. Hit by a car** on the poster board. I was responsible for taping the photo in the dream journal and appropriately labeling it with the number three and the day's date.

"All in a good night's work," said Sanger.

Dr. Sadler came up to the room.

"Why all the honking?" she asked. "Or do I even want to know?"

"We were just goofing off," said Sanger, smiling sweetly. "Harmless teenage stuff."

Dr. Sadler panned the room, as though assessing whether any of us looked drunk. The assessment appeared to bring back negative results. All the same, Dr. Sadler waved Max out.

"I'll show him to the orange room," she said over Sanger's protest that her mom was being uncool, "and make sure he has a toothbrush. It's after midnight, girls. Sorry."

Later, Sanger and I sat beneath her duvet eating Oreos. An eighties rom com was playing on television, the volume turned down low. That's when I told her about puking on Max. She laughed. Then came the contrition.

"Dude, if you'd told me, I wouldn't have invited him over. I thought you might just be intimidated by his good looks."

"Yeah. Well."

"He *is* fine looking, isn't he?"

"Yes," I agreed, and then I worried I'd said it too quickly. Sanger looked at me. She chewed her Oreo slowly.

"What?" I said.

I focused on the screen. The movie had cut away to a mouthwash ad.

"You like him?"

"Not as much as you do."

"What's that supposed to mean?"

I shrugged, fumbling with the plastic packaging of the Oreo container, trying to dig out one more cookie. I'd upped my insulin dose beforehand specifically with some Oreo indulgence in mind.

"You picked him up instantly," I said. "It's like, he can do no wrong in your eyes."

"Oh, come on. That's not true. His favorite composer is *John Effing Williams.*"

"You still seem to like him a lot."

"I like him because he's one of us," said Sanger. "He's a fringe schooler."

"Fringe schooler" was a term Sanger and I had invented back in middle school as a palatable alternative to the dreaded H-word. The term included not just homeschoolers but anyone who wasn't exactly in the mainstream high school scene: army brats, shy kids, artsy weirdos who went to the performing arts magnet school. Basically, any other teens on the fringe, like us.

"What?" I pounded the duvet in disbelief. "Sanger, he's *nothing* like us. He drives a fifty-thousand-dollar car. His dad's a CEO. He's one of those guys who's going to ship off to Yale and join a men's a cappella group."

"So," Sanger said slowly, "he's *rich.* Dunno if you noticed, Nicks, but I'm rich too. Doesn't make me less of a human."

"It's not that he's rich," I said, desperate. "He just—I don't know, he acts entitled. It's like he assumed I would agree to be his accomplice, or whatever. He told me I had nothing better to do as a homeschooler."

"He said that? Seriously?"

"Well. Not in so many words."

I still hadn't managed to extract an Oreo. I gave it up as a lost cause and shoved the package across the bed.

"Oh my God," Sanger said. "You're *jealous*. That's what this is. Stevie, don't be that way."

Sanger was laughing, but she'd used my first name. I knew she was serious.

"I'm not jealous," I said. "You just suddenly like him a lot. You don't suddenly like a lot of people. I mean, you used the freakin' BFF card for him."

Sanger looked at me, her eyes suddenly dim, unreadable. She said, "I didn't use it for him."

"Then why?" I asked. "Why is the list so important to you?"

Sanger shook her head. Just like that, the dimness was gone from her gaze, an easy grin back on her face. "No questions asked."

"You suck."

"Mhm. Just try to keep in mind, we're best friends. He's a guy. Sisters before misters."

"That is the stupidest phrase."

"Yeah, but it made you smile." Sanger dug an Oreo out of the package. She handed it to me. "I don't think of him that way, you know. Romantically."

"Why not?"

"Oh, so you *do* think he's attractive?"

"Fine."

"Mkay, well, agreed, but he's not my type, which is just as well."

"What's that supposed to mean?"

"Look, Nicks, if you want me to *not* be friends with Max, then—"

"No," I said quickly. "Of course not. He's cool, I guess. He just weirds me out a little."

"Um. *You* weird me out on a daily basis, Nicks. You save watersheds for fun."

We laughed it off. Sanger turned up the volume when the movie came back on, and we watched it until the end. In the movie, a girl named Andie ends up with the popular kid, Blane, who I thought was totally wrong for her. Sanger agreed that Andie should have ended up with her best friend, Duckie. She booed and threw the remaining Oreos at the screen while Blane and Andie were making out.

"Blane is an effing loser!" she shouted.

"He's not even hot!" I added. "He looks like a fish!"

"Team Duckie forever!"

"DUCKIE FOR THE WIN."

When the lights were out, and after I thought Sanger had already fallen asleep, she pressed down the bit of pillow between us.

"Maybe," she said, "Max will be your Duckie."

"Shut *up*, Sanger." I kicked her under the covers. "You're my Duckie."

"I know," said Sanger. "I just wanted to hear you say so."

Seven

The next day, I got eight more signatures on my STA petition. That sounds like a measly amount, but it took three hours of knocking on doors. Sanger lived in a neighborhood called Cedar Bend, which was more like a conglomeration of estates than an actual neighborhood. It was a good five-minute walk from one doorstep to the next.

Even though Max was now technically responsible for my fifty signatures, I still felt responsible for doing some of the work. There was nothing wrong with getting *over* fifty signatures. After all, what I cared about wasn't Leslie's Petition Challenge; it was saving Barton Springs.

Together, Sanger, Max, and I knocked on doors, and Sanger eagerly pitched the petition spiel, which was basically "Save Barton Springs or you're an evil human being with no social conscience whatsoever." We cut across lawns at first, but after our fifth stop we ran into a difficulty.

"Guys," Max said, pointing across the lawn. "Peacock sighting."

All I saw was a somewhat large, ordinary-looking bird strutting toward us.

"It's just a fat hen," I said.

"No," said Sanger. "I heard Mrs. Kemp say the Joneses own a peacock. They bring it out for pool parties."

"Is it supposed to be out of its cage?" I asked. "Does it *have* a cage? Maybe we should go back and tell the Joneses it's running wild."

I didn't particularly want to go back and tell the Joneses. Mr. Jones had answered the door but refused to sign the petition. He'd said he wouldn't for complex political reasons that we would understand when we were older.

"What, go back to that condescending douche?" Sanger said. "No way. He deserves for his precious little peacock to go missing."

"All the same," said Max, "we should steer clear of it. Peacocks can be territorial."

"And how do you know something like *that*, Maximilian?" Sanger asked.

For whatever reason, Sanger had been using Max's full name with gusto all that morning.

"My friend got attacked by one," said Max. "He was at this botanical garden in Prague. The sign said not to touch the peacocks, but he did anyway. Eventually, they had to bring in this dude with a Taser."

The peacock was getting closer, and I could now make out the vibrant blue of his breast. His telltale plumage was in hiding, and in my defense, he still looked like a large hen.

Suddenly, the peacock stopped strutting. He tilted his head. He made a howling noise. He sounded like a cat in heat.

Sanger grabbed my elbow. "Maybe Max is right. We should walk on the main road."

We veered toward the road, but there was still a lot of lawn to cover between him and us. The peacock howled again. I started snickering.

"You guys," I said, "this is so weird."

Max looked over his shoulder. "Oh my God," he said. "It's coming after us."

I thought he was just trying to scare us. Then I looked for myself. The peacock wasn't just coming after us. He was flapping out his wings and taking off from the ground.

"Oh my God," said Sanger. "Oh my God, oh my God, what do we do?"

"Maybe pick up the pace?" Max suggested.

We ran fast and hard. I sneezed three times in a row and remembered then, at the most inconvenient of times, that I hadn't taken my allergy pill that morning. When I looked over my shoulder again, the peacock was back on the ground. He had fanned out his full plumage, and he emitted the howling sound once more. It was hard to comprehend how something so beautiful could make such a horrendous noise.

We didn't stop running until we reached the cedar-lined road. There, we disintegrated into laughter. It was the hard kind of laughter—unattractive and overloud and straight from the gut.

The peacock howled again, but he had stopped his chase. He turned and strutted back in the direction of the Joneses' house.

"Can we add *that* to the list?" I asked later. "Death by peacock?"

"It's very Hitchcockian," Sanger said approvingly, "but there's no documentation. We'd have to go back, try to reenact it on camera."

"No way," said Max.

"Why not?" I said. "You stood in front of a moving vehicle last night. How's this any different?"

"Listen," said Max. "There's crazy, and then there's *crazy*. Even I know the difference."

The Drs. Sadler-Hamasaki signed the petition too. Another ten names wasn't fifty, but I felt good about them. I was also looking forward to telling Maribel the story about the peacock. She loved stupid stories like that.

On the drive back to Austin proper, we listened to a symphony so loud that the speakers shook with every pound of the timpani. The brass part was repetitive, which Max picked up on. Midway through the piece, he began doing his own rendition of the French horn. Sanger turned down the music long enough to say, "For someone as hot as you, Maximilian, you sure act like a moron."

Joel was sitting on the front lawn when we drove up to my house. He was re-netting his lacrosse stick.

"Hide your children," Sanger said. "Lacrosse season is upon us."

"Sanger," I said. "It's been upon us for months."

"Has it?"

"Yeah."

"Impossible. My douche radar hasn't been disturbed yet."

Sanger had this theory that the doucheyness of the guys at homeschool co-op spiked during spring lacrosse season. She claimed the sport brought levels of aggression and pointless competitive spirit to an all-time high, thus resulting in an excess of fights and generally douchey behavior.

She now explained the theory to Max.

"It's like summer and murder," she said. "It's a statistical fact that summer brings out more homicidal tendencies than any other season. Like, there are more murders in summer, across the board."

"Bad theory" was Max's assessment.

"How?" Sanger demanded.

"If anything, guys get their aggression fix on the field. It's catharsis. Anyway, that's kind of a sexist thing to say. It'd be like me accusing you of getting super bitchy around your period."

Sanger gasped, scandalized.

"See?" said Max. "It's offensive."

Joel had abandoned his lacrosse stick and trotted over to the car. He ducked his head through Sanger's open window, his nose dangerously close to hers. Sanger stiffened. She had a long-standing crush on Joel, and I thanked God every day that it was unrequited. It wasn't that I didn't want Sanger to be happy, or even that I wasn't okay with my best friend dating my cousin. I just knew Joel's track record. When the fallout came, Sanger wouldn't abandon me the way Val had; still, the fallout was inevitable.

"Stevieee," Joel cooed in a singsong. "You're in *trouble*."

So, Mom had finally graded my trig test. I looked at the plate of Alma's ginger cookies resting in my lap, knowing full well they wouldn't be enough to curb maternal wrath.

"Shove off," I cooed back at Joel.

He blew me a kiss. His chin grazed Sanger's cheek in the process. Sanger flinched again.

"Oops. Sorry, Sang," he said, drawing his head back out. He pointed at Max. "Yo, Max. Sorry my cousin barfed on you."

My cheeks burned. "Joel, I swear to God—"

"Heh heh heh." Joel actually articulated each "heh." On occasion, he also incorporated "LOL" and "JK" into everyday speech.

Sanger had recovered from the chin brush. Best-Friend Mode was now activated.

"Not classy," she said, shooting Joel a glare. "Do you have, like, any respect for the Cousin Code? You don't bring up her bodily functions in public."

Joel grinned the reprimand away. "Seriously, Stevie," he said. "Your mom wants you in the house. Prepare for your ass to be handed to you."

There wasn't much point in delaying my doom. Max handed me my duffel from the backseat, and I weaseled out the window in an unsightly, midriff-baring way.

"See you, guys," I said, knowing that I definitely wouldn't see them for the coming week at least. Getting my ass handed to me by Mom meant an all-stops-out grounding. Sanger would have to rearrange her poster board schedule. That, or she would have to induce a fake allergic reaction and a heart attack all on her own.

From the doorstep, I saw that Joel had commandeered Max's attention. He was using grandiose hand gestures and talking in his good ol' boy voice—the one that melted co-op instructors' hearts to margarine and won him an endless string of dates. I knew precisely what Joel was up to. The lacrosse team was short a decent man on the field. Max didn't attend a private or public school yet, so he was fair game for the co-op's league. Joel was recruiting.

I wondered if Max would say yes. He seemed like the type.

Mom's smackdown was a dose of the usual. I got one of these about twice a year, whenever I bombed a test or majorly slacked off on my chores. It wasn't that Mom wanted me to be perfect; she just had certain expectations, she explained to me, and missing every single question on a twenty-question test didn't meet those expectations. I understood. I didn't blame Mom, even though I was currently angry with her for revoking all Internet privileges and my right to leave the house outside of co-op.

"I can't help that I'm stupid at math," I argued, even though I knew it was a terrible excuse and factually untrue. I was mediocre at math, but I could've pulled out a B on that test if I'd actually studied instead of spending a full Saturday with Sanger at Barton Springs.

Mom didn't take my bullshit.

"You're perfectly capable," she said, folding her hands on the breakfast room table. She was in the process of coloring her hair its original brunette, and the stink of hair dye filled the room. "I'm not the Bad Guy here. If you can't discipline yourself to study, I'll take away the distractions."

We'd had this conversation several times before, but Mom still used that "discipline" argument like it was fresh and evocative. She gave me a chance to calm down and think "Oooh, yeah. She's right. I suck at self-discipline." I took the expected amount of time to calm down and contemplate my deficiencies as a sixteen-year-old.

"Do I at least get to eat supper?"

"Save the attitude, Stevie. Of course you get supper. Now, go to your room and open that trig book. If you have problems, your father is in the shop."

When Dad wasn't on the job as a landscaper, he could usually be found in a shed out back that he'd converted into a carpentry shop. Over the years, he'd produced an impressive series of Christmas gifts, including my desk chair.

I knew better than to bother Dad in the shed. Of course he couldn't explicitly tell me "No, Stevie, I don't want to help you with cosines because I'm working on a bookshelf," but he could grunt a lot and get impatient with me and keep glancing over at his tools in a longing way.

I free-fell onto my bed with a defeated *thump*. It took me a full five minutes to work up the willpower to move again. I retrieved my trig textbook from my desk and plopped it on the bed. A highlighter, pencil, and scratch pad at the ready, I set to work trying to comprehend the mysteries of the mathematical universe.

An hour and a half later, I allowed myself the luxury of checking my phone. There was a text from Sanger and, surprisingly, one from Valerie. I checked Val's first, curious to see if she was trying to make nice.

Btw, I don't want you coming to my bday party.

Nope. Definitely not making nice.

I'd forgotten that Val's birthday was the next week. I hadn't even bought her a gift or card yet. I deleted the text. Then, after a moment's thought, I went into my contacts and erased Valerie Borkowski from existence. Over the past few days, hindsight had clued me in to the fact that Val hadn't been such a great friend anyway. Now that she and I weren't talking, I remembered it was Val who always insisted on choosing the movie we saw at the dollar theater and Val who commandeered our conversations to talk about her most recent crush and Val who overdramatically yawned every time I brought up STA. I wasn't missing out on a whole bunch now that Valerie was out of my life, and I doubted she felt much of a loss either. Things might be a little awkward at co-op when I saw her around, but I'd get past it, just the same as I did with all Joel's ex-lovers.

In need of a pick-me-up, I checked Sanger's text.

What's the prognosis?

A week, I texted back.

Then I began unpacking my duffel, anticipating that Sanger's reply would take a while. I set her dream journal on my nightstand and placed the Polaroid camera on top. I looked at them for a little while, just looked, and recalled the events of the past twenty-four hours.

It had been *fun.* Really fun. The kind of fun Sanger and I had on our best weekends. I thought about what Sanger had said on the drive home, about Max being a nutter despite his hotness. I thought maybe she was right. And if Sanger was right, maybe Max really did qualify for the ranks of a fringe schooler. He was strange enough to have twenty-three fake-death wishes. Maybe he'd be strange enough to want to date a homeschooler who was bad at trig. Maybe he'd kiss me. Maybe it'd get really out of control one night, and we'd do it here, on my bed, while my parents were gone.

I wasn't exactly proud of that thought process, but it processed in just that way.

Fifteen minutes later, Sanger texted back.

Sanger: *through next saturday?*

Me: *yes*

Sanger: *But. Butbutbut death pact!!*

Me: *It's not a death pact. Don't call it that.*

Sanger: *You have to find a way around it. We have a strict schedule to keep.*

Me: *K, YOU* convince my mom

Sanger: *Tell her you have a rally; she loves your activism.*

Me: *Ha. Ha.*

Mom did not love my activism. Neither of my parents did. I mentioned earlier that while I'm a solid Normal Type, the parents are kind of borderline Blue-Jean Jumper. Like, Dad's parents were these really straightlaced puritans who didn't let him go to prom because, the horror, there was dancing involved. I don't think he ever shook that, and both he and Mom tend to be a little—*stuffy* about things. When I first told them I'd be working with STA, Dad made this fuss about it and said how people who campaigned for that sort of thing were just jobless, starving artists who spent their time getting stoned, and he didn't want his daughter hanging around "that set." Now, *that's* what Sanger would call otherist. Mom eventually convinced him to ease up, but I knew she wasn't particularly enthused about me holding poster boards downtown. That's not the sort of extracurricular a borderline Blue-Jean Jumper wants for her kid.

After three minutes, Sanger texted back.

You're at least coming to co-op, right?

I got tired of waiting for Sanger's texts. I called her.

"'Sup," she greeted.

"You are *so slow*."

"Cut me some slack. I'm driving."

"Sanger!"

"Whaaa."

"Just be careful," I said. "You don't want your last words to be 'LMAO.'"

"Maybe I do, Nicks. Maybe I want those very letters carved into my headstone." There was rustling on the other line. Then, "Hang on a sec."

I chipped at my nail polish as I listened to Sanger's transaction with a drive-through attendant. She came back on after paying for a double bacon cheeseburger.

"I'm rude," she said, as though I didn't already know. "Where were we?"

"Don't text and drive."

"Yes, thanks for the PSA. So, did you check out that Max and Joel action earlier? It looks like the Wolverines have got themselves another man."

"Wait. He really convinced Max to join the team?"

"It's Joel. You think Max withstood his mad powers of persuasion?"

"Probably not," I admitted.

"So this burger is getting cold and I don't want to gross you out with my moist chewing sounds. Mind if I hang up and eat?"

"No." I sounded pretty dejected.

"Chin up, Nicks. Everyone gets grounded."

This was an insensitive thing for Sanger to say. She'd never been grounded in her life.

Eight

When I was eight years old, I had my own near-death experience.

It was late May, one Monday after co-op. Sanger had come home with me to play. We were sitting in my backyard, in the hammock, our weight pulling us together and mushing our shoulders in a mix of sunscreen (mine) and sweat (ours).

Mom had sent us outside with juice boxes and a package of strawberry licorice. We giggled and ate and compared knee bruises. Then Sanger started tickling me. I laughed at first, and then my laughs grew weak, and then I passed out.

I don't remember what happened next, of course, but apparently Sanger started screaming bloody murder. She ran inside and got my mom. I was rushed to the hospital, and the nurses and doctors did their magic. I was released from the ER late that night.

After that, I underwent several tests involving needles and lived in a general state of terror. I was only eight. I had never, ever before faced the idea of my own mortality. And just like that, I became convinced that I was going to die.

A week after the trip to the ER, a bearded doctor sat down with my parents and me in a small, sterile hospital room and officially diagnosed me with type 1 diabetes. His beside manner sucked. My parents kept asking him to clarify words, and he kept telling them they wouldn't become diabetes experts overnight, as though that was a cutesy, solve-all line. After we left the doctor's, I still thought I was going to die. I cried a lot. I began having night terrors. My parents explained to me over and over again that yes, I'd have to get used to shots, but no, I wasn't going to kick the bucket.

I eventually pretended to believe them, but for a long time I thought they were hiding something from me and that one day soon I was going to pass out again, just like I had in the hammock, only this time I wouldn't wake up. My sleep pattern didn't return to normal until I was nine.

Sanger had it rough too. Both my parents and hers explained what had happened that afternoon in the hammock, but Sanger still believed she had been personally responsible for almost killing me. She never tickled me again.

When I was eleven, I started to give myself my own insulin shots. I made up a scenario where I was one of the mutant kids from X-Men. I had the ability to catch fire and destroy everything in my wake, and the only thing that could keep my abilities under control was insulin. Each time I gave myself a shot, I told myself I was taming the beast within and protecting humanity from myself.

On co-op Mondays, I had to excuse myself from the lunch table and give myself the shot in the bathroom, just so I wouldn't gross anyone out. I felt proud about it, especially after one of the older guys said he was afraid of needles.

"You just get used to them," I said, sage that I was. "It's a way of life."

I thought I was pretty hot shit back then.

Still, it was better than believing my death was imminent or fixating on the fact that unlike the other kids, I had to prick my finger every day and make regular trips to an endocrinologist.

I went through the Unfair Phase when I was fourteen. Why was I the one cursed with a lifelong disease? Why did I have to go around attached to a pump? (The pump stage didn't last long; I begged to go back to injections after a year of feeling like I was half-robot.) Why did I have to explain, whenever someone pointed out I wasn't fat, that being fat or skinny had nothing to do with type 1 diabetes?

I came to terms with it by sophomore year. This is how I reasoned it: Some kids are born with bad teeth. Some kids are born with bad eyes or bad lungs or bad coordination. I was born with a bad pancreas, and I could have been born with something a lot worse. I wasn't particularly lucky, but I wasn't particularly unlucky, either. And I just had to be okay with that.

Mom announced my grounding during supper, for Dad's benefit. He gave me an unsmiling look, which I took to be paternal disappointment. I nodded, properly chastised, and kept forking at my salad.

Midway through supper, I announced that I'd gone door-to-door that morning and obtained ten more signatures on the STA petition. For some reason, I thought this would serve as a blow to Mom. Like, "See why your daughter didn't get a perfect trig score? She was too busy caring about the environment and being an involved citizen. Now, don't you feel bad for grounding her." But even after the big news, Mom continued to look unaffected by my plight.

Joel announced he'd recruited a new member for the co-op's lacrosse team. I pretended to not care, even when Joel kicked me under the table.

"Come on, Stevie," he said. "I know you've been dying to see Garza in uniform."

I shrugged. "I didn't know he played."

"Well, he doesn't play, *technically*, but he's got the build for it, and he looks like he'll be fast on the field. The best part is that he's fair game. No school affiliation. The place he's going this summer doesn't have a team, so that could mean he's ours indefinitely."

"Congratulations," said Dad.

Joel beamed. "We've been short a decent midfielder for a month, ever since Rob Perry broke his ankle. We're going up against Austin Christian next month, so we're going to need all the help we can get."

Austin Christian was the biggest private school in the region and *the* team to beat in the Austin Area Private School Division. Their lacrosse team had slaughtered ours for five years running. It was possible Max wouldn't help the team, but it was impossible for him to hurt it.

After supper, I returned to the temporary prison that was my bedroom. I was so over trig for the day. I turned on *Gilmore Girls* and punched the volume down to the lowest tick in case Mom walked by and deemed watching DVDs too much fun for a grounding.

I tugged Sanger's dream journal from my nightstand and turned to the only marked page. The photograph of Max's limp body looked even creepier than it had the night before.

I found myself wondering what it would be like if someone discovered the book, not knowing the context. They'd probably turn me in to the police. Maybe, I decided, it wasn't a good idea to leave the journal out in plain sight. I opened the nightstand drawer and shoved the journal inside, then covered it up with a couple crumpled receipts.

I fell asleep fully clothed. When I woke, Snoops, my stuffed elephant, was stained with lipstick and a dewy patch of drool.

I thought I'd woken myself up, but when I pushed into a back stretch, I found Sanger staring at me through my bedside window. I didn't scream, but a paralyzing shot of adrenaline sizzled through my veins. When I recovered, I opened the window.

"You scared me half to death," I hissed.

"That was the general idea," said Sanger. She climbed into the room with a backpack slung over her shoulder.

"You *cannot* stay over."

Sanger swung the backpack onto my bed. She began unzipping it. "Your mom never said you couldn't have friends over, did she?"

I thought about this. "It was implied."

"Well, it doesn't even matter. I'm not staying over."

She started pulling things out of the bag: a flashlight, a black fleece blanket, a rubber mask.

I picked up the mask and turned its cut-out eyes toward Sanger. "Abraham Lincoln?"

"This one's even better," she said, pulling out another mask.

I couldn't quite place the face.

"Ummm," I said. "George Bush?"

"Prince Charles. Get the Polaroid."

I put the pieces together. "Scaring to death?"

Sanger grinned. "Scaring to death. Do you know which bedroom window is Max's?"

"Um, no. Sanger, I'm not sure this is a good idea tonight."

"It is an *excellent* idea tonight," Sanger retorted, her voice turning muffled as she pulled the Prince Charles mask over her head. "I thought about it, and I'm not gonna let your grounding stand in the way of our schedule."

"I think this is your bacon cheeseburger talking."

"Is that a fat joke?"

"No."

"Then put on your mask, Abe."

"But," I said, "I have no idea which room is Max's. And if my parents see me out—"

"They won't."

"Yeah, but if we're going to scare Max, it's going to make a lot of noise."

"You mean, *he's* going to make a lot of noise," Sanger said, drumming her fingers together. "He is going to go soprano. He's going to wet himself."

"I hope not. That would be embarrassing for everyone."

"Stop stalling, Nicks. We'll make this quick. I'll scout the perimeter first. Then, if it's all clear, I'll come back for you. Your primary responsibility is documentation. Your secondary, scaring."

"Sanger—"

"BYE."

She climbed out my window and disappeared into the night. Once she was gone, I realized I'd sounded like a whiny little kid. I told myself to buck up. All I was doing was sneaking out a mere house away. My parents could have *such* a worse kid. I could be shooting heroin or sneaking into clubs with a fake ID or having unprotected sex. I was one of the best kids a parent could ask for, and if I wanted to put on an Abraham Lincoln mask and scare the living daylights out of my next-door neighbor, then so help me, I was going to do it without whining.

I put on the mask. By the time Sanger returned, I was a new woman, ready to taste the sweet fruits of rebellion.

"Did you find him?" I asked.

"Back patio door," said Sanger. "He's playing guitar. Did you know he played guitar?"

"I've known him for two days, Sanger."

"Mhm. Well, thank God he was doing something G-rated."

"You're nasty."

"Guys are nastier," she said. "Got the Polaroid?"

I held up the camera.

"Excellent. If we play our cards right, this photo could be priceless."

I checked the clock. It was after eleven, which meant Mr. Palomer was probably asleep. I hoped he wouldn't wake up at the sound of his grandson's screams. I really didn't want to accidentally kill that poor man.

Sanger draped the black fleece blanket around her shoulders and pinned two corners at her throat with a jumbo safety pin.

"To add to the air of mystery," she explained. She shoved the flashlight back into the bag. "We won't need that after all. Ready?"

"Should I be wearing black?" I asked.

I was wearing shorts and a camisole. One cup of my orange bra was peeking out from the camisole lace. I adjusted the straps and tugged the neckline higher.

"You look fine," Sanger said. "Very hot. I mean, if Max is a leg guy, whoo-*whoo*."

I looked at my legs. I hadn't shaved in three days. My thighs were a war zone of brunette stubble.

Sanger climbed back out the window, and I followed her like a pro. I had practice from all my Fiat gymnastics.

Unlike Sanger's neighborhood, the space between houses here was minuscule. Dad sometimes joked that if a house twelve doors down caught fire, we would all go up in a blaze within the hour.

The Palomer house was, like ours, a seventies-style ranch. Mom had updated our place as best she could; she'd painted the trim and bought new shutters back when I was in sixth grade. Dad always kept the garden looking classy and well groomed. Mr. Palomer's place, on the other hand, still looked like something straight out of *The Brady Bunch*. The front door and shutters were all a peeling, tangerine color. Bordering the driveway was a long wall built from concrete flowers. I could only guess that this had been a "groovy" structure back in the day. At present, the wall served as a cover for Sanger and me as we rounded the driveway to the backyard. We crossed through Mr. Palomer's succulent garden and sneaked up to the brick patio.

Sanger waved for me to stop. She crouched behind the corner of the house that bordered the patio, where we could see through the patio door without being seen back. Light flooded out, illuminating the figure of Max inside. He sat on green shag carpet, strumming an acoustic guitar. It was all just as Sanger had reported.

"The attack has to be practically instantaneous," Sanger whispered, readjusting her mask so that the mouth hole was better aligned. "The moment we leave this cover, we'll be visible, and scaring a person to death is, of course, all about the element of surprise."

"So," I said, "we run toward the patio door as fast as we can?"

It seemed like a weak plan of attack, but my heart was hammering in my chest all the same.

"Yeah, that's all I got," Sanger admitted. "Only *I* run up to the door, just me, while you sneak behind. I'll pound on the glass and, like, make Freddy Krueger noises. You'll be there to take a picture of Max's reaction. It should be enough to scare him but not freak him out so bad that he calls the cops. He'll figure out it's us right away."

"You mean," I said, "right after we scare him to death."

"Precisely. Okay. Ready?"

I made sure the Polaroid's Velcro strap was snug across my hand.

"Ready."

Sanger made a run for it. I bounded after her, trying to remain in the shadows, preparing the camera for action. Sanger pounded her fists against the glass door and howled like a lunatic. Max threw his guitar from his lap. Horror was carved deep into his face as he did a fumbling, backward crab walk.

"Take it, Nicks!" Sanger yelled.

Hastily, I peered through the viewfinder and ran forward a few steps to get a closer shot. I took the photograph, the Polaroid wheezed, and just as it did, I lost my footing and careened to the ground.

Pain burst in my knees. The heel of my hand skidded across rough brick. My other hand lost hold of the camera, and it went toppling in a series of *clunks*. For just a moment, all was very still. Then Sanger was by my side, helping me sit up, shouting at the sight of blood.

"Arghhh!" Her voice was hoarse. "Arghhh, where is all the blood coming from?"

I pointed. Both my knees were skinned badly. Blood trickled down my right leg. I looked at my hand. It was chafed, but the skin wasn't broken.

A cold blast of air hit me. Max had opened the patio door. "Stevie? Sanger?"

"I'm okay," I said. "I'm fine, I'm fine."

To prove that I was, in fact, fine, I started to get to my feet.

"You're bleeding, though," said Max, offering me a hand.

I accepted the help, and Max pulled me up like I weighed no more than an empty milk carton. His hand was cold and dry. And missing two fingers.

"Really," I said, struggling to peel off my mask, "I'm totally fine."

I removed Abraham Lincoln's face with a grunt of satisfaction, glad to be free of the humid close quarters and the pungent smell of rubber. My peripheral vision restored, I noticed the Polaroid lying at the far end of the patio. I retrieved it. Gingerly, I turned it over in my hands, preparing myself for some sign of irreparable damage. But as far as I could tell, the camera was miraculously unscathed. The photo was at my feet. I picked it up, flipped it over, and shook out the developing image.

"Camera's okay too," I said, rejoining the others. "See? So everything's good. I'm just an idiot." ˙

Sanger, who had chosen to remain in her Prince Charles mask, heaved a sigh.

"Thank God. That camera's an old present from a friend that I really, *really* care about."

I grinned at Sanger.

"You guys are insane," said Max.

"You're welcome," said Sanger. She grabbed the photo from me, took a look, and cackled. "Nicks, this is perfect. Totally worth the sacrifice of a good knee."

It *was* a perfect picture. Even I was surprised by how well it had turned out, considering the total lack of coordination that followed it. I'd caught Max mid-crab-walk, every edge of his face pulled back in pure terror.

"What a fun way to die," I said.

"Not nearly as fun as I thought it'd be. My heart. Ugh. My *heart*." Max clutched dramatically at the vital organ, then stooped, his hands on his knees. "You could've warned me."

"You wouldn't have been scared if you saw us coming."

"Yeah," said Sanger. "And we saw what an adrenaline junkie you were last night. Figured you could take it."

Max straightened back up. "It's just—you can't show those photos to anyone else, okay? Or sell them to the press. Or put them online."

"I make no such promises," I said, tucking the photo under my bra strap.

It was probably the most scandalous thing I'd ever done. Max smirked at me. I blushed.

"Anyway," said Sanger, "we had to bring the party to you because Nicks got herself grounded."

"What?" Max laughed in disbelief. "What do homeschoolers have to do to get grounded, watch cable on a Sunday?"

"I'm failing trig," I said.

"But you're *homeschooled*," said Max. "How can you fail anything?"

"Yo, Twenty Questions," said Sanger, snapping her fingers in Max's face. "She's bleeding out. Do you have paper towels? A Band-Aid?"

My right leg looked a lot worse than it felt. The entire lower half of it was coated in streaks of sticky blood. It resembled something that belonged on a hook in a slaughterhouse.

"So you practically break into my house," said Max, "and then you demand first aid for damages incurred while breaking into my house?"

"She can't very well sneak back into her bedroom bleeding on everything," said Sanger. "How's she supposed to explain that to her parents? 'Sorry, Mom. I scraped both of my knees by falling out of bed'?"

"Just hang on," said Max. "I don't know where anything is in this house."

He went inside and disappeared down a hallway. Sanger turned to me with triumph in her eyes.

"Two down," she said.

"Two down," I replied.

"Really, sorry you fell."

"All for the cause."

Max came back out with a roll of toilet paper, a bottle of hydrogen peroxide, and a giant fabric Band-Aid. I put them all to good use. Before I could stop him, Max gathered the trash, blood-soaked toilet paper included.

"Oh. Gross. You don't have to touch that," I said.

Max shrugged. "You don't have diseases, do you?"

"Unless you count diabetes."

Max raised a brow. "Really. I thought only fat, old people got that."

"You're so otherist," Sanger told him.

"What does that—?"

Sanger raised a hand to silence him. "No time for chitchat. Nicks here has gotta get to the home base before the parental unit gets savvy."

Sanger sounded like she was trying to imitate a character from a movie. It wasn't worth telling her she sounded ridiculous.

"How long are you grounded?" Max asked.

A week, I told him. Then Sanger and I got up to leave. Max caught me by the elbow. It wasn't a creepy grab or anything. It was more like a brush, because his fingers fell away the moment I turned.

"So," he said, "maybe I could have your number? You know, in case I get any bright ideas about the list and want to text you?"

I had no idea why I said what I said next. Maybe it was slipping that photograph into my bra strap that gave me the boldness.

"If you want to get ahold of me, I'm just next door."

I smiled pleasantly at him. Then I turned and crossed the yard.

It wasn't until we were back in my bedroom that Sanger let out a low whistle.

"Playing hard to get, are we?" she asked.

"What? *No*."

I really hadn't intentionally played hard to get. I'd just said what I'd said without half knowing why I'd said it.

Sanger unpinned her makeshift fleece cape. She rolled it up and stuffed it into her backpack, along with the masks.

"He really likes you," she said.

"He just asked for my number, that's all."

"No, no," said Sanger. "He asked for your number *after* you barfed onto his person. And after he cleaned up your *blood*. Your very blood, Stevie. *Your diabetic blood.* Oh. He is into you. That's basically true love."

"There's no such thing as diabetic blood," I said. "And he's just desperate for friends right now. He told me so himself."

"Or desperate for *luuurve*."

I smacked Sanger. I'd been aiming for her shoulder, but she moved, and I ended up hitting her chest.

Sanger froze. "Girl, did you just punch me in the boob?"

"Oops," I said, smiling. "And look, Max is not into me. Even if he was, did you hear all that crap he was saying? 'Durh, you're homeschooled. Har, har.' 'Ooh, aren't all diabetics fat? Har, har.'"

"You sound like Homer Simpson," said Sanger, "not Max Garza. And yeah, he's otherist, but you can always cure otherism if said otherist is malleable. Max is totally malleable. You know why? Because he *wants* you."

"Well, I don't know if *I* want *him*," I said.

It was the truth. I'd never come close to dating a boy before. I'd never met a boy I even remotely *wanted* to date before. It was pretty slim pickings at the homeschool co-op. I didn't know how I was supposed to be feeling. In the past couple of days I had been around Max, I'd spent half the time willing him to look at me and half the time freaking out when he did.

Was that what *wanting* a boy looked like?

Sanger shouldered her backpack. She gave a long-suffering sigh and trudged to the window.

"Just figure it out, okay?" she said, climbing outside.

"Figure out what?"

Her disembodied voice slipped in from the thick darkness outside, like a ghost's.

"What you want."

Nine

There were a ton of overachievers at homeschool co-op. I was not one of them. I was a solidly average Normal Type. I didn't sass the teachers, and I turned in my assignments on time. I wasn't elected to student council, but I wasn't pond scum either. That would suck pretty bad, to be pond scum in the *homeschool* hierarchy. Most of those types belonged to the Last-Chance Charlie category. One of them, a senior named Lacey Edmonson, had gotten pregnant a year earlier. The leadership board met with her and her mother one Monday, and after that Lacey didn't show up at co-op again. Ever.

The "leadership board" was really just a group of five homeschool moms who'd agreed to do administrative grunt work. They all went to the same church, and their children were mostly teenagers who had formed an incestuous friend group that ran through more intergroup-dating permutations than a CW show. The leadership-board kids were the upper echelon of the co-op's high school crowd. Valerie Borkowski was one of them. Joel was part of the upper stratum because of his charming personality. Now that he and Valerie had split, however, there was bound to be some division in the ranks.

Not that I really cared how it panned out. The only person at co-op I liked unreservedly was Sanger. Since fourth grade, she and I had registered to be in all the same classes together, right down to the last period.

Junior year, our schedule started with art class. The whole idea of co-op was for students to learn supplementary subjects and extracurriculars their parents had no clue how to teach. So, for example, if your parents didn't have a creative bone in their bodies, you could take an art class from Mrs. Hernandez, who was a famous local sculptor. Co-op was also a place for group activities you couldn't do at home unless you belonged to one of those families with eleven siblings. We had a choir, drama club, dance team, yearbook committee, student council, and, of course, sports teams.

I had registered for art because Sanger wanted to take the class. For me, Mrs. Hernandez's studio was a chance to prove to myself, once and for all, that I sucked at art in all its sundry mediums. Sanger returned the favor by enduring a community service class two periods later, which I liked but she didn't; she called it the Bleeding Heart Hour.

Anyway, that day in art class we were doing charcoal drawings. I'd forgotten my acid-free notebook, so Sanger tore out one of her own sheets for me to use. We worked as Mrs. Hernandez proctored the room and answered questions, making vaguely encouraging comments like, "Excellent strokes" and "Good method!" Once, Sanger had told me that all of Mrs. Hernandez's comments could be translated to a sexual context. I'd never been able to hear them the same way after that. Occasionally, when Mrs. Hernandez said something like, "Keep doing what you're doing!" Sanger and I would both burst into hiccuping laughter.

When it came to my work, which I knew was invariably bad, Mrs. Hernandez would still say something nice like, "That's a unique perspective, Stevie." Sometimes I wished she'd just say, "I've seen drunk chimpanzees create better art with their toes, Stevie." I preferred honesty, even if it was brutal. Maybe that's why Sanger made for such a good friend.

"What happened to you?" Sanger asked me, focusing on the bowl of fruit in the middle of the table, which we were supposed to magically replicate using nothing but a stick of charcoal and our boundless talent. "You totally fell off the grid. You haven't been answering any of my texts."

"My mom must have heard me talking to you Saturday night," I said, "because she decided it wasn't a true grounding unless she confiscated the phone."

"Sad."

I'd been trying to draw an apple stem for five minutes straight. It looked a lot like a stem, actually, but then, it's pretty hard to screw up an apple stem.

"Maybe you should attach some fruit to that," Sanger suggested.

"Yeah," I said, but I didn't. I just stared at the paper, not wanting to ruin it with any further marks.

When I looked up, I hooked eyes with the girl sitting across from us. It was Jessica Parrish.

"Hey," I said.

I tipped forward in my chair to get a better look at her drawing. Jessica had started with the fruit bowl, which was probably a better approach.

"That looks good," I said conversationally.

"Oh. *Oh!*" Jessica looked down at her artwork as though surprised by its existence, as though it wasn't the whole focus of our hour-long class.

"Just wait," said Sanger. "Mrs. H is going to come over here and tell you that you have a 'good method.'"

She winked at Jessica.

Jessica just sat there, looking like a petrified kitten. She didn't seem to know what to do with Sanger. I didn't blame her; most adults didn't know what to do with Sanger either.

"So," I said, drawing Jessica's fearful gaze back to me, "are you going to submit anything to the exhibit?"

At the end of May, the co-op held an exhibit of science fair projects and artwork and photography and other student-generated content, like haikus. There was also something called Senior Showcase, where each of the dozen or so graduating high school seniors put together a triptych poster presentation of all their greatest accomplishments—ribbons, medals, pictures with friends and family, the acceptance letter to their top-choice college. Later that night, after the exhibit, there was a big assembly. The elementary and middle school kids put on a musical, and the high school drama club performed a series of skits. The whole night was supposed to be a Look How Far We've Come celebration, but it usually just made me feel like a total failure who wasn't doing enough with her free time.

"I won't be there," Jessica said. "I'll be in Oklahoma visiting family."

"But you could still have your work on display," I said, "even if you aren't there."

Jessica smiled unenthusiastically. It was tough work, trying to keep up normal human interaction with the girl. I wasn't sure why I'd tried talking to her in the first place, but I decided to give up the effort and finally add an apple to that stem of mine. Somehow, the apple turned out boxy. In the end, it looked more like a wedge of cheese with a toothpick poking out the top.

Sanger and I were partners in chem lab. Dr. Hampstead, our teacher, was a professor at Austin Community College, but he also homeschooled his two sons. As a favor to the homeschool populace, he'd offered to teach chemistry to those of us who couldn't replicate a lab experience at our kitchen counter. Every Monday, he managed to turn a Central Methodist Sunday school classroom into a decently equipped lab.

This particular Monday, Dr. Hampstead had brought in three centrifuges and a bunch of test tubes. We were going to centrifuge peanut butter, he explained, and analyze its various components. Because there were only three centrifuges, and because Dr. Hampstead could only stagger our experiment phases so much, we had to combine lab partners to form groups of four. And so it came to pass that Sanger and I were forced to join up with Aaron Weiss, son of the leadership board's recently elected president, and none other than Valerie Borkowski.

"Mergh," I groaned for only Sanger to hear, watching Aaron and Val's ominous approach to our table. "Where's the hydrochloric acid when you need it?"

"Aaron and I have discussed it," said Valerie even before she took a seat, "and we think it'll be more efficient to split up the experiment. He and I will do the centrifuging, and you two can record the data."

She delivered this line entirely to Sanger.

"Dr. Hampstead said we had to do the full experiment together," said Sanger. "Didn't he, Stevie?"

"He won't know the difference," said Aaron.

What Aaron meant was that his mom was president of the leadership board and Dr. Hampstead would therefore turn a blind eye to any disobedience at our table.

"Damn, Weiss," Sanger said. "You're gonna make a great politician one day. Like daddy, like son."

Aaron's dad was a state representative. I knew from research that he'd voted against the bill Springs for Tomorrow Alliance was now working so hard to get passed in the Senate.

"At least I *have* a dad."

Aaron said it under his breath, as an aside to Val. Valerie promptly chuckled, and I pondered briefly why I was ever friends with her. No wonder she was Joel's shortest relationship to date.

"Oooh, burn," said Sanger. "Good one, homophobe. What, are my mommies going to hell?"

I placed a hand on Sanger's wrist, out of sight, under the table.

She knew as well as I did that Aaron was just trying to get a rise out of her.

Usually, the homeschool community was a welcoming place. Most of us knew what it was like to be the odd one out. We were a bunch of freaks from all walks of life, with as many backgrounds as there were families and as many reasons for homeschooling as there were kids. It followed that given our diversity, we would be open-minded. And most homeschoolers I knew were.

But there was this certain offshoot. There were some who, like Jessica, protested in front of the capitol that the earth was only six thousand years old and that anyone who believed otherwise was an amoral pagan. Sanger and I called this faction of the co-op MURICA. It was composed primarily of Blue-Jean Jumpers, but also some Normal Types.

Aaron, for example, was for all intents and purposes a Normal Type. He was an only child, he watched MTV, and he was captain of the co-op's lacrosse team. He was usually on good terms with me. Not that we ever hung out or anything, but I'd never sensed that he actively disliked me until now. Apparently, Val had won him over to the Dark Side after the Joel breakup.

Aaron scratched his buzz cut and said, "I didn't say anyone was going to hell."

I unscrewed the peanut butter lid and began lining up test tubes and measuring instruments.

"We need a pipette," I announced, in an attempt to change the conversation.

No one paid heed to our lack of pipette.

"You're kidding me," Sanger said to Aaron. "You mean you're not God?"

"All I'm saying," said Aaron, "is that your parents should've met with the board way earlier. Mom says there have been complaints for years."

At this point, even I forgot about the pipette.

"What are you talking about?" I asked Aaron.

"Sanger's parents are talking to the leadership board today," he said. "About the complaints."

"What complaints?"

"It's nothing," Sanger said. I watched her carve her name into the upper right-hand corner of her assignment paper. Her pencil lead snapped on the first *a* of "Hamasaki."

"It's nothing," she repeated. "Aaron's just being a supreme douchebag."

She fixed Aaron with a tight smile. He crossed his arms and leaned back in his folding chair. On the wall just above his head, a series of primary-color cut-out letters read: PROVER S 3:5. The *B* had come loose and fallen to the linoleum tile floor. I wondered what Proverbs 3:5 said. I hoped it was something like, "Thou shalt not be an asshole, nor let thy hateful attitude smellest up the land."

Sanger hadn't told me anything about her moms meeting with the leadership board, but maybe she'd just learned about it. Maybe that was what she'd been texting me about the day before, after Mom confiscated my phone. Whatever the case, I wasn't going to get any real information from her until we were out of lab.

"I guess *I'll* get a pipette," I said, shoving back from the table.

The experiment was rough going. Val wouldn't talk to me, and Sanger wouldn't talk to Aaron. It was like one of those convoluted team-building camp games, where one teammate looks at a hidden picture, then runs across a field and describes the picture to their teammate, using nothing but hand gestures. Inevitably, important stuff gets lost in translation. We eventually ended up doing close to what Val initially suggested: Sanger and I worked out the calculations while Aaron and Val handled the test tubes and measurements.

I tried to make nice with Aaron, just once, at the height of the experiment's awkwardness, when Sanger and I had done all the number work we could.

"I heard you all found a new player for the team," I said.

I conveniently left out the fact that Joel had been the one to find Max Garza and recommend him to Coach Whitt.

"Doubtful" was Aaron's reply. "He's never picked up a lacrosse stick in his life, from what I've heard. Though lack of talent hasn't kept plenty of *other* people from making the team."

That was a low blow, and unfounded. I knew for a fact that Joel had the best offensive record on the team. I didn't say that, though. My aim had been to diffuse the tension, not start another fight.

"Have you ever asked Joel about his other hobbies?"

I shot my head up to see that it was, indeed, Val who had asked the question and who was now impatiently waiting for an answer, drumming her pink-polished fingernails on the table.

"Uh, hello to you too," I said.

I returned my attention to the worksheet, even though it was already complete.

"Well," Val said, "*have you?*"

I set down my pencil. I folded my hands.

"I don't grill my cousin on his extracurricular activities."

"Really?" said Val. "Like, you don't know anything about his letter-writing skills? His pen pals? It's really fascinating. You should ask him about it."

I gave Val a weird look. Pen pals? What the hell was she talking about? And how was this in any way relevant to centrifuging?

"Yeah, okay, whatever."

Sanger was looking at Val strangely too. "Are you high?" she asked.

That's when Dr. Hampstead clapped his hands together— our equivalent of a school bell—and dismissed class. Sanger and I turned in our assignments and headed down the hallway toward the exit, out of earshot from Val and Aaron. We pushed through the double doors that led to the church parking lot. A humid breeze tickled my arms and blew back my bangs.

"Sometimes," said Sanger, "I think Dr. Hampstead is an agent of the underworld, sent to torment us."

Sanger, I knew, was expecting me to smile at that. I didn't.

"Why didn't you tell me?" I asked. "About your moms and the leadership board?"

Sanger squinted toward the horizon. She kept walking.

"Yeah, it's not a big deal."

"It's a big enough deal for Aaron to be an ass about it."

"Aaron is an ass about everything."

We stopped at a concrete median, waited for a minivan to pass, then continued our walk toward the large stretch of grass that bordered the parking lot. The field was church property, bought with the intention of Central Methodist's continued growth into megachurch status. For now, it was only a field, and the church allowed the co-op to use it for lacrosse practices and matches.

Coach Whitt was already on the field with his assistant, an overzealous homeschool dad named Mr. Vanderpool, who had three sons on the team and a temper to rival Bobby Knight's. Last year, when we lost to Austin Christian, Mr. Vanderpool turned over the water cooler and punted the lid onto the field, where it nearly hit a player.

Central Austin Homeschool Cooperative took its lacrosse very seriously—out of necessity, because we didn't have any-where near a big enough student population to assemble a decent football team. Guys like Aaron acted like hotshots, but Sanger and I agreed it was due to an inferiority complex. High school football was, and always would be, the Texan sport of choice. Anything else, lacrosse included, was subpar.

Sanger and I took a seat on the edge of the field, in a patch of clover. She stretched her legs out and began picking at a scab on her shin.

"You know how Mrs. Weiss has been changing stuff around," she said. "All that effing dress code nonsense?"

I knew the effing dress code nonsense all too well. Backed by half the leadership board, Mrs. Weiss had proposed a new dress code, intended to go into effect at the start of the coming school year. Some of the proposed regulations:

No V-necks for girls.

No skirts above knee length.

No tank tops or otherwise provocative blouses.

This proposal did not go over well with anyone in the co-op who was not of the Blue-Jean Jumper persuasion, and especially not with us high school girls.

"None of that is going to pass," I said. "If they want it so bad, they can start their own Pilgrim colony."

"But didn't you hear, Nicks?" Sanger deadpanned. "We can't lead our fellow brethren astray with our 'otherwise provocative' clothing. They're too weak to resist our supple bodies, and if we don't cover ourselves up, they'll have no choice but to violate us on the spot."

The words "otherwise provocative" had caused a lot of indignation in the student body. So had the fact that the dress code targeted girls and only girls. So had the fact that Mrs. Weiss blithely ignored that we lived in the middle of Texas, where, nine months out of twelve, tank tops were necessary for survival.

"What does this have to do with your moms?" I asked.

Sanger picked harder at the scab. It flaked off and dropped into the clover. A gush of blood prickled to the surface of her dark skin.

"They were called in on a VD."

"*What?*"

If you tried hard enough, it was possible to get yourself suspended or expelled even from a homeschool co-op. How you did this was by receiving a values demerit, or VD. According to co-op policy, VDs were warranted for "behavior not in keeping with a healthy and wholesome learning environment." VDs were rare, but they did crop up occasionally.

Demerits were for rowdy students or for crazy parents

like Mr. Vanderpool, who had demolished that water cooler at the Austin Christian lacrosse game. They weren't for people like Sanger's moms, who had done nothing but contribute to the healthy and wholesome environment of Central Austin Homeschool Cooperative.

Sure, the Drs. Sadler-Hamasaki weren't an exemplar of parental involvement like some moms, who made costumes for the elementary musical and whipped up five dozen homemade pies for volleyball fund-raisers. They both worked full-time. But just because the Sadler-Hamasakis didn't show up for parent meetings or serve on a co-op committee didn't mean they deserved a VD.

I realized now what Sanger had meant by bringing up the dress code. Those new regulations had all been the doing of Mrs. Weiss, the new board president. So it must have been Mrs. Weiss who had now found some sort of bizarre fault with Sanger's moms.

"So, what?" I said. "Are your moms supposed to pay penance for a lack of bake sales?"

"It's not a big deal," said Sanger. "Mrs. Weiss is just going a little haywire. Mom says she's drunk with power. And Mam is an expert negotiator. Whatever it is, they'll work it out."

"Well, it's stupid" was my incisive reply. "The only reason any of those other moms are involved at co-op is because they stay at home all day."

"There's nothing wrong with staying at home. Mam did for five years. Your mom's still doing it."

"I *know*," I said, irritated that Sanger was missing my point. "I just mean, Mrs. Weiss can't punish your moms for not 'contributing,' or whatever. They're contributing to society as a whole."

Sanger pressed her thumb against her slow-bleeding wound.

"See," she said, "this is why I didn't tell you before. I knew you'd go all activist on me and blow it out of proportion."

"Aaron just pisses me off."

"Speak of the devil . . ."

As though summoned by the mention of his name, Aaron Weiss walked onto the field. His lacrosse stick was slung over his back and threaded through his raised arms—the ultimate posture of lacrosse doucheyness.

He was accompanied by four other guys, all geared up and laughing loudly. Coach Whitt shouted an indiscernible order at them. Joel hadn't shown up yet. I wondered if it was because he'd agreed to meet Max beforehand. At that thought, and for no identifiable reason, my stomach did a twist.

Most Mondays after co-op, Sanger would drive the two of us to Hamasaki House. Or sometimes, when the weather was really nice, Sanger and I would make the three-mile walk to my house. Today, neither of those options was a possibility. I was still grounded, and Sanger's Fiat was finally in the shop for passenger-door repair. I had to wait for Mom to pick me up after Joel's lacrosse practice, and Alma was picking up Sanger for an optometrist appointment.

Alma was from either Sweden or Norway—I could never remember which—and had come to Austin six years back as an au pair for Sanger, then stayed on at the Sadler-Hamasakis' as their cook. She was tall, lithe, and blond, and she was always baking adorable stuff like scones and calling Sanger and me "love."

Sanger and I had spent a few minutes giving Aaron the evil eye from our perch when Alma showed up. She rolled down the window of her tan Corolla and shouted to us from the curb, "Eye time, Sanger, love!"

"You heard her: *eye time*." Sanger did a perfect impression of Alma's lilting accent.

"What's this?" Alma called as Sanger headed to the car. "Stevie, love, aren't you coming too?"

Sanger turned back to give me a pouty face. She traced an invisible tear down her cheek. I noticed that her shin was still bleeding. Alma would have a Band-Aid on hand. She was a veritable Mary Poppins, always producing napkins or hand sanitizer or tampons whenever Sanger and I ran into a crisis.

Sanger got in the car, and I watched her explain my grounding to Alma. In response, Alma leaned over Sanger and made a sad face in my direction. I shrugged, displaying the appropriate amount of shame for a girl who couldn't pass homeschool math.

"Text me as soon as you get your phone back!" Sanger instructed.

Alma sped off.

Back on the field, a handful of other players had shown up and were in various stages of stretching. I tugged my iPod from my backpack, set myself up with a playlist entitled "CHILL," and propped my American Government textbook on my knees. Just as I reached a gripping passage on the Federalist Papers, something touched my back. I ripped out my earbuds and looked up.

Joel stood smirking over me. Max was by his side.

"Enjoying the view out there?" Joel asked.

"Seven more weeks," I replied.

"We get a car in seven weeks," Joel explained to Max.

"Both of you?" asked Max.

"Yeah," said Joel. "It's kind of a joint custody situation."

"But we've already worked out a detailed schedule of who gets it when," I said.

Max nodded, and as he did I noticed the hollow of his throat. It was an idiotic thing to notice, but I kept staring at it. The curve of delicate bone, the way his tanned skin stretched tautly across—

"You know," said Max, "I've got my own car. So if this whole lacrosse thing pans out, I could drive Joel back after practice, and your mom could pick you up earlier."

I realized that by "you" Max meant me.

"Oh." I nodded. "Thanks."

I didn't tell him I usually had a ride with Sanger, or that

even when I didn't, my mom still couldn't pick me up earlier because she had a weekly co-op committee meeting during lacrosse practice.

Joel was grinning goofily at me. Every time I crushed on a guy, Joel could always tell, and he'd smile in that goofy way, thus achieving his goal of making me feel supremely uncomfortable.

"Okay, well, you should go practice," I said, sounding meaner than I intended.

Joel blew me a kiss and jogged out to the field. Max stayed behind.

"So," he said, toeing the clover with his sneaker, "Sanger's come up with this idea for the allergic reaction. Ever heard of a ghost pepper?"

"I'm guessing that's a very hot pepper."

"Oh yeah."

"Sorry I'll miss it."

"Me too."

Max crouched beside me. His knees popped, and his calf muscles bulged under the strain. I was feeling supremely uncomfortable again, but not in a pissed-at-Joel way; it was an exhilarating kind of uncomfortable.

"You don't have to play on Joel's team," I said. "He can be really persuasive, but—"

"I don't do stuff I don't want to do," said Max. "Anyway, it looks like fun."

"Okaaay," I said, returning to my textbook, where a two-inch-by-two-inch portrait of Thomas Jefferson stared up at me.

"Stevie."

I looked up. It was weird hearing Max say "Stevie," his postpubescent voice deep and free of cracks. I wasn't used to hearing my name said that way.

"Yeah?" I said.

I was helplessly aware that my cheeks were heating up.

"I'm kind of nervous."

"About what?"

"Tell me it's pathetic to be nervous about joining a home-school lacrosse team."

"It's just new kid jitters," I said. "Don't worry about it."

"Okay."

He didn't move. I didn't move. A breeze blew back several pages of my textbook.

"Can I kiss you?" he asked.

I thought I'd misheard. I thought I'd gone into a dream state, or that maybe Max was joking and if I said anything serious in reply, he'd never let me live it down.

So I didn't say anything.

"You know," Max said, "for luck? But if you don't want to—"

"Yeah," I said.

"Yeah" was such an ugly word, I reflected. It would've been better to say "yes." But that didn't seem to bother Max, because he put a hand on my collarbone, and he leaned in and kissed me.

It was short, simple. I'd only just begun to move my lips when he pulled away. At first I thought I'd done something wrong, and I wondered if Max could tell it was only the second time I'd ever kissed a guy. But then I saw that he was grinning. I realized I was grinning back. He laughed a little. I laughed too.

"Did that help?" I asked.

"Definitely," he said.

He got back to his feet, and his knees popped again. I shaded my eyes against the sun glare so I could see his face.

"I'll see you when you're not under house arrest?" he asked.

"Definitely," I said.

"Cool."

He ran out to the field then, and I watched. I decided to walk the three miles home. If I stayed until after practice, I'd have to see Max again, and I was afraid that would ruin things.

He'd kissed me, and I'd said "definitely," and he'd said "cool," and I wanted to keep it that way.

Ten

It was the worst possible time to be grounded.

All I wanted to do was tell Sanger about the kiss, but all outlets of communication were on lockdown for the rest of the week. I started to think in the way criminals must, assessing all possible ways around the law. I thought about setting my alarm for three o'clock in the morning, sneaking into the kitchen, and using the landline to call Sanger, or getting on the computer and sending her an e-mail. I considered bribing Joel into letting me use his phone.

All of these illicit plans had their shortcomings. This wasn't the kind of news I wanted to have to whisper while crouched on the kitchen floor. It definitely wasn't news I wanted to send Sanger in an e-mail, where emoticons wouldn't do my feelings justice. If I begged Joel into letting me use his phone, he would ask questions, and he wouldn't relent until I told him the truth about Max. If I did tell him, Joel would make snide, innuendo-laced remarks for the rest of the month.

So really, I didn't have much of a choice. I was forced, for 120 hours straight, to keep the kissing incident all to myself. Given this quandary, I had no other recourse but to journal.

I wasn't the journaling type. My thoughts always raced faster than I could write, so by the time I was finished penning one sentence, my head was already a paragraph ahead. I did, however, own three blank journals, all birthday gifts from relatives. I kept them on the top shelf of my closet, too guilty to throw them out or give them away. But now, at last, I finally had use for one—a Vera Bradley blank book that my cousin Bridget had given me two years back. It was bright and preppy, just like Bridget. I would never be caught dead with it in public, but it seemed fitting for my current situation.

I filled five pages, front and back, on the topics of Max and lips. Afterward, I read over my musings and noted that a) I had slaughtered the sacredness of the exclamation mark and b) if Max ever got his hands on this journal, he would think I was a total nutcase. But then, I guess that's the point of journaling: You tell a journal all the things that, said aloud, would make you sound like a driveling madwoman.

Tuesday through Friday, there was a glaring lack of Max in the neighborhood. Not that I was stalking him or anything crazy like that. I did study on the back porch more than I would've under normal circumstances, and I occasionally looked out the window at the Palomer house during supper.

No Max.

I began to fear that maybe my subconscious had made the whole kiss up, as a form of wish fulfillment. And that was when I realized the kiss *had* been a fulfillment of a wish, which meant I had wanted that kiss, and I had enjoyed that kiss, and I definitely wanted it to happen again, only longer and deeper and wilder.

I was officially into Max Garza.

I thought back to how I'd practically hated him a week ago, how I'd been irrationally jealous that he and Sanger got along so well. I wondered if I was only into him now because he'd kissed me. I wondered if that made me an awful person.

He only cropped up in conversation once, Thursday night, at supper.

"He's a natural," Joel said, "so that makes me the team's savior for finding him. He scored twice on Aaron, and that's unheard of. It was fate he moved in next door."

I snorted at that, and the creamed corn I'd been eating went down the wrong way.

"You don't believe in fate?" Joel challenged.

"Sure," I said. "Call it fate."

On Friday, I asked Mom if I could get back my phone for good behavior. She said no. So I added a page in the Vera Bradley journal about how my mom was a domineering overlord, and no other kid in this nation would get their phone ripped away just because they failed a trig test. It was a cliché gripe, but it was therapeutic.

It really was the worst time to be grounded, because not only did I want to talk to Sanger, I wanted to go to Barton Springs. I didn't just go there to swim. I went there to think, went there to watch, went there to *be*. For just a two-dollar admission fee, I could sit on that grassy knoll and be an anonymous human. Not a sixteen-year-old. Not a homeschooler. Not a diabetic. Not even a Normal Type. Just a girl thinking.

I did some of my best thinking on that knoll. There at Barton Springs, I'd decided to go to summer camp in the sixth grade, decided to chop off my hair to a bob cut in seventh, decided to join the co-op yearbook club in eighth, decided to *leave* yearbook in ninth. Maybe it was all in my mind, but that poolside gave me clarity. I could sit there, stripped of all labels and preoccupations. Just sit there and think a thing through. And Max Garza was a thing I wanted, *needed*, to think through.

By the time Saturday finally rolled around, I was in rough shape. Mom gave me my phone back over breakfast, and I weeded through a dozen texts and nine missed calls, most of which were from Sanger and the rest of which were about co-op homework assignments and the upcoming STA rally the next week.

I called Sanger. It rang, then went to voice mail. I hung up and called again.

She answered.

"Rescue me," I said.

"Yeah. Okay."

Her voice sounded clouded up, like she was sick with a head cold.

"Are you all right?" I asked.

"Fine. I'll be there in thirty."

• • •

When the Fiat pulled up in the driveway, I half expected to see Max fling open Mr. Palomer's front door and wave at me and say, "Hello, neighbor!" like a total goon and then run across the yard and kiss me, right there, in front of Sanger, who would squawk in glee and lay hard on the car horn until we cut it out.

But Max didn't make an appearance.

I shoved my duffel through the passenger window and prepared to follow suit.

"It's fixed," said Sanger.

She was wearing a pair of oversize sunglasses. Her voice didn't sound foggy anymore.

I tried the handle.

Sure enough, the auto wizards had done their magic. The door swung open, good as new. It made me a little sad.

"The end of an era," I said.

Sanger just nodded.

"So, no death list today?" I asked as we pulled out of the driveway.

"No," said Sanger. "I thought you heard, Max is in Dallas."

"How would I have heard that?"

"I dunno." Sanger shrugged. "Maybe if you'd given him your number when he asked, you would be savvy about these important developments. He texted me Monday night and said he'd be up there for a week. It's something legal. Apparently his parents are suing his school, and Max is testifying or talking to reporters or *something*."

"Oh," I said, feeling a blissful assuagement of that week's fears. Max hadn't been avoiding me; he'd just been out of town.

Sanger noticed me smiling.

"What is wrong with you?"

"Nothing," I said. "So you didn't get to do that thing with the pepper?"

"When he gets back," said Sanger. "*Why* are you *smiling* like that?"

I didn't want to tell Sanger like this, when we were in the car. I wanted to wait until we were in her bedroom, where we could properly squee and shake each other's shoulders and glut ourselves on potato chips. But thirty minutes stood between me and Sanger's bedroom, and I couldn't hold it in that long.

"He kissed me."

Sanger turned down the piano solo on the radio. She screeched to a stop, even though the traffic light ahead had only just turned yellow.

"What? Max? He kissed you?"

I nodded.

"Dude."

I nodded again.

"And here I thought you hated him."

"I never said I *hated* him."

Sanger gave me a look, and even with the sunglasses covering half her face, I sensed its snark.

"Okay," I admitted. "I didn't like him that much. But I

definitely like him now. It's just, I don't even know if he likes me like that, or *what* he wants. He said the kiss was for luck, so maybe that means he was just testing the waters?"

"Wait, wait, wait," said Sanger. "When did he find the time to kiss you?"

The car behind us honked. The light had turned green. Sanger shoved her middle finger out her open window. She waved it around glibly for a full five seconds. Then she hit the gas.

"It was right before lacrosse practice," I said. "On Monday."

"AND YOU'RE JUST NOW TELLING ME?"

I reminded Sanger that I had been restricted from all forms of communication with the outside world.

"Whatever," she said. "You could've found a way to let me know. You could've, like, called me in the middle of the night or gotten ahold of Joel's—"

"I thought about that," I said, "but I didn't want to tell you that way."

"No," said Sanger, "what you mean is, you didn't think it was worth the risk to tell your *best friend* about the *second kiss of your entire life.*"

"Sanger, shut up. I wanted to tell you in person."

"God, I can't believe you."

She turned up NPR. Loud.

I glared over at her. She kept her eyes on the road. I crossed my arms and slunk down in my seat.

We didn't speak the rest of the way.

She turned off the highway onto the feeder road, then down the long stretch that led to Hamasaki House. Cedar trees flitted by. Most of the bluebonnets had died off, leaving only long grass behind.

Sanger passed the driveway to her house.

I punched the radio button, cutting off a progression of pounding octaves. All other sound became loud and crisp— the hum of the car engine, the rush of wind outside the open windows.

"What are you doing?" I asked. "You missed the house."

My voice was soft, but it was plenty angry.

"I don't want to go there yet."

"Why not? What's *wrong* with you?"

Sanger wrenched the Fiat off the main road, into a gas station parking lot. The red and blue of the Chevron sign were faded, and the mini-mart doors were clouded with dirt. The station had been out here far longer than the residential development. Sanger had told me once that there was a big to-do with the neighborhood association trying to pay off the owner. But the owner had refused, and the gas station had remained, and Sanger and I had walked out there from her house many times to buy movie candy before a sleepover. I had good memories of the place, so I was now angrier still at Sanger for pulling us over there, in the middle of a fight.

"Are you jealous?" The possibility hadn't struck me until I asked the question, out loud.

Sanger cut the engine. She looked at me with disgust.

"No, Stevie, I don't want your effing eight-fingered crush."

"Fuck you."

It was the first time I'd ever said that to Sanger. It was the first time I'd said it to anyone, period.

I threw open my now perfectly working door and slammed it shut after me with enough force to break it again. I headed toward the mini-mart, wiping tears from my cheeks.

A rusting cowbell announced my entrance. I didn't make eye contact with the old man at the register who was busy horking on a wad of chewing tobacco. I slipped into the candy aisle, rubbing at the gooseflesh that the nearby AC window unit raised on my arms. The cowbell clanked again. I brushed away the remaining tears from my face and made a hard-eyed study of the candy bar selection.

"I'm moving."

Sanger stood in the middle of the aisle, arms out, palms up, as though to show me she was harmless.

I stared at her.

"What?" I asked.

"I'm moving."

"*Moving* moving?"

Sanger poked at a hanging packet of beef jerky. "Pennsylvania moving."

"*What?*"

"Moms just made it final."

"When?"

"Start of summer."

I gave up trying to rub out the gooseflesh. My entire body was prickling now.

"No," I said, because it was the only word clanging in my brain.

No, no, *no.*

"Can we go outside?" she asked. "Please?"

I understood. This wasn't a conversation I wanted to have in an overcooled gas station, within earshot of a tobacco-chewing attendant.

But then, it wasn't a conversation I wanted to have anywhere.

We stepped outside, into a blast of warm air. We didn't get back in the car. We leaned against the hood, and the hot metal burned my bare thighs. Cicadas croaked in the cedar trees overhead.

"How long have you known?" I asked.

"Get this: Mam got the job offer two weeks ago. You know when she flew out for that engineering conference? Turns out she was interviewing for a faculty position at UPenn."

"Wow," I said. "Wow, that's—that's pretty prestigious, isn't it?"

"The whole thing is ridiculous. Mam already has an awesome job, everyone loves Mom at the hospital, and I've grown up here. But last night, Mom was going on and on about how

Mam supported her all through med school and how we need to be a symbiotic family unit, because this is Mam's *dream* job. I didn't even know she wanted to go into academia. Academia sucks. She's taking a pay cut, and Mom will have to find a new hospital, and I'm supposed to spend my senior year in Philadelphia, being *symbiotic.*"

"What did you tell them?"

"What do you think? I refused to go. I came *this close* to playing the in vitro card."

The in vitro card was something that came up every time Sanger's moms did something she deemed grossly unfair. She'd threaten—to me, not actually to her moms—that she was going to run away and find the sperm donor who had "knocked up" Dr. Hamasaki and who Sanger swore was stand-up comedian Donald Glover, despite the fact that this was chronologically impossible. I, of course, would be coming along for the adventure, and Sanger assured me that it would be the most epic road trip story of all time. Jokes like that were as close as Sanger ever came to talking about what she called her "man genes."

"I came close," said Sanger, "but it's no use. They're serious. Mam's already found a townhouse to rent and a private school for me to attend. *Private school.*"

"You've been to private school before."

Sanger's parents weren't the type who homeschooled for die-hard ideological reasons. They just did whatever they currently thought was best for Sanger's education. She'd gone to

Montessori school when she was very little and a private school until third grade.

"That doesn't count," said Sanger, "and it's not the point. They're uprooting my life, and it couldn't be worse timing. I'm happy here. I've got you, I'm doing well at school, and I probably make more money coding than I'll make after I get a college degree. It's like they've been lying in wait, thinking 'Hmmm. When would be the best time to disrupt Sanger's emotional, social, and academic development? Oooh, I know: summer before her senior year!'"

Sanger was irate. I knew this because she was acting like a typical moody teenager, and usually Sanger was cool and debonair, even about unpleasant things. There wasn't a hint of the debonair about her now. She sounded petulant, and much younger than usual.

"There's not a chance they'll change their minds?" I asked.

Sanger rubbed an errant tear from her cheekbone. "Mam's accepted the position. It's final."

I closed my eyes. I was suddenly irritated with the sun for warming my skin, with the cicadas and their croaking, with the passing traffic, with the strong scent of gasoline.

"So that means you're leaving when? Like, in a month and a half?"

"The first of June."

Sanger scratched at something coated on the Fiat's left headlight. It looked like bird poop.

"It snows there," she said, her voice folding over in a sharp crease. "I don't do snow. I don't do Yankees. They're rude."

"*You're* rude," I said, trying to smile, because what else was there to do? Sanger's fate was sealed, and no amount of railing against the adult world would change that.

"I don't want to start over," Sanger said. "I haven't made a new friend since I was, like, eight."

"You mean, since me."

Sanger nodded morosely.

"That is so not true. You make friends with plenty of people. Take Max, for example."

"Yeah, but he's not my *friend*," said Sanger. "Not like you, the way a friend counts. Anyway, about three quarters of the reason I even tried with him is because he told me he had a crush on you."

I stepped away from the car. The metal was suddenly burning too hotly into my skin.

"What?"

Sanger smiled, though to herself, not at me. "Yeah. He walked straight up to me and said, 'I really like Stevie.' And I was like, 'Cool dude.'"

"Why didn't you tell me that?"

Sanger shrugged. "Because you acted like you loathed him. I didn't want to give you another reason by telling you how he basically begged me to set you two up. But, you know, now it all seems to have panned out for you, so whoo-hoo."

I absorbed this information with a frown. I shook my head.

"It's just a year, you know," I told her. "Then you can go to college anywhere. We can choose the same place. Though I probably can't get into Rice."

Rice had been Sanger's top-choice school since she was twelve years old.

"It's still a year," she whispered. "Do you know what it was like, how bad it was, just waiting between yesterday and today, when I was dying to tell you everything?"

"Yeah," I said. "I know what it's like."

"We've got a year of that. At least. And do you want to hear the worst part about it?"

I didn't, but I nodded.

"Mam says she was still on the fence about the job until the meeting with the leadership board at co-op."

"What does that have to do with anything?"

Sanger smiled grimly. "It wasn't about bake sales."

"Then what?"

Sanger's grim smile became less of a smile and more of just a grim.

Then I realized. Aaron's snide comment at chem lab on Monday replayed in my mind, and I knew.

"No," I said. "*No.* They are *not* playing the gay card. They can't do that."

"Co-op's a private organization," Sanger said, shrugging. "They can do whatever the hell they want."

"But your moms are great. You're great. No one's had a problem with it for all these years."

"Apparently," said Sanger, "they have. There's, like, this whole coalition of them. Most of them go to that gigantic church in the Hill Country, and the pastor's been driving it home that the gays are out to destroy the family as we know it. They've basically signed a petition."

"Saying what?"

"What do you think? That my moms don't represent healthy values, or whatever."

"That's so—"

"It doesn't matter what it is. The leadership board just blindsided them with it at this coffee shop. They were like, 'We really appreciate your membership, and Sanger is a jewel, but this is for your own good.' I think the direct quote was, they were 'calling them out *in love.*'"

"What did your moms say?"

"I mean, what can you say to that? What would you say if Mrs. Weiss stared you down over a latte and was all, 'You're a dear, Stevie, but you need to reevaluate your conflicted feelings about Max Garza'?"

I did think I needed to reevaluate my feelings toward Max Garza, but I didn't mention that. It would ruin Sanger's example, and I knew what she was getting at.

"So my moms basically said 'screw you' in a classy way and pulled me from co-op, which pisses me off, because that's just what those harpies wanted in the first place. Mam had been sitting on the job offer for a week by then. She said it's what nailed the coffin shut. She took it as a sign we were closing a chapter here, something bogus like that."

"I'm not going to co-op again," I said.

"Sure you are. Your parents will make you. Tuition isn't refundable."

"They won't make me after I tell them what happened."

I glared straight into the sunlight reflected off the nearest gas pump.

The first of June.

June 1.

The day Max went to school. Our death-list deadline.

"You never answered me," I said. "You never said how long you've known."

"That it was a possibility?" Sanger sighed. "Since Mam interviewed."

"Two weeks ago."

"Yeah."

"That's why you played the BFF card," I said, closing my eyes. "You knew this might be happening. That June first could be it."

"I couldn't tell you. It wasn't definite then, so what good would it do getting you worked up over nothing? But I had a bad feeling. Then Max shows up with this insane list, and I guess I thought it was a chance for us to, I don't know, have a last dose of fun before everything goes to shit. I just needed you to be part of that. And if you remember, you weren't too fond of Max back then, so I had to give you a nudge. No questions asked."

I nodded, final understanding burning through my body.

"Stevie?"

"Yeah."

"Don't get grounded again, okay? It really sucks with all lines of communications down."

"I'll try not to."

"Do. There is no try."

"Fine," I promised. "I'll do."

I wasn't thinking about my promise, though. I was thinking of what Sanger had said earlier: A year was still a year.

Eleven

That afternoon at the gas station was the angriest I ever saw Sanger about moving. In the days that followed, she fizzled back down to her usual wry, unruffled self. She resumed her excruciatingly slow text conversations. She published the Critters and Twitters website. With me by her side, she stalked the online profiles of her future classmates at Germantown Friends School in Philadelphia. And above all, she devoted herself to Max's fake deaths.

I realized then that Sanger meant for Max's list to serve as more than even he'd intended. It was a last hurrah. It was a form of defiance. Its deadline also coincided perfectly with her move-out date. Now I got why Sanger had fervently vowed that we would cross out all of Max's fake deaths by June 1. I got the energy. I got the urgency. And now I shared it.

The list was also a distraction, for me at least. I wanted to think and do and plan anything that didn't remind me of Sanger's imminent departure. The list fit the bill perfectly. It meant plans and action, all hurtling toward a climactic spontaneous combustion on May 31. It meant a constant need for Sanger Sadler-Hamasaki in my life. Okay, and Max Garza.

He called my cell the day after Sanger dropped the big news. I didn't recognize the number, so I let it go to voice mail. In the message, his voice was chipper, and I could hear clinking silverware and voices in the background.

"Stevie Hart. Hello. This is Max Garza, your neighbor. I've felt kind of like an asshole this past week, which isn't *technically* my fault since you're grounded and I'm out of town, and you were too coy to give me your digits. But Sanger said I have a chance with you, and she gave me your number, so don't hate me forever. This is just me telling you I'll be back in Austin on the thirteenth. That is a Thursday. When I get back, I would really like to talk-slash-fake-die-slash-kiss with you. Kiss with you? Damn. This is the third time I've left this message, so I'm not doing it again or you'll think I'm deranged. Unless Sanger's wrong, and you don't like me, in which case you already think I'm deranged and this is the worst voice mail I've ever left. What the hell. I shouldn't have told you this was my third message. What the hell am I even doing?"

I played the voice mail to Sanger over the phone.

"Sooo," said Sanger, "what's the verdict? Creepy or cute?"

"I thought you would know," I said.

"He's trying too hard, but that might just be because his phone persona sucks."

"A lot of people suck over the phone," I acknowledged.

"Mhm. Especially sex-line workers."

"Sanger."

"Har har. Okay, no, but seriously, I wouldn't respond imme-diately. Wait until Wednesday, call him up, and invite him over to my place Friday night for more deathscapades."

I decided to take Sanger's advice.

From Sunday to Wednesday, I tried not to think about Max or about Sanger's move. Instead, I poured myself into school.

On Monday, I told Mom my sugar was out of whack and that I was feeling too light-headed to go to co-op. I knew I shouldn't have lied about something like that, but there was no way I was going to co-op after what Sanger had told me, and I still hadn't worked out a way to explain the situation to my parents.

I got an eighty-eight on Tuesday's trig test, which Mom graded immediately after I took it. I basked in the sweet, sweet glow of redemption.

On Wednesday, I chickened out and didn't call Max.

Thursday afternoon, I got another e-mail from Leslie Cobb, heralded by three urgent exclamation marks.

Subject: Next Meeting & Rally!!!

Hello, Fellow World Changers,

How are those petitions coming along? I've received great feedback from many of you already. Let's keep up the fight!

I'm pleased to report that our bill is FINALLY set to come up for introduction in the Senate this coming Monday. It's been a long and tedious process, but Senators Rowan and Maldonado have just recently lent their support to our cause.

Keep working on those petitions. **Every signature counts.** *Our job is to present constituent voices to our lawmakers and bring about REAL CHANGE.*

The rally begins this Monday at 6 PM. We will congregate at our customary meeting place, the Texas Rangers Memorial. Those who arrive early may be able to catch a seat in the gallery. BUT REMEMBER: Be quiet and courteous at all times. We want to give the very best impression of Springs for Tomorrow Alliance.

Leslie Cobb

Founder, Springs for Tomorrow Alliance

"Carry out a random act of kindness, with no expectation of reward, safe in the knowledge that one day someone might do the same for you."—Princess Diana

I marked my calendar. Then I texted Sanger.
Me: *Going to call Max. Friday @ 5:30?*
Sanger: *yea*

Me: *Okay. So I'm going to call him.*

Sanger: *so do it*

Me: *I will.*

Sanger: *you're stalling. Suck it up and call him.*

I called Max, praying it would go to voice mail.

He picked up.

"Oh my God," he said. "You *don't* think I'm a creep. Or else you're calling to warn me about the restraining order."

"I don't think you're a creep."

"That was the worst voice mail in the history of voice mails. Please don't use it to blackmail me."

"I make no promises."

I was aware I sounded flirty. I wasn't trying to be flirty. Did Max just bring out the flirty in me?

"Are you back in town?" I asked, and then worried I'd crossed over from flirty to desperate.

"Leaving in an hour. I'm packing up."

"Oh. So, um, why exactly were you in Dallas?"

"Yeah, sorry," said Max. "I forgot to mention this when we were making our death schedule. My parents are suing St. Michael's for negligent something or other. Personally, I think it's stupid. The parents are already loaded good and plenty, you know, and it's Death's fault, not St. Michael's. But anyway, they scheduled me to talk to some local news reporters. You're allowed to think that's as cool as it sounds."

"Was it hard?"

"Stevie, that hurts. It's like you don't even know me. I'm a natural-born public speaker, remember?"

"I meant, was it hard to talk about the accident?"

"Oh. Honestly?" Max went quiet for a long moment, and all I could hear was rustling on the other end. "I was more pissed off than anything else. Just that it happened, and that they never found my fingers, and that Zach Brandt is probably wearing one of them in his nose as we speak. I was just angry about that. And when we got back home, Mom was going on about how brave I'd been, but, like, how brave is it to just tell it like it is?"

"Yeah," I said, not sure I agreed with Max. Sometimes it could be extremely hard to tell it like it was, especially when whoever you were talking to didn't want to hear how it was.

"Anyway," said Max, "Mom's been bawling all day. I think this has been rougher for her than me. And Dad's out of town on business, which is typical."

"Are you an only child?" I asked, wondering if you should know that about a boy before he kisses you.

"Technically? No. Mom's got two other kids from her first marriage, but they're in their thirties. They live in New England, so I only see them for Thanksgiving in Boston."

"Oh."

"Yep."

"Um, well, Sanger and I had this idea. Like, if you're not busy tomorrow."

"Why would I be busy tomorrow?" asked Max.

"I don't know. I thought you could've had plans."

"You're my plans."

I went very quiet and very still. It was a moment just like the moment he'd kissed me, where my brain felt untethered from my body and not at all certain of present reality.

"Stevie?"

"Yeah! Yeah, I'm here."

"Sorry. That sounded way more romantic than I meant it to."

"So you didn't mean to sound romantic?"

"Damn. No. I didn't mean that either. It is as romantic or unromantic as you want it to be."

"Okay."

"So Friday."

"Um, yeah. Sanger and I thought you could come over to her place around five thirty and we could knock some more of those fakes off your list."

"I'm so down. Though I already told Sanger I would."

"Wait. Sanger called you?"

"Texted. Yesterday. Is she always that slow of a texter?"

"Always."

"My gramps texts faster."

"So Friday at five thirty."

"It's a date."

I smiled wide. "Did you mean that romantically or unromantically?"

"Oh. Romantically, no doubt."

I smiled wider. "Okay."

"You know, I could drive us there. Instead of Sanger driving all the way out to pick us up?"

"That works."

"Leave at five?"

"Great."

"Right. Well, see you then."

I hung up.

I squealed. I jumped on my bed. I literally jumped on my bed. I felt idiotic and juvenile. I proceeded to grin without reprieve for minutes straight.

Then I texted Sanger.

Me: *You already asked him?!*

Sanger: *didn't know if you'd have the adequate lady parts to call.*

Me: *I really like him.*

Her final reply came after a full thirty minutes.

Yea, I know

Friday at 4:50, the doorbell rang. I shouted at Joel not to get it. He got it anyway.

I found him and Max talking lacrosse in the front room. Joel was bemoaning Max's notable absence from practice that past week. Max was saying how much he was looking forward to the coming Monday, which I knew was just Max being polite, because who looks forward to Mondays?

I set foot in the room, and Max looked in my direction, and I realized that there was no way of keeping this from Joel. All it took was that look between Max and me and, with the help of his sixth sense, Joel knew exactly what was up.

"Mhm," he said, scratching at his chin. He smirked at Max. He smirked at me. "*Mhm*. Well, I guess I'll leave you two alone, then."

"We're going to Sanger's for the night," I said. "Mom already knows."

"Sanger's *for the night*?" Joel frowned. "How come you never invite me on your big adventures?"

"Because you've never wanted to hang out with a couple of girls," I said.

I was paraphrasing a grand insult Joel had made three years back, when Sanger had included his name with mine on her birthday party invitation. Sanger had a big crush on Joel even then, before he got taller and trimmer and more confident. She had been bummed that he hadn't come to the party, and his dismissal ("It's a *girl* party") lived on in infamy.

"It has been eons since that happened," said Joel. "Aren't you gonna drop it?"

"Never," I assured him.

Joel smiled in a funny, non-smiley kind of way that made me say, "You can come if you want."

"No." And suddenly Joel was smiling the right way. He laughed. "No, I'm just messing with you. Have fun." He pointed at Max. "Be safe."

Then he left us alone.

"Hi there," said Max.

He was wearing jeans and a red V-neck shirt. It was the least preppy I'd seen him. It was also the first time I got a good look at his collarbone. It was one nice collarbone. He was tanner than I remembered him too, and in a moment of imbecility, I wondered if the UV rays in Dallas were more intense than in Austin.

"You look good," I said, giving way to my Max-triggered instinct to flirt.

"You look better," he said.

I laughed, half-sure I sounded manic.

I'd tried on seven variations of the sundress-and-boots getup I was currently wearing, and I'd paid extra attention to my eyeliner application. It was nice to get a pat on the back for the extra effort, however hokey a pat it was.

"It's supposed to rain tonight," Max said on the way there.

Through the windshield, I could already see clouds crowding onto the skyline, tinged orange from the setting sun. That's the thing with Texan sky: It's so big that nothing can hide, not even slow-brewing storms an hour in the future.

"Uh-oh," I said.

"What? Storms freak you out?"

"No. It's just, we've still got a long way to go, and you've already resorted to talking about the weather."

"I'm not bored. Are you bored?"

"No."

"I was genuinely concerned about the weather. There's no telling if it'll interfere with tonight's plans."

"Sanger hasn't told you what we're doing either?"

"I know what's on the agenda," said Max. "But the method remains a mystery."

"I think Sanger wants it that way."

"You're lucky, you know," said Max. "To have a friend like that."

"I know," I said, before giving Max's profile a good looking at. "Do you still keep in touch with your friends back home?"

Max shrugged.

"I mean, you must've had a lot of friends in Dallas."

"What makes you say that?"

Because you're freakin' adorable.

"You just seem like you'd have a lot of friends."

Max made this phlegmy sort of honk.

"I mean it," I said. "So do you still talk to anyone?"

"I told you what happened after the accident, remember? No one checked in on me. No one. Not even Dylan, who I guess was supposed to be my best friend. But I don't know, I've never really been one for best friends. I mean, no one I would call up and be, like, hey, I want your opinion on this. You know?"

I shook my head, because I honestly didn't know. Sanger

and I had been friends for so long, I couldn't remember a time I hadn't been able to call her up and ask her opinion on anything, from whether I should go to summer camp to what brand of tampons I should buy. I didn't know what it was like to not have a best friend. It seemed as strange to me as the concept of not having parents.

"Yeah, well," said Max. "Point is, I'm kind of pissed at the whole lot of them, and I don't even know if I have a right to be."

I wanted to ask it. I knew it was probably a mistake, but I *had* to ask it.

"What kind of friends would you say Sanger and I are?"

"Uh. Is it really lame if I say . . . you're the best friends I've got?"

I stared at Max. His eyes flitted over to me.

"Maybe a little," I said slowly. "But it's sweet enough to make up for the lameness."

"It's just, back in that dark funk of mine, I realized something else. One day, Death really is going to catch up to me. I'm not stupid enough to think I'm immortal. And when that happens, I want to go out knowing I have friends who actually care. I want to go out really living, one hundred percent."

"And that's why you're trying so hard with me and Sanger?"

"You make it sound so unattractive."

I grinned. "If it were *that* unattractive, I wouldn't be here, would I?"

• • •

It took longer than usual to get to Sanger's place, because Max stopped at yellow lights rather than sped through them and because he went the speed limit, not fifteen miles over it.

At last, Max pulled up in the driveway of Hamasaki House and cut the engine. We sat there for a moment, neither of us going for the doors.

"Does it freak you out?" he asked abruptly.

"Does what—?"

Max raised his three-fingered hand.

I was honest.

"It did at first," I said. "But it's fine."

I was partly honest, anyway.

"But, like, is it repulsive?" Max pressed. "Do you get the heebie-jeebies thinking about it when you picture us making out?"

I smirked. "Who said I picture us making out?"

Max shrugged.

"I just don't want you to be disgusted by me," he said at last.

I frowned a little. Max seemed unsure of himself in that moment, and so, so small.

"I'm not disgusted."

"Okay," said Max, getting out of the car.

He didn't look entirely convinced.

Sanger came galloping out to the driveway.

"Thank God," she said. "I thought I was going to have to pull you two off each other."

I felt my cheeks heat, even though this was Sanger, and she and I had gabbed about hypothetical make-out sessions plenty of times before. Maybe it was weird now because things were no longer hypothetical. Sanger was talking about me, and she was talking about Max and about something that just he and I could share—even though we hadn't.

Not yet.

Sanger pressed her hands together in a reverent way, as though she were about to enter a meditative state.

"We have a lot—and I mean *a lot*—to accomplish, my pretties. We've been put behind schedule by Stevie's delinquent behavior and Max's journey to the wasteland of Dallas. But we've reconvened on this auspicious day to make up for lost time."

Sanger was doing that thing again where she sounded like she was imitating a movie character. Her smile scared me.

"And *so*," she said. "So it begins."

Twelve

Max sat in an armchair as Sanger unwrapped a single pepper from a produce bag. It was called a ghost pepper. It was bright red and shriveled and the length of Sanger's index finger. She held it by the stem, presenting it to Max with great pomp and circumstance.

"The ghost pepper," she announced, "is one of *the* hottest peppers in the world. Technically, the *Guinness Book of World Records* says the Carolina Reaper is the hottest, but I couldn't find one of those. Anyway, the ghost pepper possesses a Scoville rating of over one million."

"That number means absolutely nothing to me," said Max.

"I think," I said, "it means you're going to be in a lot of pain. Probably go red in the face. Writhe around. It'll resemble an allergic reaction."

"But it's *not* an allergic reaction," said Max. "It's just a stress response to your body's pain reactors going berserk. Or something."

"Thank you, Bill Nye," Sanger said. "I'm aware that it's not *actually* an allergic reaction. But what else are we supposed to do when you don't have any allergies?"

"No *known* allergies," said Max.

"Yeah, well, we don't have a lifetime to figure out if you're allergic to a rare herb," said Sanger. "We just have until the first of June. Capisce?"

Max shrugged. "Capisce."

I winced. The first of June. I knew that was our deadline. I'd known for a while. But the words had a different flavor to them now that they weren't just an end date for Max's list. Now the first of June was the day life as I knew it ended. The day Sanger moved away. And it seemed so much sooner now than it had when we'd made that poster board schedule in Sanger's bedroom.

"Okay," said Sanger, oblivious to my internal discomfort. "Stevie will record a video and take the photograph of your untimely demise. I will be on hand with milk and bread."

She pointed to the coffee table, where a pint container of milk and half a baguette sat at the ready.

"Have people done this before?" Max asked.

"Of course they have," said Sanger. "How do you think anyone found out its Scoville rating?"

Max reached for the pepper. "Okay. Give it."

"Just remember," Sanger warned, "don't touch your eyes or anything afterward. Stevie, ready?"

I started the video-recording on Max's phone.

"Ready."

Max stuck the whole pepper in his mouth, bit it clean off

the stem, and chewed. Sanger and I stood transfixed. I could tell Max was trying to tough it out. He grinned a lippy smile at us both, chewing all the while. But then he swallowed, and the smile faded into a look of intense concentration.

Max's face didn't turn red, like I had predicted. He didn't scream or hop around or fan his mouth, saying "hot-hot-hot." He just looked monumentally uncomfortable. He gripped his fingers hard into the armrests of the leather chair. Tears began to leak from his eyes.

I stopped the video. It didn't really look like Max was having an allergic reaction, just more like he'd eaten a pepper with a Scoville rating of one million.

Max hadn't said anything for a full minute. He started to hiccup.

"I think he should drink the milk," I said. "Max, do you want the milk now?"

Max hiccuped. He nodded.

"Wait," said Sanger. "The photo."

I grabbed the Polaroid. I focused in on Max's agonized face. He was noticeably sweating. His curly black hair had plastered along his ears. I took the photo. Sanger handed Max the milk, lid unscrewed. He hauled in a huge gasp. Then he chugged the milk, all of it, in one go.

"Bread," he demanded. "Please. Oh God, *bread*."

Sanger handed him the bread.

"What does it feel like?" she asked. "Describe it."

Max shook his head. "Can't. Talk."

He demolished the half baguette.

"Need air," he said.

He pushed past us and made for the veranda doors. Sanger and I chased after him. Outside, Max walked in circles, hands atop his head, puffing out breaths as though he'd just run a marathon.

"My throat," he said. "My throat is melting."

"Maybe he needs to eat something else," I suggested. "Like pudding? Ice cream?"

Sanger nodded and went back inside.

Max sank down on one of the patio chairs. He stomped his feet on the ground. He pressed his fist to his chest. I decided it was best to keep my distance. I'd begun to feel a little bit sadistic. What if Max really *did* have some kind of allergic reaction? What if his throat sealed up? The nearest hospital was at least fifteen miles away. What if Sanger and I went down in history as teen killers who dared a peer to eat a ghost pepper and watched as he died in agony?

Sanger came out with a lidless carton of strawberry ice cream. She handed it to Max, along with a spoon. He shoved a heaping serving into his mouth, closed his eyes, and groaned.

Sanger leaned over and whispered to me, "I wonder if that's what he sounds like in bed."

"That helps," Max said. "That helps, like, a lot."

"You sure you're okay?" I asked, venturing a little closer to where he sat.

Max looked like he was on the edge of an answer. Then he seemed to change his mind. Then change his mind again. He shoved another spoonful into his mouth. He closed his eyes and lowered his face over the open ice cream container.

"Why did I do this?" he wheezed.

"It'll pass," I said. "Just hang in there."

Max shook his head. "There is *no way* childbirth can be more painful than this."

"Okay, now you're just being stupid," said Sanger. She didn't look nearly as scared as I felt.

"I might puke," Max added.

When he lifted his head back up, a sheen of sweat covered his cheeks.

"Puke on Stevie," Sanger suggested. "It'll be poetic justice."

"Sanger, shut *up*, would you? He's really in pain."

Max retched once, and by instinct I jumped back. I for one was not a believer in poetic justice or karma or any variation thereof.

But Max didn't puke. He pressed a palm to his mouth, he shook his head, and he let out a long breath. When he opened his eyes, the tinge of panic I'd seen there before was gone.

"Doing better?" I asked.

"Getting there. Mind over matter, right?"

Sanger started to cry.

"What's wrong?" I asked.

"Dammit. I touched my eyes."

. . .

Ten minutes later, Max was in better shape, though it was hard to tell if he was completely better or if he was still acting tough. The hiccups were gone, at least, and he had stopped sweating, and I was no longer worried that his throat was going to close.

Sanger spent three minutes flushing out her eyes in the kitchen sink.

When it was all over and everyone had recovered, we went up to Sanger's room. Max grabbed Sanger's green poster board and, with unquestionable relish, marked through **8. Allergic reaction**.

"There had to be a better way to do that," he said.

"Yes," said Sanger, "but aren't you glad you did it, all the same?"

Max didn't look anywhere close to glad.

"If I have indigestion for the rest of this week," he said, "I'm holding you responsible."

"So maybe," said Sanger, "you want to take a break?"

"Oh no," said Max. "Bring it."

The next death on our agenda was **10. Freeze to death**. It required a field trip to H-E-B, the purchase of thirteen ten-pound bags of ice, and the transport of said ice from grocery to Fiat to one of the massive freezers in the Hamasaki-Sadlers' garage. It was one of those chest freezers, the type that's perfect for casserole pans.

Or, as Max glibly pointed out, "It's the place where guys like Hannibal store human body parts."

Then he made a nasty slurping sound between closed teeth, and I laughed, even though it made me a little uneasy when Sanger hoisted open the lid for the three of us to assess the freezer's contents.

But of course, this particular freezer didn't contain body parts. There was just a plastic tub of pistachio gelato and a few tube Popsicles. We placed the food on the hood of Sanger's car and then set to work cutting open the thirteen bags of ice and emptying them into the deep freezer. When we were through, Sanger climbed inside and used a fire poker to break up the ice on top.

"We've got to cover you up a little," Sanger explained to Max, "for full effect."

"I don't know," Max said. "It seems kind of . . ."

He trailed off, staring out of the garage. The storm clouds had reached us hours ago, and it was raining, the night sky cast in a dim, gray funk.

"Kind of what?" Sanger demanded.

She stood up in the freezer and tossed the poker to the concrete floor, a jarring *clang*. Her bare knees looked raw and wet from cold.

"Kind of *lame*," Max said at last. "I mean, it's not exactly what I had in mind."

"Then what did you have in mind?" Sanger asked, using my shoulder for balance as she climbed out of the freezer.

"What, did you want to fly out to the Arctic and get deposited in the wild, amongst the snow dogs?"

"No."

"Then propose an alternative."

Max sighed. "I guess I don't have one."

Sanger clamped her hands on Max's shoulders. "He who has no alternative has no griping rights. Now, get in the effing freezer, Maximilian."

Max said, "Yeah, yeah, okay."

But he still stood there, motionless, looking at the one hundred thirty pounds of ice.

I realized something.

"You're afraid," I said.

It wasn't an accusation. I hadn't meant to make Max feel embarrassed. It was just a thought so sudden and clear that it pushed down from my firing synapses and off my tongue, before I had the chance to let it sit.

Max's eyes flashed to mine. He shifted from one foot to the other.

"No, I'm not," he said. "I'm just working myself up. It's going to be damn cold, lying there for a half hour."

"You don't have to do it this way," I said. "We could always figure something else out."

"Like hell we can," said Sanger. "Who bought all this ice? Me."

I could've reminded Sanger at this point that she had insisted on buying all the ice, that she'd been the one to conceive a scheme involving bags of ice to begin with—but Sanger was not in a mood compatible with reason.

"Well," I said, "he doesn't have to stay in there for a full thirty minutes. He might get, like, frostbite."

"No, he won't," said Sanger, waving her hand dismissively. "Max is in the prime of life. He's got thick skin, remember? He'll be fine."

Max looked ill at ease. He was wincing, as though he was hearing a high-pitched noise. I couldn't figure it out. Just days ago, he'd stared down a speeding car as though it were nothing. Just *minutes* ago, he'd told us to "bring it." What had changed?

"Max," said Sanger, "are you gonna flake, or what?"

"*No,*" he said, with a sudden vehemence that made even Sanger raise her eyebrows. "No, of course not."

In one fluid movement, he hurdled over the side of the freezer. He situated himself in the bed of ice, face up. The freezer was long enough—and Max short enough—that he only had to bend his knees slightly to fit. He licked his lips, then puffed out a sharp jut of air.

"Cover him," said Sanger, reaching in and scattering loose chunks of ice over Max's torso and arms. I covered his legs, and I noted that at least Max was wearing his sneakers, so it was pretty unlikely his toes would get frostbitten.

"You okay?" I asked when we were done.

Max was still wincing, though this time it was clear why: He was in pain.

"Don't worry," said Sanger. "You'll go numb soon enough. I think."

"Thirty minutes," I said. "I'm timing. But if you need out before then—"

"Stop coddling him, Nicks," Sanger said, hitching up a seat on the hood of the Fiat. "He wants an almost death by freezing, and that's what he's going to get."

She ripped open an orange tube Popsicle and offered me a strawberry one. I joined her on the Fiat, but not before giving Max an encouraging thumbs-up.

"How many people do you think have gone this way?" Max asked. His voice was breathy, strained.

"Frozen to death?" asked Sanger. "Who even knows. A lot during the caveman era, I bet. A whole lot."

"You don't really want to think about that right now, do you?" I asked.

I bit wrong on my Popsicle, and a chunk of it fell onto my shorts, staining the right cuff pink.

"I don't know," said Max. "I have a whole lot of sympathy for them now, that's all. I thought cold would just be *cold*, not . . . I mean, it *burns*. What a weird thing for cold to do."

"Here's a question," said Sanger. "Would you rather die from cold or heat?"

"Heat," Max said immediately. "Definitely heat. Heat sounds excellent right now."

"But put it into perspective," I said. "At least you'd

eventually stop feeling things in the cold. You'd go into shock, or a coma. But heat, like desert heat? You'd feel it all. You'd smother to death. And all the while, you'd be burning to a crisp in the sun."

"*You* would burn to a crisp," Sanger corrected.

"It still wouldn't be pleasant," I said, "whatever your melanin levels."

"It's like that Robert Frost poem," Max said. "About the world ending in ice or fire, you know? And at first he's like, fire, no doubt. And then he thinks about it more and is like, but ice is pretty bad too. You know, how people like Dante thought that the deepest layer of hell would be cold? Like, frozen over?"

"That's bleak, Max," said Sanger. "Is that what they teach you at prep school?"

"Yes," he said, and Sanger snickered.

"What?" I asked.

"It's just funny that the poem's by Robert *Frost*. You know? Because—"

Sanger's bad joke was cut short by a sudden, terrifying *slam*.

It was the noise I registered first. The slam. Then a clank. Then the sound of a muffled shout.

The freezer lid had fallen shut.

"Oops," said Sanger, jumping off the car hood. "Oops, *oops*. Sorry, Max! Hang on!"

She pushed the lid, then frowned. She heaved at it again. It didn't budge.

I dropped my Popsicle and slid off the car, hurrying to Sanger's side.

"What, is it too heavy?" I asked.

Sanger licked her lips. She shook her head. She was pointing to something at our feet. It was a long metal handle—the source of the clanking noise.

I looked at the freezer's latch, which was now nothing more than warped metal. The handle must have broken off from the force of the slam. Max yelled again.

"Both of us," I said, gripping my fingers under the lid and nodding to Sanger. "Come on, push."

"It won't work," Sanger said, shaking her head. Her voice was stretched thin. "Look at how the handle broke off. It won't work."

"Just *try!*" I yelled.

We tried. We pushed at the lid, and we pushed again. It didn't budge.

"Oh my God," said Sanger. "Oh my God, oh my God. We're going to freeze him in there. Or he's going to suffocate. Or, whatever, he's going to *die.*"

The next time Max yelled, I could make out his words.

"Not this close to death!"

"It won't open!" I shouted back. "Don't panic, we're going to figure something out!"

Sanger had gotten on her knees and was tugging on something at the garage wall. The plug. She was unplugging the freezer.

"There's still tons of fresh ice in there," I said.

"I know, I know, I know." Sanger was shaking as she got to her feet. "I know, I'm just trying to do *something*."

"It's the latch," I said, stooping to inspect the hewn metal. "It got cut off weird. Look. Look here."

Sanger stooped beside me as I pointed. The lid had been constructed with a latch on top, a handle on the bottom. A clean break would've simply broken the handle off but left the lid free to open. But this hadn't been a clean break. We had left the handle bent down when we opened the freezer, and the slam had smashed it loose, warping the remaining metal up in a vise grip over the top of the lid.

"Look," I repeated. "See? It's not that bad. We just need something to pry the metal down. Like, um, like a crowbar."

I looked around, surveying the garage. At the far end, a few hammers and wrenches hung from a pegboard. I headed toward it, eyes still scanning. Sanger followed, fast on my heels.

"Where would you keep something like that?" I asked.

"Like a *crowbar*?" Sanger barked a hollow laugh. "Do I look like a carjacker?"

"Those," I said, spotting a large pair of pliers that hung on a peg out of my reach. "Those could work."

I grabbed a nearby box marked *Halloween* and rammed it against the wall, climbing atop to reach the plier handle tilted closest to me.

"Keep looking for something else," I told Sanger. "Something bigger. Any kind of pry, okay?"

Back at the freezer, I knocked on the lid.

"Max? Max, it's okay. We're going to get you out."

There was no reply. Panic burst under my skin and screeched through my veins.

"Max? *Max*?"

Nothing.

"Oh my God," Sanger wailed.

"Keep looking!" I shouted.

I opened the mouth of the pliers, positioning them over the most accessible shred of metal bent over the lid. I closed the mouth down and wrenched back, my body slanting from the effort. It was easier than I'd anticipated. The metal didn't bend easily, but it did bend, curling back under the grip of my pliers like the snap of a soda pull-tab.

"It's working," I said, more to myself than Sanger.

There was only a little metal left obstructing the lid, a quarter's width across. I tried positioning the pliers at its edge, but when I closed down to grip, I lost hold. I stumbled back, swearing loudly. Then I tried again, coming at the metal from the other corner. This time, my grip held. I bent the metal shred back like I'd done the one before it, and the lid was free. I pressed my sweat-soaked palms against the edge of the freezer. I pushed up. The lid gave way, swinging up toward the wall with such force that it came careening back down. Sanger reached me just in time to help catch the lid and, this time, guide it safely to an open resting place.

Max sat up, ice clattering down from his body. He looked at Sanger, then at me. He said nothing. My body slackened with relief.

"Why didn't you answer me?" I demanded.

"I was conserving oxygen."

"That was bad," said Sanger, covering her face with her hands. "That was so bad."

"But you're okay?" I asked.

Max looked at me again, in silence.

And he started laughing.

It was a wild laugh—clunky and staccato, the kind of laugh you can't control. The kind of laugh that hits you in the middle of a lecture or during a moment of silence, when, of all possible times, you're not supposed to find anything funny. And that, of course, is when the laughs hit you the worst. Max gripped the edge of the freezer, laughing in that uncontrollable way, his face going purple from the exertion. Or maybe his skin looked purple for other reasons.

"We should get you out of there," I said, glancing nervously at Sanger.

"Is hysteria a symptom of, like, hypothermia?" Sanger whispered, but loud enough for Max to hear.

Max just laughed in a clunkier, wheezier way. He waved his hand at us.

"I-I'm not hypothermic," he said. "I'm not. And you haven't taken the photo yet."

The photo. How could Max be thinking of documentation at a time like this?

"Take it," Max said, more insistent than before.

I grabbed the Polaroid, but I was still watching Max in a leary way.

"We take the photo," I said, "and then we get you out of there."

"Mhm," said Max, lying back down on the ice.

This time, there were no sharp breaths, no protestations of pain. He just remained still, eyes closed, waiting for me to snap the picture.

When I did, Max burst into the jagged laughter again.

Sanger touched my elbow and said, "I think we've broken him."

"We're really, really sorry, Max," I said. "I mean—that was, like, a freak accident."

Max sat up, his body shuddering.

"Are you kidding?" he said. "That was the whole point. An almost death? We couldn't have planned it better if we'd tried."

"That could've been some serious shit, though," said Sanger. "You get that, right? If Nicks here hadn't gone all Bob the Builder on you—"

"But she did," said Max. "She always saves me."

Then he looked at me in a steady, unblinking way that turned the contents of my chest to liquid. Only I couldn't figure out if I *liked* that sloshy, heated feeling inside of me. I

couldn't figure out Max. He'd sounded panicked enough earlier, when he'd been locked in that freezer, yelling for release.
And before that, his reservations, his uncertainty—I'd never
seen him like that. But he was laughing now, and he was
looking at me *that* way.

Max climbed out of the freezer, his skin damp and off-
colored. He'd only taken one step when he stumbled and
grabbed hold of a utility shelf to right himself.

"Whoa there," said Sanger. "Take it easy. Let's get you
upstairs. I'll start a warm bath or something. A warm bath,
right?" she asked, looking to me as though I were the WebMD
page on severe chill. "That's what you're supposed to do in
cases like this, right?"

"Yeah," I said, stooping to lend Max my shoulder. "I guess."

Sanger shoved the gelato and Popsicles into the freezer. She
plugged it back in and shut the lid, causing me to jolt. Then
she disappeared into the house, while I devoted my attention
to Max.

"Hey," I said. "Are you okay? You can breathe okay, right?
You're not getting dizzy or anything?"

"I'm fine." Max straightened with the help of the utility
shelf and my hands. "My legs are just weak from the cold, I
guess."

I walked in step with Max. He moved carefully from there
on out, and he didn't stumble again, not even on our way up
the steep stairs to Sanger's bedroom. We didn't speak. Max was

swallowing raspy, erratic breaths that I hoped were only the side effect of having laughed too hard.

We passed through the yellow onslaught of Sanger's bedroom and into the adjoining bathroom. Sanger was sitting on the closed toilet lid, chin in hands, watching the tub fill with steaming water.

"Still with us, Maximilian?"

"I'm cool," he said.

Then he started to snicker again.

Sanger grabbed a pink floral towel and shoved it at his chest. "I'll leave you to it, then. Get warm. If you feel like you're dying, give us a shout." She paused on the threshold, wearing a wicked grin. "I mean, unless you want to scrub him down, Nicks."

Heat poured over my body, pinking my skin. Max was looking at me, eyebrows raised.

"Yeah, no, I'll just let you do your thing," I said, jetting to the door and shoving Sanger out of the way in the process. I yanked the door shut, then gave Sanger a death glare.

"Ho hum," she replied.

Then she dove onto her bed and retrieved a jumbo bag of M&M's from under a throw pillow. When I joined her, she nudged the bag toward me.

"I shouldn't," I said.

My sugar had been consistently high for the last few days, which was due solely to the fact that I'd lapsed on watching my food intake and insulin levels. We'd eaten penne and marinara sauce after the pepper incident, and I knew that hadn't helped the situation.

"Moms are going to be none too pleased about that freezer when they get home."

"Oh no," I said. "Do you think one of them might actually *raise her voice?*"

"Hey, I can't help that I don't get punished. Anyway, it's not like I got a DUI. I broke a freezer. And I can totally just blame it on a manufacturing issue. Faulty handle."

Sanger clicked on the television to a sitcom, and we watched in silence for a while.

"Joel wanted to come along today," I said.

"What?"

"He was acting all injured because we didn't invite him."

"*What?* You could have invited him. You know my situation!"

"Yeah, I know your situation. That's why I didn't invite him. He's great as a cousin, he's great as a friend. But the moment you two start messing around, he'll be a total jerk to you."

"Nicks," said Sanger, grabbing me by the shoulders and giving me one firm shake. "I don't want to marry and settle down with the asshat. I just want to kiss his perfect mouth."

"I'm fighting the urge to puke on you. And I've got a track record, so just watch out."

"We should invite him one day," Sanger said. Then, with much feeling, "I'm going to invite him."

"He probably wouldn't get what we're doing," I said, now fervently repenting of having ever mentioned Joel. "He'd think it was weird. You know, he's super mainstream like that."

"You don't know that. I'm inviting him." Sanger pleadingly tilted her head in my direction. "Unless you forbid it."

"Like I could stop you," I muttered. "I'm just telling you, it's a bad idea."

We went back to channel surfing. Outside, the rain picked up, and lightning occasionally lit up Sanger's sheer-covered windows. We still hadn't talked about the recent terror we'd both felt, or about how we could've very well killed Max Garza in that chest freezer. But after a while, Sanger turned to me with a simper.

"So, that sexual tension between you and Max," she said. "*Meow*. I could cut through that like soft cheese."

"Sanger, just no."

It was a "no" to the fact that she'd meowed, but it was also a "no" to the fact that she'd used the term "sexual tension" in reference to Max and me. "Sexual tension" was a phrase I reserved for One True Pairings from television shows and book series. Sexual tension was *not* what was going on here. Sure, Max and I had shared some weird smiles and lingering looks, but that was far better classified as "highly awkward, confused, and hormonally charged exchanges."

I told Sanger as much. And then Max came back into the room, and Sanger kept talking as though he hadn't, and I pelted her with a handful of M&M's.

"How're you feeling?" I asked Max.

"Grand," he said.

He was wearing the same damp clothes as before.

"That can't be good for you," I said.

"Oh, yeah," said Sanger. "Sorry. I'd offer you a change, but we don't believe in man clothes in this household."

He shrugged. "I'll just strip down when I get to the orange room. Speaking of which, I should probably head there now. . . ."

I checked my phone. Sanger's moms weren't back yet, but it was twelve fifteen.

"Oh, hey, Max," said Sanger. "Would it be okay if we invited Joel on one of these expeditions? I think he could be a big help on the Death by Delusions of Grandeur one. You know, like a special guest star."

Max shrugged. "Sure, I guess."

"Fabulous," said Sanger. "I've got to pee."

Then she hopped up and left us alone in the most blatant display of matchmaking known to humankind. I got up from the bed so Max didn't have to look down a good two feet.

"That was fun," he said. "We should do it again sometime."

"Sixteen to go," I reported. Then, "Are you really feeling okay?"

I didn't want to sound overbearing, and I certainly didn't want to sound like a mom. But I'd been way more afraid in that garage than I'd let on, and the only expressible emotion I had left to me was concern.

Max nodded. I stuttered on.

"And," I said, "and—you're sure your mouth is okay?"

"My taste buds may have been thrown off-kilter permanently, but I'll have to wait until tomorrow to see if sweet stuff
tastes sour and spicy stuff tastes bland."

"You don't have to wait until tomorrow," I said, picking up
the bag of M&M's and handing them over. "Try it out now."

Max gave the candies a cursory glance and set them down
on Sanger's vanity.

"Okay," he said. "I'll try it out now."

He kissed me.

He did it in a way I'd seen before on television. He hooked
one hand around my waist and tilted my chin, and he kissed
me. And I did what I'd seen on television: I wound my arms
around his neck and stood on tiptoe, even though I didn't need
to. I wondered, even as our lips moved, if we *looked* the way
that people on television looked. It was, by far, my longest kiss.
The only one I'd had before Max had been Greg Herrick my
freshman year, and that experience had felt more like Greg was
hungry and my lips were a fudge brownie.

This kiss, this *real* and *long* kiss with Max, wasn't bad, just
different. I felt my cheeks flame up as he pulled away, and I
wondered if I should've tried using tongue, or if the guy was
supposed to start something like that.

"Your face is bright red," said Max. He looked pleased
about it.

"You still smell like pepper," I said, even though he didn't. Then, as he headed for the door, I asked, "Do *you* think there's sexual tension between us?"

It was totally the wrong thing to ask a guy you'd just kissed, I knew, but I felt like I could ask Max. I felt like I could ask Max a lot of things I wouldn't normally ask a guy. Maybe it was because he'd fake-died in my presence six times now, and fake deaths built up confidence.

"Oh," he said. "Definitely."

After Max left, and with precise timing that could only mean she'd been waiting for him to go, Sanger whisked back in from the adjoining bathroom.

"Told you," she said, and she smiled like a cat that had swallowed a whole flock of canaries.

Thirteen

Sunday night, I spoke to my parents.

A week before, after Sanger had told me her news, I'd asked them if we could convene for a family meeting. It had taken this long to get Mom and Dad with me in the den. I didn't want Joel to be there, but he was anyway. He sat on the couch, stringing his lacrosse stick, and he refused to leave when I asked him.

"Is this a private matter?" Mom asked me, which sounded more like she was asking, "Is this dirty?"

And of course I had to say "no," because if I said "yes," Joel would try to taunt it out of me afterward.

So Joel stayed on the couch, and Mom and Dad settled down beside him. I sat on the edge of the recliner, across from them.

"I don't want to go to co-op anymore," I said. "And I know you're going to try to convince me otherwise, but I've made my decision, and I won't change my mind."

Whatever my parents had expected from me, this clearly was not it.

"Where is this coming from?" asked Dad.

LUCKY FEW • 221

In the lamplight, I could see the dirt still caked on his fingernails—lawn nails, my mom called them.

I had hoped Dad wouldn't be the one to get the conversation rolling. I loved him, and I knew he loved me, but he never paid much attention to what was going on in my life. I didn't blame Dad; he had a taxing job, and he worked sixty hours most weeks. He would tell me stuff like, "I'm proud of you, sweetheart," and he meant it, but the truth was, he didn't know anything about my most recent art project at co-op or when I had appointments with the endocrinologist or what *STA* even stood for. He wasn't the kind of dad who coached my soccer team or took me on father-daughter ice cream dates. We just weren't close in that way. I was fine with that, really, but it was for that reason I didn't want to be carrying on the brunt of this discussion with Dad. He just wouldn't understand.

I looked to Mom in a pleading way.

"Is this about the Sadler-Hamasakis?" she asked.

"What do the Sadler-Hamasakis have to do with co-op?" asked Dad.

He really was trying.

"Have they not told you yet?" Mom asked him. "They're moving. In June. To Pittsburgh."

"Philadelphia," I corrected.

"They haven't mentioned it," said Dad, looking upset. "Whoever buys that house is going to ruin the carp ponds."

"There was a meeting with the Sadler-Hamasakis a couple

weeks back," said Mom. "The leadership board asked them to leave the co-op."

"I see," said Dad.

He didn't ask why, and Mom didn't elaborate, but I was sure they both knew the reason.

"It isn't right," I said, "what Mrs. Weiss did to them."

"Wait," said Joel, looking up from his lacrosse stick. "What happened?"

"They got asked to leave because they're lesbians," I said.

"Wait, *what*? Seriously?"

"Honey," said Mom, "that's a very harsh way of putting it."

"It's a very *true* way of putting it," I said. "Sanger told me everything."

Dad scratched his cheek, leaving behind a smudge of dirt. Mom adjusted the hem of her skirt.

"Well, it's *wrong*," I said, trying to get a bigger response out of them. "I don't want to go to a co-op like that. That's blind hatred. It's disgusting. The doctors are way more talented and better parents than any of those other moms."

"I'm sure the women on that leadership team don't see it as hatred," said Mom. "They have a reason for their decision. They think they're acting out of love."

"Yeah," I said, "well, if that's their idea of love, it's majorly screwed up."

"I'm sure it wasn't an easy decision," Mom cut back in, "and yes, I think it could've been handled better, but that isn't even the reason the Sadler-Hamasakis are moving. Dr. Hamasaki was offered a job. You know that."

"But she might not have taken it if the leadership board hadn't treated them like a couple of reprobates."

"Whoa," said Joel. "Vocab."

"Shut *up*, Joel."

"Hey!" said Dad, raising his hands in a peacemaking gesture. "Let's bring it down a notch."

"Why aren't you taking this seriously?" I demanded of Mom.

"I am, sweetie. I just think you're blowing things out of proportion. You need to realize this is a much more complicated—"

"What's complicated about *hate*?"

"Stevie." Mom pinched the bridge of her nose. She sighed. "This isn't one of your rallies."

I grew still. "What's that supposed to mean?"

"You get so worked up over things. You demonize the other side. Mrs. Weiss and the rest of the leadership board aren't monsters."

"This isn't a rally," I said. "It's *Sanger*."

"I know you and Sanger are close," said my dad, "but I think you need to look at the big picture."

"What big picture?"

Mom placed a hand on Dad's knee, a warning of some kind. When Dad spoke to me again, he leaned in closer and softened his voice.

"There are several studies," he said, "that demonstrate the

importance of having a mother and a father in the household."

Dad was right: I didn't want to hear that. I couldn't believe I was hearing that. I shook my head at him, incredulous.

"So, what, you think Sanger is messed up or something? You think she had a faulty childhood because she grew up with two moms?"

"Don't make it personal," he said.

"It *is* personal!" I shouted, jumping from the recliner. "I thought you liked the Sadler-Hamasakis. You always say they're your favorite clients. But, what, when they're not paying you, you sit around *judging* them?"

"We know you're upset," said Mom, "but deciding not to go to co-op is not the right approach."

"It is. It's *my* right approach. I don't want to go there after what happened. I don't want to be there if Sanger's not."

"Sanger *is* Stevie's only friend," Joel pointed out.

"Why are you even here?" I shouted at him. "Can't you fix your damn net somewhere else?"

For the first time since I was eleven years old, my parents sent me to my room.

Mom knocked on my bedroom door later that night, while I was reading *The Great Gatsby*. It wasn't part of my English curriculum, but I'd heard it was a book most kids read in high school, and I wasn't going to be *that girl* who knew nothing about Jay Gatsby in her college English class.

"Hi there," Mom said, taking a seat at the foot of my bed.

"Hi."

I put the book down, keeping my eyes trained on Mom as though she were a predator and I was prey. I was ready to jump out of harm's way.

"I love you," she said.

I wondered if this was some kind of trap.

"I love you?" I said back, cautiously.

"I love how deeply you care about the things that are important to you."

I studied Mom's clear brown eyes, then the laugh lines engraved around her mouth, then my bedspread.

"I sense a 'but' coming," I said.

"No 'but,'" said Mom. "When I was your age, I didn't care about anything. I had a severe case of teenage ennui."

"Really? You were an emo kid?"

"I wore quite a bit of black, if that's what you mean. When I turned fifteen, I surprised Nanna by dyeing my hair magenta."

"You owned Doc Martens, didn't you?" I asked, getting excited. "You would've been, like, a total Fall Out Boy devotee."

Mom smiled. "Maybe. My point is, I shouldn't have faulted you for caring. Though I think you might still be acting hastily, and you might be oversimplifying the issue. Not everyone in that co-op is a hateful bigot."

"I know," I said. "I get that. It's just the principle of the matter."

"I'm here to make a deal with you."

"Okay. Shoot."

"I've thought it through," she said, "and I've talked it over with your father. Considering there are only four weeks left of co-op, I don't think the lack of chem labs or art classes will affect your transcript. If it really means that much to you, I won't force you to go to co-op. However, I do expect that you'll do a full day's worth of schoolwork in its place. I'll be monitoring your assignments and the goal chart."

I nodded eagerly. "I swear, Mom, I can pay you back the money you lost in tuition. I will, once I get a summer job."

"I don't want money," said Mom. "I just want you to promise me that when the new school year comes around, you'll consider going back."

"I'm not going back."

"You have to promise you'll reevaluate that decision," she said. "That's all I'm asking. You're already on the roster for the next school year, and I don't want you to make a rash decision now that you'll regret when August rolls around."

"I won't regret it."

"The co-op is the easiest way to take your science labs and electives. If you don't go back, we're going to have to work out another solution."

"Fine," I said. "I'll look at other co-ops. I'll look at community college classes. I'll have the car by then, so I'll drive myself. If it's more expensive, I'll pay the difference. I'm just not going back *there*."

"Make the promise."

"I'm not going to change my mind."

"Stevie."

"Fine," I groaned. "Whatever, I promise."

Mom nodded. She patted my foot.

"I can't believe Dad said that stuff," I said. "About scientific studies?"

But in a way, I could believe Dad had said those things. I'd already identified my parents as borderline Blue-Jean Jumper. I just didn't realize how borderline. Okay, maybe they were *past* the line. Or maybe there wasn't a good way of categorizing it. Maybe I shouldn't have been trying.

I was thinking about what Mom had said too, about how this was one of my rallies. And I wondered if that was how my parents saw *me*. As a rally-er. As totally Granola. As a girl who just got worked up about causes for the sake of getting worked up.

God, I hoped not.

"Stevie," said Mom, breaking me out of my worries. "You're going to disagree with me and your father plenty of times. You have to pick your battles. And you have to learn that disagreement doesn't equal disrespect."

I narrowed my eyes. "Did you just sneak a parental lecture in there?"

Mom rose from the bed.

"That's what I'm here for," she said.

• • •

So Monday morning, I stayed at home. Joel went to co-op. He did not, he said, have the same moral scruples as me. I didn't hold it against him; I knew how much the lacrosse team meant to Joel.

It panned out as a typical school day. I worked through my assignments, math first and English last, making careful documentation of my work in the assignment notebook that Mom checked at the end of each week, along with my tests and quizzes. I finished reading *North and South* that day. It was underwhelming. I started an SAT vocab version of *Oliver Twist*, where three-syllable Latinate words were bolded in the text on the right-hand page and their definitions given on the left.

Max drove Joel home from lacrosse practice. I came out on the front porch while they practiced tossing. According to Joel, Max had excellent form, and though I didn't know and couldn't care less about the rules of lacrosse, I had to agree: Max had *very* excellent form. As I sat there on the front steps, playing my Top 40 playlist, I indulged myself in thoughts of how much closer I wanted Max's excellent form to mine.

Mom brought out a big plastic bowl of watermelon, and the guys took a break to join me on the steps, where we crammed our mouths and spat seeds and stickied our hands.

Afterward, Max and I headed to his car. He'd offered to take me to the STA rally. I warned him it would be a snoozefest.

He said, "I'll bring a pillow."

It took us a while to find a parking spot downtown, but

that was mainly because Max refused to parallel park between two cars. It was after he passed the second open space that I caught on.

"You can't parallel park," I said, "can you?"

"Sure I can."

I grinned in disbelief.

"What?" said Max. "Sure I can!"

"Okay, then do it."

"Not today."

I laughed. "What is *up* with you, Max Garza? You're a seventeen-year-old guy. You're supposed to be the most irresponsible driver out there. You're supposed to be, like, doing doughnuts in parking lots and paying a bajillion dollars in car insurance as a result."

"That's just not me."

"Why not?"

Max didn't answer.

The rally was more of the same. The Senate gallery had been full upon our arrival, so the STA members stayed outside. We went to the street and racked up about twenty more signatures on the petition. Maribel liked Max a lot. Behind his back, but not out of earshot, she referred to him as my "lover." I giddily reprimanded her.

Nothing exciting happened that day, except that unlike last time, the bill really was introduced in the Senate. As Leslie Cobb explained to us before we dispersed, now wasn't the time to ease up. We should call our senator, or write a letter, or both, and we should keep on collecting signatures for the petition, which would be presented to whichever Senate committee was assigned the bill.

In the car, I asked Max what he thought about the experience.

He said, "Very informative."

By then, the sun had set and the streetlights had guttered on. He parked his car a block away from our cul-de-sac. He unbuckled his seat belt, and he turned to me, the cracked leather *thurrp*ing with the shift of his weight. I thought he was going to kiss me. Maybe he thought so too. He leaned in, just a little, but he stopped. His breath smelled like Maribel's homemade lemon squares.

"What is it?" I asked.

"I'm not a complete lame ass when it comes to driving," he said. "It's just, when I was nine, my mom flipped our car."

I strained my eyes in the dark to check Max's expression. Frustrated by my lack of success, I punched on the overhead light. My eyes stung, then adjusted as Max talked on.

"It was when we were living in Montreal," he said. "She hit a patch of black ice. We were both fine. Mom broke her wrist, and I was pretty bruised up. But we were fine."

"I didn't know," I said, a pointless observation.

"I didn't handle it well," he said. "I didn't even get what death *was* before that, you know? Danger that big. The kind

that stops you short? It messed with me. I wouldn't go anywhere in a car after that without kicking and screaming. They
ended up sending me to a therapist."

I was quiet for a while. I poked at the glove compartment
handle with the rubber edge of my sneaker.

"I'm a horrible person," I finally said. "Sanger and I both
made fun of you for driving like a grandmother." I sighed,
pointed at my face. "Told you, failed the empathy test."

"You didn't know," he reminded me. "It's not something I
like to talk about because, I don't know, I don't like mentioning
the therapist part? I was nine. I was old enough to just get over
something like that. It was embarrassing."

"Is that what you meant back when I met you? You said
Death had messed with you one too many times."

"Twice is too many."

"Yeah, but I still don't see how that's Death screwing you
over. If anything, Death must like you. He let you live, right?"

"Yeah," said Max. "About that."

"What?"

"I may have kind of fudged about why I wanted to do the list."

I waited for him to continue. After a long space of silence,
he did.

"When I was ten, my therapist did this thing called exposure therapy. It's for people with anxieties, phobias. To get over
your phobia, you have to face the thing that scares you, straight
on. Only, like, in a safe environment."

"Sounds awful."

"It is," said Max, "but it's effective. It's how I finally got myself into a car again. We spent some therapy sessions out in the driveway where all I would do was build up the courage to get inside the car and sit down."

"So, the list?"

"It's my exposure therapy. Because if I didn't do it, I think—I don't know, I think I'd always be terrified of death. Something snapped after the accident in shop. I was like, this has happened twice. Both times I was just minding my own business, doing life, and *wham*. Some stupid accident blindsided me. So who was to say it couldn't so easily happen again? After that, I'd be shaving, and all I could think about was how the blade could slip. I'd be eating and think how easily I could choke. And even when I was doing nothing, just on the computer, I'd think, now's the prime time to have an aneurysm. I didn't want to live that way. Something like that, that way of thinking—it can paralyze you."

"Max," I said.

"I know. It's fucked up. But I found a way to fix it. The list, it's been great. The more deaths I face, the stronger I get, you know? It's my own exposure therapy."

"Max, are you seeing a therapist now?"

"Mom set me up with this woman here in Austin, but she's totally incompetent. And I think, why do I need a therapist when I've got my own method? And it's working, Stevie. It's really working."

I nodded.

"You think I've lost it, right?" he said.

"No," I said. "It makes more sense now."

I thought about the freezer incident, about the wary way Max had looked at the ice, the way he seemed so hesitant one moment and daredevil the next. Max wasn't just trying to take on Death for kicks; he was trying to shake himself of Fear.

Then I told Max about my near death at the hands of diabetes. I told him about the night terrors, everything. And maybe I wasn't fixated on death with a capital *D*, wasn't racked by anxiety that it was coming around every corner, but I at least got what it meant to be shaken into mortality when you're only a kid. I got that entirely.

"I made fun of you for your diabetes," said Max. "So I am also a terrible person."

"I guess that makes us even?"

"Deal."

"Maybe," I said, "we should be grateful to Death. If you think about it a certain way, it's like Death has brought us together. Death is our common ground."

"Death is *everyone's* common ground."

I splayed my fingers out from my head, indicating that Max had blown my mind. Then he really did kiss me, and I kissed back, and this time he used tongue, and I wasn't an expert, but I was pretty sure it qualified as a grade A kiss.

Fourteen

Death became our weekend ritual. We did almost everything at Hamasaki House, because it had the most resources and Sanger's parents were usually gone and, above all, because in less than two months it wouldn't be Sanger's house anymore.

We kept to a schedule of three fake deaths a week, sometimes more. At the rate we were going, there was no question we'd meet the June 1 deadline. Sanger even suggested we add to the list, but Max and I both vetoed that idea.

"The moment you do something like that," I said, "one of us will catch walking pneumonia."

"Yeah," said Max. "It's Murphy's Law."

So we kept to the list of twenty-three.

By May, we had checked off more than half the deaths and begun to tackle some of the more elaborate ones, like **5. Bitten by a brown recluse**. Max actually wanted a spider to bite him, just not a fatally poisonous one. In pursuit of such an arachnid, the three of us scoured the basement of Hamasaki House, then the attic. We finally found a suitable spider holed up in a box of Christmas china. It was no bigger than a penny, and colored gray.

We'd first speculated, then googled how to get the spider to bite Max. In the end, we had to drop it on his arm and collect it again a total of seven times before Max proudly displayed a set of tiny pinpricks just below the elbow.

"What if it turns out that it really was poisonous?" I asked Sanger, after Max had gone to the orange room for the night. "What if Max dies in his sleep?"

"Don't be silly," she said. "He can't die in his sleep yet. Natural causes is number twenty-three."

Occasionally, we went on field trips. Max insisted that **16. Starve in the wilderness** really had to take place in the wilderness. So we drove to the Greenbelt and hiked out for thirty minutes into as good a wilderness as we could scrounge up. We walked off the path into a copse and Max, who had been fasting for a full forty-eight hours, slumped against a tree trunk, assuming a forlorn expression for the camera.

"Hey!" said Sanger. "Do you think maybe he tried eating his own arm first?"

"YESSS," said Max. "Why didn't I think of that?"

So Max insisted we drive all the way back to his place, where he concocted a fresh batch of corn syrup–based fake blood. Then we drove all the way back to the Greenbelt and hiked all the way back to the "wilderness." There, Sanger set to work on Max's arm, and when her masterpiece of gore was done, I finally snapped the photo.

"It's a really awful way to go," I said on the dusky hike back.

"That's why we're rubbing it in Death's face," said Max. "He deserves a taunting after putting real people through that hell. What a sick bastard, Death."

On these ventures of ours, whenever conversation lagged, the topic always came back around to **17. Spontaneous combustion**. Max was serious about this being the fake death to end all fake deaths, and as such, he claimed, it would require weeks of forethought and planning. So far, the plan involved gasoline, baking soda, vinegar, firecrackers, and a recording of Tchaikovsky's *1812 Overture*. The whole thing seemed wildly improbable and idiotic to me, but I kept quiet when Max and Sanger jabbered about it. They fed off each other like two alpha dogs barking across the street, attempting to top the other's most recent manic idea.

"Yeah, and then you'll cram a whole roll of Sprees in your mouth and chug a two-liter of root beer!"

"And then there'll be, like, fire— Hey, no, wait, do you think anyone in town teaches fire-breathing lessons? You know, like what they do at traveling circuses?"

That kind of talk made me nervous. I liked to think they were joking about most of the stuff, but this was Max and Sanger. I couldn't be entirely sure. I wanted to tell them to stop, but I couldn't place exactly what it was that made me uncomfortable. Maybe it was the idea of Max flirting that hard with danger. Or maybe it was that every time they mentioned **17. Spontaneous combustion**, all I could think about was what came after it, on June 1. Sanger would be gone. Max would be in summer school. Even Joel would be moving on to all things college related. Max's last death would be fake, but the combustion would be real. I didn't like to be reminded of that. I didn't like to think we were speeding toward the end of the list, because we were also speeding toward the end of everything. I wondered if Max and Sanger ever saw it that way. I wondered if it scared them as much as it scared me.

We had to modify **15. Fall off a building** to **15. Fall off a cliff**. And it wasn't really a cliff. It was just the concrete edge of the pool at Barton Springs. This alternative was, Sanger admitted, a paltry substitute, but our commitment to the authenticity of number fifteen was tempered by the fact that it was Saturday, and it was sunny and seventy-eight degrees. There was no excuse on earth to pass up Barton Springs on a day like that, not even a death list.

Max stood at the water's edge, feet curled over the concrete. Sanger kept lookout, waiting until enough swimmers had cleared from the water below before she gave Max the go-ahead. I stood at a distance, positioning the camera at just such an angle that I couldn't see the water below Max and it looked like he really was falling from a cliff.

Sanger gave the signal and screamed to the swimmers, "BELLY FLOP!"

Max free-fell.

I snapped the picture just in time.

We joined him after that, swimming and racing and diving until our limbs ached with the fantastic soreness that only comes from swimming. Hours later, we lay out on the grassy bank, using the beach towels Sanger had brought from her place. We forced Max to take the bubblegum-pink Hello Kitty towel. We snickered at the men who shouldn't have been wearing Speedos and at an unsavory bit of PDA a few towels over.

"Can we get pregnant watching this?" I asked.

"Oh my God," Max said. "He's totally getting her off."

We all craned our necks. The girl was covered in a towel from navel to knee, and the guy's right hand was conspicuously under cover.

"Austinites are so sleazy," Sanger concluded.

We all snickered again, but in a different way than before—in a nervous, breathy way. I was reminded of the time I accidentally found Sanger's homemade birthday card for me in her dresser drawer, a full week before my birthday. I felt that same way all over again—embarrassed and a little sad, though no one and nothing was at fault.

I reapplied sunscreen. When I lay back down, something brushed my thumb. I opened an eye and found Max squinting over at me.

His hand—the three-fingered one—covered mine.

I flinched.

It was only a little, and I hoped Max hadn't noticed. To make up for it, I smiled, and I squeezed his hand, and I closed my eyes back up.

I didn't exactly feel like smiling. I knew Max was trying to be cute, to be romantic, but something deep inside me curdled at the sight of his hand on mine. The fact that he was missing two fingers didn't bother me, I told myself. Not, at least, in an important way. It bothered my instinct, the part of me I couldn't control, the part that *just liked* bluebonnets.

"When you have kids of your own," said Max, "do you think you'll homeschool them?"

"*If* I have kids."

"If?"

"I don't have childbearing hips," I said, waving a hand over my celery-stick form. "Seems like it'd be extra uncomfortable."

Max was quiet. Sanger had fallen asleep, and as a joke, I'd placed a glob of 85 SPF on her nose.

"*If* I had kids," I said, after thinking it over, "I guess I would homeschool them. I mean, I've liked it. I get to read all the time, and my family can go on vacation off-season. When I was seven, we went to Disney World in December, while everyone else was taking tests or finishing school. We didn't have to wait in long lines. Plus, the weather was great."

"Huh," said Max. "But don't you get sick of your parents?"

"Not really. Dad's always at work, and Mom and I are pretty close. I like being at home. I like being alone, too. Not everyone's like that. So if I had a kid who wanted to be around people all the time, maybe public school would be better for them. It just depends. Homeschooling is hard work. Especially when I was younger, my Mom had to do a lot of prep. I don't know if I'd be up to that. Maybe I'll be too busy with another job."

"You don't feel like you're missing out, though?" pressed Max. "On a normal school experience?"

He wasn't giving me the judgy face. He was just asking.

"Well," I said, "there is one thing."

"What?"

"You're going to think I'm so shallow."

"*What?*"

"Prom."

"Aaah. Promenade."

"Is that really what it stands for?"

"See, if you were a normal school kid, you'd know."

"I know it's ridiculous. It's probably severely overrated. It's just, in all the movies—"

"Oooh, all the movies."

Max was enjoying this too much.

"I didn't have to tell you," I said. "I just entrusted you with some vulnerable information, and you—"

"I'm sorry. *Sorry.* But it *is* totally overrated, in my limited experience. Then again, I'm a prep schooler. Maybe both of us are missing out on a state-funded extravaganza."

"It's possible."

"Don't *bad* things usually happen in movie proms? Public humiliation? Telekinetic disasters?"

"You're clearly watching the wrong movies. The prom I have in mind is, like, the slow-dance scene where they're playing 'Time After Time' and they finally kiss."

"Who's 'they'?"

"It doesn't matter. They're just a stand-in for you and whoever your crush is at the moment."

"So, what, your homeschool group doesn't do prom?"

"Half the people there think dancing is a cardinal sin."

"See, I get to thinking you're somewhat normal, Stevie, and then you say something like that."

"*I* don't think it's a cardinal sin," I said crossly.

"So prom. You feel like you're missing out."

"Who knows."

Max propped up on an elbow. The sun caught hold of his black curls, giving them a plasticky sheen.

"You know what?"

"Hmm?"

"We haven't really been on a date yet. Unless you count the rally, which I don't."

"Me neither."

"I suck, don't I?"

"Little bit."

"Okay, well, Saturday night. How about we do something Saturday night? Just the two of us."

"What do you want to do?"

Max didn't answer, so I opened my eyes to get another look at him.

"It's a surprise," he said.

"Meaning you have no idea."

"No," he said. "Meaning it's a surprise."

We got back into the water for **2. Drown in a public pool**. We had waited until after nine that night, when the lifeguards left their posts and the "Swim at Own Risk" warning went into effect. There were far more swimmers out tonight than there had been back in April, when we'd first met Max. A group of college kids was playing a tipsy version of Marco Polo at the deepest end of the pool, and the bank was dotted with stargazing couples.

We positioned ourselves closer to the shallow end, where we had relative privacy. We didn't want anyone asking questions or freaking out the way that I had when I'd thought Max was actually drowning. Max had, of course, been attempting **2. Drown in a public pool** the night we met, and it was because of my interruption that he now insisted on a "do-over."

The deal with drowning is that it's a progressive kind of death, not instantaneous like getting guillotined or shot in the head. It's possible to have "been drowning" in your life without having actually drowned. So the key to fake-drowning Max was, of course, to find the fine line between "been drowning" and "drowned."

Sanger and I sat at the pool's edge while Max floated on a foam noodle, a few feet out in the water. Sitting there in the still of night, under the glow of the overhead lights, I felt different. Maybe it was the way the fluorescents hit my skin, or maybe it was that Max had nothing to do but look up at my body. Whatever the reason, I suddenly felt exposed in a way I hadn't earlier in the day. My limbs looked extra pasty, and I noticed for the first time that I'd missed a huge patch of hair above my scabbed right knee.

And then there was the boob thing. Sanger and I joked regularly about the significant difference between her cup size and mine. I was, and feared I always would be, a 32A. Sanger was a C, pushing a D, and her "gals," as she called them, didn't show any sign of letting up. I'd never been so aware of the boob difference as when Sanger and I were sitting there, side by side, in front of Max. Sanger had effortless cleavage spilling out of her paisley bikini top, and I crossed my arms over my padded but still insubstantial chest.

I knew Max noticed. Of course he had to notice. I wondered if it bothered him, and I wished I wouldn't wonder. I shouldn't have cared. I was actively trying not to care, just the same as I actively tried not to care that none of the glossy girls staring me down at the grocery checkout aisles were a 32A or had pasty thighs.

Not that Max was that fit himself. He didn't have any defined muscles on his torso, and a thin ridge of flesh spilled over the waistline of his plaid trunks. That made me feel a little better, though I still hated myself for having to feel better in the first place.

But then.

Then I caught Max looking at me with a half smile. I half-smiled back at him, and I felt a *lot* better.

"What's your record for holding your breath underwater?" Sanger asked Max.

"I don't remember."

"Then we're about to find out. And if anything goes wrong, Stevie knows CPR, don't you, Stevie?"

I nodded. In addition to the rescue classes at Barton Springs, I took a Safe Sitter certification class every year, which kept me in good standing with the co-op moms as a well-qualified babysitter.

Max's half smile turned into a whole smile.

"That's not good incentive for me to resurface still conscious," he said.

"Ew," said Sanger.

To carry out my duties as Documentarian, I had to a sit on a towel at the pool's edge and hold Max's phone at a safe distance from the water. When I was ready to record the video, I gave the customary thumbs-up.

Max slipped off the foam noodle, which Sanger grabbed

to keep it from floating away. Then Max went under.

I started the video.

Sanger counted.

Max made it to eighty-one seconds.

He surfaced, breathing hard. Sanger extended the noodle, and Max grabbed hold, still heaving in breaths and swiping water from his eyes. He asked how long, and Sanger told him.

"Pathetic," he said, spitting out a mouthful of water and shaking his head. "That's embarrassing."

"It could be better," said Sanger.

"What are you talking about?" I said. "That was over a minute. That's good."

Max shook his head. "No. No, I've looked up how long people can stay under. Do you know how long? Up to *eleven minutes*."

"Yeah, but people who can do more than a couple minutes are professionally trained," I said. "Scuba divers and swim team kids."

"I was on swim team in fifth grade."

"It doesn't matter," I said. "Sanger and I don't think you're a pansy for not staying under longer. I think eighty-one seconds is totally respectable."

"That's because you play tonsil hockey with him," said Sanger. "I for the record think you're a pansy, Maximilian."

I shot Sanger a dirty look for several reasons, but primarily for the use of "tonsil hockey."

"Sanger's right," said Max. "I can do better."

"The point," I said, "is to have an almost-death experience, not beat a scuba diver's breath-holding record."

"Then all the more reason for me to try again," said Max, "because that didn't feel like an almost death to me. It was completely lame."

"You don't have to—"

But Max had already released the noodle and gone under a second time. I didn't bother videotaping. I wasn't in the mood. Sanger still timed. Max only made it to fifty-three seconds.

"How much was that?" he asked, once he'd regained breath.

"Uh," said Sanger.

"You're losing momentum," I said. "You've already used up the best of your energy. Give it a rest."

Max only plunged under the surface again, this time kicking himself deeper into the water.

"This is ridiculous," I said, glaring at Sanger.

"What? He's right. The whole setup is lame. He's just trying to liven it up."

"He's going to knock himself unconscious."

"Maybe he *wants* to knock himself unconscious."

I stared hard at the blackened water. Air bubbles popped on the surface in fast succession, then slowed and, at last, gave way to glassy stillness.

"That's enough," I said.

I put down the phone, yanked off my sandals, and jumped into the water. I pushed past the bracing chill and toward Max's body. My hand slammed hard into bare skin, and I made quick work of hooking my arms around Max's waist. He struggled against me, forcing my hold loose as we floated upward. I surfaced to the sound of Max's watery chokes.

"Don't you *dare* go under again," I sputtered.

Max was still horking out water and hauling in air, but I saw him shake his head.

"Come on," I said, and I swam to the pool's edge, keeping in stroke with Max, watching him closely, afraid that if I took my eyes off him for a second, he would go rogue and try drowning himself once more.

But Max didn't try anything funny. He climbed out of the pool, and as I followed I pretended not to notice Sanger's annoyed expression.

"I think we've all passed our peak," I said, grabbing my towel and drying down my legs. "We should just go."

I was trying not to sound angry, because I knew I didn't really have a right to be. Weren't we all just playing the game? This was how the list worked: Max almost killed himself, while we sat by making photo documentation and providing commentary. I knew I wasn't supposed to interfere, but what Sanger had said scared the shit out of me.

Maybe he wants to knock himself unconscious, she'd said.

And as I watched Max towel himself off, his chest still juddering out phlegm-speckled breaths, a terrible suspicion slammed into my brain.

. . .

We headed up the bank, which felt like running a gauntlet of PDA—a big sonic swath of lips on lips and whispered sweet nothings from the stargazing sweethearts. Maybe if I were a bigger person, like a poet, I would've found something beautiful about that walk. But I was just sixteen-year-old me, and I only found it to be gross and mildly unsettling.

Sanger was angry. She hadn't said a thing, but I knew. I knew *because* she hadn't said a thing. Still, I wasn't too worried. This wasn't an irresolvable angry. It was the same kind of angry I was feeling—an emotion that would slide off both our backs in the next few hours and that we wouldn't mention again.

"I'll see you two later," Sanger said once we reached the parking lot.

I watched as she headed for the Fiat, knowing next time she and I saw each other, we'd pretend like our last parting hadn't been as abrupt as this. We'd both just chalk it up to being tired. And maybe that was all it really was.

Max and I got into his car. He turned the ignition but didn't shift into gear. He sat staring out the windshield. The air in the car felt thick with the weight of something unsaid. I turned the AC up a notch.

"Look," said Max, "I was just trying to . . . You know, they say when it happens, your lungs burn. They say your thoughts fizzle away completely. That's what I've heard, anyway. I was trying to get it that far. I was— I don't know, maybe I let it get too morbid."

My tongue was itching with the question.

"Max," I said quietly. "Is this one hundred percent for you?"

"What?"

"You told me before, you didn't have close friends in Dallas. That Sanger and I are as close as you've got. And you said if you were going to die again, you'd want to go out living one hundred percent, knowing people cared about you."

Max stared. I wasn't sure if he knew what I was getting at. I wasn't sure I wanted him to. But then he grabbed my hand and held it tightly, squeezing out the remaining moisture in our palms. When I looked up, I knew he got it entirely.

"Hey," he said. "I have plenty of problems, but I'm not suicidal. Promise."

"It's just, sometimes I kind of wonder what we're doing here."

"I told you. I told you the real reason. It's my exposure therapy."

"And you're sure that's it?"

"Stevie, I'm *sure*."

"It's just, I know we're taking things to the edge. That's the whole point of this. I get that. But I don't want this to end badly."

"Like, you don't want to accidentally end up as an accessory to a murder."

I gave Max a hard look. "Like, I don't want you to *die*. For real."

"I won't."

We sat in a heavy, exhaust-scented silence.

I said, "I'm not sure you should do number seventeen."

"What?"

"I don't like the way you and Sanger talk about it. It just gets more and more dangerous, and—"

"But that's the whole point! It's the *pièce de résistance*, remember?"

"Oh, don't use your stupid French pronunciation on me!"

I glared at Max. He glared back. His bottom lip was trembling. So was mine.

We began laughing at the same time.

I covered my face with my hands and breathed in one damp breath.

"Stevie," said Max, once the laughs had puttered out. "Nothing bad has happened. Nothing bad is *going* to happen. I'll stop joking with Sanger about the spontaneous combustion, okay? I didn't realize it bothered you so much."

I lowered my hands. I looked Max in the eye.

"Things are still going to change," I said.

"What?"

"It's not all your fault. It's just—"

"What?"

I couldn't get it out. I couldn't express how I felt like everything was going to end, how I was terrified of June 1, how I didn't want to be reminded of that damn date.

"Nothing," I said. "But that is the last time I jump into Barton Springs to save your life."

A slow grin wound up Max's face. "Understood."

"Good."

"So, it's good to know you don't hate me for going a little haywire back there," he said. "But even if you *did*, I would've at least had some leverage."

He reached into the back and fished something out of the passenger seat pocket. He set it in my lap—three pieces of paper, stapled together, worn and curled on the edges. It was the STA petition. I flipped over the first page, then the second. It was three pages' worth of signatures, some in blue ink, others in black, a few in pencil.

"Sixty-four," he said. "Almost as good as my drowning time."

I stared some more at the signatures. Then up at Max. He was beaming like a third grader who'd just made a clean sweep at the National Spelling Bee.

"That should put you in good with the folks at Hot Springs Troupe Forever and Always."

"Springs for Tomorrow Alliance," I corrected, grinning.

"Mhm. What I said."

"Thank you," I said, holding the petition close to my chest.

"Careful. You don't want the ink to bleed."

"Shit. Oh yeah." I pulled the paper away from my damp shirt. "Sixty-four. That's . . . Thank you. Seriously, Max, thank you."

"Are you crying?"

252 •   KATHRYN ORMSBEE

I punched Max in the shoulder. Then I wiped away the tears.

"No judgment," he said, rubbing his arm. "I mean, I see why you love this place so much. I get why you want to save it now. It's worth saving."

"It is," I said, my voice swollen. I didn't say anything else, because I was pretty sure it'd start up an ugly bout of crying and that Max would think less of me, even if he wasn't judging.

Minutes later, once we were on the road and going a steady five miles under the limit, I trusted myself to speak again.

"For the record," I said, "I think I got the better end of our deal."

"You make it sound like signature wrangling isn't fun."

"It isn't for me," I said. "I hate trying to sell people something."

"Whereas that is my special talent."

"Then I guess I'm lucky you showed up."

"I'd say we're very good for each other," said Max. "Very complementary."

"Which kind?" I asked, though I knew which kind.

"Both, obviously. The kind that goes, 'You look absolutely gorgeous in that brown one-piece, which so excellently matches my eyes.'"

I snorted and said, "You're so stupid."

Which was as close as I'd ever come to telling Max Garza just how much I liked him.

Fifteen

I had worn 85 SPF at Barton Springs, and I had reapplied four times. I'd burned all the same. No amount of cold showering and aloe vera could prevent the pain of putting on a T-shirt the next afternoon, as I got ready for the lacrosse game.

The Wolverines were playing the Austin Christian Eagles, and Joel had racked up promises from the whole family that we would attend. It would be my first time seeing the co-op crowd since I'd dropped out. I wanted to support Joel, of course, and Max too. I did not, however, want to sit through two hours of boys running around with glorified sticks while I sizzled under the stares of all my former homeschooled peers. I especially didn't want to see Mrs. Weiss there, cheering on her turd of a son.

I'd gotten a few texts since dropping co-op, from people I actually liked. I'd explained to them, in the brevity afforded by text, that I was focusing on test prep. It was a perfectly legitimate excuse, since I was taking the ACT for the first time that June. But I didn't want to feed that same excuse to a dozen other moms and acquaintances who were only on the prowl for gossip fodder. I stayed close to my mom on the bleachers and devoted my attention to my phone.

"Honey," said Mom, "don't you want to sit with Valerie or some of your other friends? I'm sure they miss you."

"I'm good," I said.

"Are you going to stare at that phone the whole time?"

"Maybe."

Mom went quiet, which meant she was giving me a stern look. I slipped the phone into my purse. Sanger wouldn't text back for at least a full minute anyway. She hadn't come with me to the game for several reasons, one of which was three bleachers down and dressed in a retina-shattering Lilly Pulitzer dress. Mrs. Weiss, I speculated, had probably been one of those sorority girls who went to Longhorn football games wearing a cocktail dress and pearls.

"Is it because it's awkward?" Mom asked. "You haven't had Valerie over in a while."

"It's not about the awkward," I said. "Trust me."

"I know it isn't my business, but I don't want you throwing the baby out with the bathwater. There are some great kids your age, and they have nothing to do with the leadership board."

"Val and I just don't get along anymore," I said. "It happened before all the stuff with the Sadler-Hamasakis."

Mom didn't look at all convinced, but she produced a tin of mints from her purse and offered me one, a silent armistice between us.

Dad sat on Mom's other side, talking lacrosse with one of the other players' fathers. I'd once heard Dad say, when Joel wasn't around, that lacrosse was just soccer for wusses. If that really was Dad's heartfelt opinion, he never showed it at Joel's games. He screamed just as loudly as he screamed when watching a Baylor basketball game—and that was *loud*.

Once, during one of their practices in the backyard, Joel and Max had tried to explain to me the rules of lacrosse. I was an attentive pupil until they started to talk about the difference between short crosses and long crosses, at which point I returned to reading *The Great Gatsby*. I knew the essentials of the game by then. I hadn't asked to become an expert. And anyway, I was at a very tense point in the book, where everyone's at this luncheon, and Tom catches on to the fact that his wife, Daisy, is having an affair with Gatsby. It was the juiciest part of the book thus far, and I was grateful that I simply got to enjoy the juiciness and didn't have to write a persuasive essay on it afterward, like most kids in public school.

As Coach Whitt gathered the team together and the refs took their places, I tried to remember my crash-course lacrosse lesson. The only thing I successfully dredged from my memory was that each team was trying to fling a ball into the opposing team's net and that Joel was an "attacker" and Max was a "midfielder." Those terms meant nothing to me. I just watched the game, cheered when the green jerseys got a shot, and remained silent when the purple jerseys scored.

At halftime, I went down to the field. Max met me. He was covered in sweat, which I'd been hoping might smell nice since it belonged to Max. But it didn't; it just smelled like normal sweat—salty and laced with body odor.

"Gross," I observed, after Max had released me from a bear hug.

Max just planted a sloppy kiss on my forehead.

"Disgusting," I said, grinning.

"I could go all halftime," said Max, "but Coach wants to talk to us."

So Max joined a huddle around Coach Whitt, and I trekked back up the bleachers to Mom and Dad, careful to avoid eye contact on the way. The game started again, and after another ten minutes, I'd exceeded my lacrosse attention span. I tugged out my phone. Sanger had texted three times.

Are you surviving?

guess so.

R u having hot halftime make out sesh with Max?

I tilted the screen away from Mom, paranoid she'd sneak a peek.

I texted back, *I'm not just here for my bf.*

I couldn't remember when I'd first started calling Max my boyfriend, or when he'd started calling me *novia*, which he claimed meant "girlfriend" in Spanish. After the first time he'd used it, I'd looked up the translation online and found out it meant "fiancée." I'd called him up and asked him what sort of joke that was.

"It means 'girlfriend' too," he'd said. "It means both. I'm not trying to get you to marry me."

"Thank you," I'd said.

After that, every so often, when we were both in a particularly good mood, Max would call me "fiancée."

Anyway, I couldn't pinpoint exactly when we'd started to call each other those things. It was somewhere in the springy mush of those April and May weeks. All I knew was that I was not at the lacrosse game simply because my *novio* was playing. I didn't want either Joel or Sanger to think that.

Moms packed up the basement today, Sanger texted. *It's muy depressing.*

Whenever Sanger or I brought up the move, which was rare, we always couched it in phrases like that: "it's depressing," "doesn't it suck?" "I just can't believe it", "it's so unfair." For some reason, we felt the need to remind ourselves of what a horrible thing the move was. As if we didn't already know.

I was texting Sanger back when Mom grabbed my arm. The phone went flying out of my hand and clattered to the bleacher below. I scooped it back up, casting a nervous glance around, afraid I'd annoyed the surrounding crowd. No one had even noticed. They were all fixated on the field. Coach Whitt had called a time-out, but instead of the usual huddle formations on either side of the field, there was a tight pack of green jersey players all shouting and pointing at a spectacle just a few yards off from the water coolers. Two of the green jerseys were on the ground, rolling, aiming punches, *fighting.*

One of them was Aaron Weiss.

The other was Joel.

And even I, so poorly versed in the rules of lacrosse, knew this wasn't supposed to happen.

Coach Whitt and Mr. Vanderpool went running to the scene. They pulled the guys off each other. Aaron was screaming something at Joel, and Joel was screaming back. Some of the other Wolverine players were yelling too. The Eagles, like the rest of the crowd, were staring dumbfounded at the spectacle. Some of them began to laugh. Their coach crossed the field to speak to Coach Whitt. Mom's nails pinched hard into my arm.

"What do we do?" she asked. "What do we do?"

"Just leave it alone," Dad whispered. "Coach will bench him. It's Joel's responsibility to stick it out down there until the end of the game, even if it's from the sidelines."

Mom shook her head. "No, no. I think we should go down now. Something could be wrong. He could—he could have broken a bone, for all we know."

"He didn't break a bone."

Down on the field, Coach Whitt had been shouting an order to Aaron and Joel. They now walked away and sat themselves on opposite sides of the bench while Coach Whitt sent two reserves on the field.

"I'm serious, Harold," hissed Mom. "We should take him home."

"He's fine. We'll get the whole story after the game."

"It isn't about getting the whole story, it's about—"

I tried to tune out their words. Their loud whispers were beginning to draw the attention of the people around us, and I shrank with embarrassment. I was embarrassed, but I was worried, too. Joel wasn't the fighting kind. He'd never been in a fistfight, or at least not one I knew about. I wondered if this was about Val, but that didn't make much sense. Joel was over Val. Why would he be fighting over her, and in the middle of a lacrosse game? None of it made sense. I waited out the rest of the game with prickled skin and a twisted stomach.

The Wolverines lost, 8–15.

By the time we got down to the field, Joel was nowhere to be found. Dad spoke to Coach Whitt, who said that Joel and Aaron had been acting "shifty" around each other during practices, whatever that meant, and that he was going to organize a meeting in the coming week between both parties, whatever *that* meant.

"Hey!" I said, flagging down Luke Wert, one of the players and a friend of Joel's.

Luke gave me a leery look, but he came trotting over to Mom and me.

"Have you seen him?" I asked.

Luke nodded. "He left with Max."

"What happened?" Mom asked Luke.

Her face was just as horror-struck as it had been on the bleachers, during the fight.

"Aaron's a tool, that's all," said Luke. "Um, pardon my language, ma'am."

"What were they even fighting about?" I asked.

He shrugged. "Aaron's been ragging on Joel for weeks, trash-talking him every time we're off the field. I told you, he's a tool."

"Thank you," said Mom, before herding both Dad and me toward the parking lot. "I'm guessing," she said to me, "that 'tool' is a bad thing."

"The worst thing a high school guy can be," I confirmed.

When we got home, Max and Joel weren't there. Not that I was expecting Max to drive Joel to our house first thing, but it still wasn't easy to watch Mom pacing the front room, compulsively checking the window and clutching the house phone, as though Joel would think to call.

Joel didn't call. He came back that night, four hours after the game had ended. He wasn't drunk, and he wasn't angsty. I didn't even know he'd returned until I emerged from my bedroom for a snack and found him talking to Mom and Dad in the den, at which point I forgot about obtaining Doritos and backtracked. Unlike Joel, I didn't like listening to conversations I hadn't been invited to join.

A little later, I got a call from Max.

"Is he doing okay?" he asked.

"He's been talking with my parents, and no one's yelled yet."

"Good."

"What was that all about?"

"Honestly? It wasn't really clear. I just know Aaron's been a real prick to Joel lately, and he must've gone too far today."

"Thanks," I said, "for whatever you did for Joel. It's put him in an okay mood by the looks of it."

"I took him to a strip club."

I said nothing.

"Kidding," he said. "*Kidding*. We went to Zilker Park. We walked around. We fed ducks."

"Strip club was more believable."

"I'm serious, Stevie. We fucking fed ducks. I'm not even joking. We bought a loaf of bread at Central Market, and we fed the ducks. Ducks are crazy. Like, vicious, too. One of them nearly took a bite out of the other one's wing trying to get to the bread first. Canniducks."

"What?"

"You know, cannibal ducks? Canniducks?"

"Why Central Market?" I asked. "Everything's super overpriced there."

"Whoa, enough with the criticism. What happened to the gratitude for babysitting your angry cousin?"

"Joel is older than you," I said, "and he's not usually angry. Anyway, I thought you liked him."

"I know, and I do. And just in case you didn't know, he cares a lot about you. When he found out about *us*"—Max drew out the word in a sibilant way—"he gave me *the Lecture*."

"No, he did not." I started to smile.

"I assure you, he did. He used the words 'tongue' and 'condom' and 'beat you to a pulp.' Like a greaser from a fifties movie: *beat you to a pulp*."

Condom? Joel had said the word "condom" to Max in reference to me. I grabbed Snoops, my stuffed elephant, and pressed his plush belly on my face, as though this were in any way an effective method of absorbing my humiliation.

Sex wasn't something that had come up between Max and me, not *actually* and *physically*. It came up sometimes in conversation, but in the most generic ways, like when Max said that he and I had sexual tension or when we'd been at Barton Creek and snickered at the PDA couple.

Max and I had only talked about sex in *that* way, and it had only been around Sanger, because over the past weeks, all of our time had been spent with Sanger and the death list. As Max had recently pointed out, we hadn't even been on an official date. We talked and texted, just the two of us, but we hadn't been alone much. So far, I was okay with that. But now I wondered if Max was too.

I had been quiet for a while.

"Stevie," said Max. "You're not pissed at him, are you?"

"No," I said. "No, no."

"That was not my intent."

"I know."

There was a knock at the door.

"My mom wants to talk to me," I said. "Bye."

It wasn't my mom. It was Joel.

"Hey," I said, and I thought, *Beat you to a pulp.* It made me want to leap off my bed and hug him.

"Hey."

Joel closed the door and flopped down into my purple papasan. The left side of his forehead was bruised. His left eye was blackened.

"That escalated quickly," I said.

"Yeah, I'm sorry if I embarrassed you. And stole your boyfriend away."

"I didn't come to the game for Max," I insisted. Then, "Sorry you lost."

"It's whatever."

I was trying to figure out exactly why Joel was there and what he was after. I never went into Joel's room unless I wanted something out of him, and vice versa.

"So," I said. "What's up?"

"What did you hear about the fight?"

"Just that Aaron was his usual self, and you went off on him."

"You didn't hear anything else?"

"No," I said. "Why? Why are you acting all mysterious?"

"I'm not," Joel said, hoisting himself out of the papasan. "I just wondered, that's all."

"Joel. Seriously, what's up?"

"Nothing. Sorry I ruined your day."

When he slammed the door, a magnet clattered off my dry-erase board.

I texted Sanger, *Can guys get PMS?*

An hour later, as I was nodding off to sleep, she texted back.

Max or Joel?

Joel, I wrote.

Then no. Joel is perfect.

The exchange had knocked me out of my sleep drift, so I got up to pour a glass of water in the bathroom and, on my way back through the den, decided to check my e-mail.

Leslie Cobb had written.

Subject: WE DID IT.

World Changers:

That's right! For those of you who didn't already hear today's exciting news, the Cleaner Environment bill passed the Senate by a vote of 21–10.

I am SO PROUD of each and every one of you who contributed to this monumental success. Every name on that petition, every call or letter to your senator, every hour you spent volunteering for STA paid off in the end.

Nick Esquivel and I had the honor of bringing the petition before the Senate committee, and we were both present in the gallery during today's vote. Now all that remains is for Governor Vincent to put his John Hancock on this baby so New Systematic Solutions can feel the consequences of their careless and unsustainable practices.

This serves as an invite to a celebratory get-together THIS SATURDAY EVENING @ 5:00 PM. Feel free to come and go as you please. It'll be a casual potluck picnic—bring a dish or two!—and we will hold it, of course, at the Texas Rangers Memorial! Nowhere else would be quite as fitting. :)

A gigantic thank-you to all members of STA. I'm privileged to share this moment with ALL OF YOU.

Leslie Cobb

Founder, Springs for Tomorrow Alliance

"Two roads diverged in a wood, and I—I took the one less traveled by, And that has made all the difference."—Robert Frost

I read over the e-mail twice. When it had all fully sunk in, I clicked out of the window and squealed.

Mom poked her head in from the kitchen.

"I thought you were asleep."

I felt like I was glowing, like I was radioactive.

"We did it!" I said. "Barton Springs isn't going to turn into a toxic waste dump."

Mom took a break from wiping down a baking pan to give me a thumbs-up.

"I'm very proud of you," she said, "but celebrate on your way to bed. You've got school in the morning, even if it's not co-op."

I went to bed happy. I went to bed picturing myself on the grassy knoll at Barton Springs, free to be my anonymous self and think my clear thoughts whenever I wanted, in perpetuity. And as stupid as I thought Leslie's inspirational signatures were, one of them now framed my very way of thinking as sleep washed into my system. I'd been the change I wanted to see in the world—or at least, the change I wanted to see in Austin, Texas.

Sixteen

I knew what Sanger was up to the moment I spotted the yellow envelope in our mailbox. There was no return address, but Sanger's handwriting was unmistakable—precise and slanted leftward. The letter was addressed to Joel.

Ever since Sanger had received Max's blessing to invite Joel along on one of our deathscapades, I'd been waiting to see just how she would wrangle him in. Would it be coercion? A secret message passed along through my hands? Or maybe she'd just blindside him one of the days she picked me up at the house. My mind had bubbled with possibilities at first, but then weeks passed and still Sanger made no move.

Eventually, I figured she'd chickened out. But when I removed that envelope from the mailbox, I knew. What could be more perfect than this? Sanger was sending Joel yet another party invite, daring him to reject her again, like he had on her thirteenth birthday, simply because she was a cootie-ridden girl.

"Special delivery," I said, dropping the letter on the coffee table, where Joel was finishing a conjugation assignment in his Spanish textbook.

Joel set down his mechanical pencil. He stared at the envelope with distrust. He made no move to pick it up.

"There's no glitter in there," I said, "if that's what you're worried about."

Though I had no idea if that assurance was true. It was Sanger. There could be a baby squid inside that envelope for all I knew.

Joel glared at me. "Why're you hovering?"

"I just want to see you open it."

"Yeah, well, it's none of your business, is it?"

What was going on? Joel could be nasty every so often, but it was usually after I did something like slander the name of his favorite band. It was never like this. Never unprovoked.

"Fine," I said, backing off with a snarl to match his. "It's none of my business. Calm down."

"Whatever," said Joel, ripping into the envelope.

Luckily, there was no glitter. It was just a hot pink square of card stock. From where I stood on the living room threshold, I could make out the metallic heading of *You're Invited!* scrawled at its top. Sanger's unpredictability was terrifically predictable. Of course this was how she'd do it. My glare transformed into a smirk as I watched Joel read the contents of the invite. He was clearly confused. He flashed the card in my direction.

"What's this about?"

"Sanger wants you to hang out with us," I said. "And you know she can't ask like a normal person."

Joel frowned back at the card. "It says 'bring goggles.' What's that supposed to mean?"

"I imagine it means 'bring goggles.'"

He tossed the card on the coffee table and sank into the couch, covering his face with both hands. Only then did I realize his arms were shaking. Only then did I realize: Joel had been expecting a letter from someone. Someone other than Sanger.

"Joel?" I ventured, creeping a few steps back into the room. "Everything okay?"

"Yeah," Joel said, face still covered. "It's fine. Tell Sanger I'll come."

"Really?"

Joel didn't answer. I didn't press it. There was something happening here, something weird and weighty that I was not a part of. I left Joel alone with his thoughts and his shaking arms.

Things were back to normal that night. At supper, Joel talked about some upcoming freshmen at UT-Austin he'd met through an online group and how they were planning some get-togethers over the summer. Mom expressed her concern about Joel meeting in person with people he'd met on the Internet. Dad backed her up, saying it sounded pretty shady, and why didn't kids these days just make friends at orientation? I backed Joel up with a grand pronouncement that this was the age of the Millennials, and how else were we supposed to make sense of integrating into a freshman class of eleven thousand? Joel gave me a grateful wink.

So everything was okay again, and we were both in chipper spirits on Friday afternoon as we piled into Sanger's Fiat and headed to our next death-list destination: the W Hotel, downtown Austin. Sanger's moms had decided to do some renovations on the condo they owned there before leaving for Philly, which meant the place was currently vacated of its tenants and fair game for deathscapade number twelve, **Delusions of grandeur**.

"Why haven't we been using this condo for all our ventures?" said Max.

Sanger said, "It's possible the parental unit doesn't know about my possession of the condo keys."

"You *stole* them?"

Joel was sitting behind Sanger, his long legs bent against the seatback in a circulation-cutting V shape. He sounded impressed with Sanger, and for her sake, I hoped she'd heard it.

"We're not going to wreck the place or anything," she said. "It's just, us paying a visit is a little on the risky side. A one-time event. Meaning we should make the most of it."

"And what are we doing there?" asked Joel.

Sanger said nothing. Max and I exchanged a look in the rearview mirror. Though Joel knew the three of us hung out a lot, we'd never clued him in to what we did. And now that it came right down to it, I didn't exactly want to explain the situation. How could I? Every way my brain phrased it, it sounded wrong.

Max is pretending to die.

We're engaging in reckless and morbid behavior.

We've been plotting a fake spontaneous combustion for the past few weeks.

"We're just . . . taking some photos," I said.

"Photos of what?"

"It's just a project," I said. "Shut up, Joel."

"You guys are creeping me out. Photos of *what*? And why am I supposed to have these?" Joel waved a pair of swimming goggles.

"Oh, you actually brought some!" Sanger cried, just as she turned into a chrome-covered parking garage. "Bless you, child.".

"That's not an answer," said Joel. "I need answers."

We didn't give him answers. What had begun as awkward inability to voice the nature of our current mission had now turned into something much more enjoyable: toying with Joel's emotions. Our silence alone was driving him over the edge.

"Seriously, what's up? Is this some sort of initiation into a cult? Is this a surprise birthday party?"

"Your birthday's not for another five months," I told him, patting his hand consolingly.

"An intervention, then."

"Why, Joel?" said Max, turning in the passenger seat. "Are you engaged in behavior that requires intervention?"

"I wouldn't know. Isn't the whole point of intervention to, like, point out something I'm not aware of?"

"Score," said Sanger, pulling the car into a parking space right next to the elevator. "Joel, chill. All will be revealed in due time."

We got out of the car, Joel last of all and most reluctantly. He watched in meek silence as Sanger opened the trunk and pulled out two large triangular kites. One was rainbow patterned. The other bore the face of the Incredible Hulk. They'd been duct-taped together at their tops; their tails fluttered out on opposite ends.

"My son," said Sanger, turning reverently to Max and holding out the conjoined kites. "Your wings."

"Fucking A," said Max, accepting the proffered gift with a mad grin.

Joel stood close to the car. One of his feet was still solidly planted on the backseat floorboard. He clung to the car door as though it was the only thing keeping him upright.

"What. Is. Going. On."

"Just follow us," said Sanger. "We'll show you things."

She gave him a big, brave wink. Then she headed for the elevators. Only when we stepped into the buzzing parking garage lights did I notice how nervous she looked.

"I thought you said it was Room 237?"

The elevator dinged, and the doors opened, though on the eighteenth floor, not the second, as Joel had apparently been expecting.

"He's seen the Movie, right?" said Sanger, turning to me. Then, to Joel, "You've seen the Movie, *right*?"

Max, ever the gallant one, whispered into Joel's ear, clueing him in to the fact that "the Movie" was Stanley Kubrick's *The Shining* in Sanger lingo.

"Uh, yeah," said Joel. "One Halloween, I think. Yeah."

I could tell Sanger was trying hard to withhold the judgy face.

She said, "Well then."

She led us out of the elevator and to the condo, which was really number 1805. I'd visited only once before, during a brief hiccup between leases, when Sanger and I were twelve and her moms had allowed us a supervised sleepover. The condo had looked then as it did now—bare-walled and free of furniture. Our footsteps echoed as massive clomps in the empty, hardwood-floor rooms. The appliances were elegant and space-age. The recessed lighting shone on our faces as though we were pieces of art in a gallery exhibit. Max and Joel were clearly impressed by the place, and Max bemoaned that we couldn't make Room 237 our head-quarters from here on out.

"So, we're here," said Joel. "Is someone finally going to explain what's going on?"

Max flapped the kite contraption—his wings—at Joel.

"What do you think?" he said. "I'm going to jump off the building."

He nodded to the living room's glass sliding doors and,

beyond them, a long stretch of balcony. Before us was a magnificent view of Lady Bird Lake and the whole of South Austin. The balcony was boxed in by a waist-high railing but nothing more.

"The skies are ours!" bellowed Sanger. "Camera, Nicks?"

I unzipped my backpack and removed the Polaroid. "Check."

"Thanks, man," said Max, grabbing the goggles from Joel's limp hand and fitting them over his eyes. Then he slipped on the double-lined duct-tape arm straps of his homemade wings.

Sanger slid open the balcony door, letting in a rolling gust of city heat.

"Less of a breeze than I'd hoped for," Max said. "But it'll suffice."

Joel had grown still. His eyes caught mine in a wild stare, but he was smiling a little, as though he knew, or at least *hoped*, we were just being ridiculous. Still, I guess he had to ask.

"You all are joking, right?"

I finally had the guts and general kindness to clue him in.

"It's just one of Max's fake deaths," I said.

"What?"

"Yeah, he's doing twenty-three of them. We're calling this one Death by Delusions of Grandeur."

"I do this in the name of Franz Reichelt," said Max, strutting toward us with his impressive new wingspan and goggled eyes. "Poor guy thought he'd invented wings for sure and certain. Jumped off the Eiffel Tower to show them off. It ended poorly, but he went out in style."

"Enough history!" barked Sanger, heading outside and throwing on her shades. "Let's do this."

Max took slow, dignified strides toward the open door. I followed, Polaroid in hand, wondering how I was going to hold the camera steady long enough to snap the shot, because I was shaking so badly. Not from fear. I was laughing too hard at the totally weird mash-up of Max's solemn demeanor and the rainbow-striped wing popping out of his left shoulder blade.

Joel followed us, but he didn't come out on the balcony. He remained on the other side of the glass, arms crossed. He looked unsure and, as a result, much less like himself. It bothered me, so I called into the condo, "It's just a joke!"

Joel nodded stiffly.

Sanger said, "Focus!"

I got the camera ready. Max adjusted his wings.

"Do they look good from that angle?" he asked me. "Do they look imposing enough?"

"I think you're asking the wrong question," I said.

Max thought about this and nodded. Then he cleared his throat.

"Okay!" he said. "I, Max Garza, being of sound mind, have come before you to announce that I am a world-class genius and have been granted the divine knowledge of Flight. Today,

I shall demonstrate the glorious power of these artificial wings, patent pending."

Here, he shook his wings. He looked like some kid in an elementary school play trying to wriggle out of his costume. The camera was shaking again with my laughing spasms.

"Um. So. Here goes. Look upon me, oh peons, and despair."

Max turned around. He stepped up a few inches onto the bottom rail of the balcony, wedging his sneakers between the metal bars. Then he spread his arms.

"Good Lord, Max," Sanger hooted. "Nicks, take the picture already, would you?"

I had to quickly reposition my angle, scurrying down the balcony so that I could manage a good profile shot of Max. Once re-situated, I placed my eye to the viewfinder and snapped.

Max gave a throaty shout, waving his arms above his head.

"You're insane!" I shouted. "If someone down there saw you, they'd think you were actually going to try something."

"But no one can see me!" Max cried. "No one but the angels!"

Sanger cheered. I joined in.

"You're a bird, Max!" shouted Sanger. "You're a plane!"

And then a voice boomed from the other side of the glass, startling us out of our frenzy.

"Get. The fuck. Down."

We turned.

Joel was glowering at us, his arms crossed tightly.

"What do you all think you're doing?" he asked.

I glanced at Max, who had stepped down from the railing. I glanced at Sanger, who'd gone bug-eyed and was, for once, incapable of a clever response.

"We're just having fun, Joel," I said. "This is Max's thing. Don't be an ass about it."

"What *is* this?" Joel said. "You're faking his death?"

"That's what I said. Look, we didn't have to invite you—"

"Yeah, I wish you hadn't," Joel cut in. "This is really screwed up. What else have you been doing, putting a machete to his head? Holding him underwater?"

I cast Max another glance. He was red in the face. All of a sudden, his wings looked like very frail things, no stronger than twice-used tissue paper.

"Do you get how insensitive this is?" Joel said. "There are real deaths happening every second. You guys are, like, some of the lucky few still kicking, and you want to waste your time *pretending to die?*"

"It's not like that!" I said, full of a sudden sharp anger. "You have no idea why we're doing this. Why *Max* is doing this. You don't know where he's coming from."

"Yeah, well, do you know where *I'm* coming from, Stevie? Can you guess?"

It was just me and Joel then. It was just his question in my gray matter, worming around and bringing about a terrible realization.

Aunt Lynn.

He was talking about Aunt Lynn.

That's where he was coming from. That was the real death in his life.

His mother. Real cancer. Real death.

A deluge of freezing-cold guilt poured down my nerves. My mouth made a wet, clicking sound, but words didn't come out.

Joel shook his head.

"This was a real treat," he said.

He made for the door.

"H-hey!" Sanger called. "You need a ride ba—"

"I'll figure something out."

He sounded like he'd just gargled with acid. He sounded livid. He sounded so un-Joel.

The door slammed behind him, leaving the rest of us in hot silence, peppered only by car honks from the streets below. Sanger sank into a cross-legged sit, her head bowed. It looked like she was praying.

"What was that about?" Max whispered.

I could have told him. I could've told them both what I suspected: Joel was angry because this was personal to him—something that didn't even cross my mind when we invited him along. An oversight I hated myself for now. How could I have not considered the fact that he'd find this offensive?

"It's his senior year," I said instead. "It's almost graduation. A lot of stuff is going on. I think he's just under a ton of stress.

I mean, take what happened at the lacrosse game, right?"

"Yeah," said Max, who didn't sound even half-convinced by my weak explanation.

He slipped out of his kite wings and dropped them to the ground. Then, as though we'd been cued, he and I both sat next to Sanger at the same time. I put an arm around her back.

"We're terrible people," she said into her hands.

"No we're not. I'm really sorry that happened."

"It's not your fault. You told me he wouldn't like it. And now he thinks we're these death-obsessed emo freaks."

We'd been on such a high only a few minutes earlier. Now it felt like someone had rounded up all our remaining happiness for the day and buried it in wet cement.

Max said. "I kind of feel like shit now."

"You *shouldn't*," I said, surprised by how angry I sounded. "Maybe Joel has his reasons for getting pissed, but you have your reasons for the list."

"But I invited him for the stupidest possible reason," Sanger muttered.

"What're you talking about?" asked Max, but I shook my head at him. It would do no good now to mention Sanger's unrealized dream of kissing Joel before she moved away.

A minute passed during which no one said anything. Then another. And another. I rested my chin on my knees and watched the tail of the Hulk kite—a string of tiny green bows—pick up and flutter in the wind.

I wanted to sit Joel in front of me. I wanted to make him see we weren't making light of what had happened to his mom. We were just trying to help Max. But Max's story wasn't mine to tell. Not his real story, anyway. And Joel's story wasn't mine to tell either. So I'd told the others it was stress that had turned Joel so mad. I'd told them it was just end-of-year jitters, because that's what I hoped it was. Because we weren't terrible people.

Were we?

Because I could remember having qualms about the list when we first started.

Max held up the limp pair of wings. "What do we do with these?"

"Set them free to the wind?" suggested Sanger.

"I think that's a hazard," I said, peering through the balcony railing down eighteen stories.

Max began stripping off the pieces of duct tape, one by one.

"They've got some wear left in them," he said. "We should fly them sometime. Or, like, give them to kids in need or something."

"Watch it, Nicks. You're gonna mess it up."

Sanger pointed to the toe of my sandal, where the photo of number twelve was lodged. Carefully, I tugged it free. It was an excellent photograph. Max's arms were spread in abandon, his hair whipped back in the breeze. The Incredible Hulk glared, defying any onlooker to laugh at his undignified state. And in spite of everything, I smiled. That was the required reaction to a photo like this. This was a photograph of a happy memory. I hoped that a few months from now, when everything had changed, when everything with Joel was sorted, that's how we'd remember this day.

Seventeen

"No one gets salmonella from eating raw cookie dough."

"I bet it happens," Max said. "And what a treacherous way to go. Everyone trusts cookie dough, like everyone trusts ice cream and Thanksgiving pies."

"This is ridiculous," said Sanger. "No one trusts food. You can't trust food."

We'd moved operations from Room 237 to Hamasaki House. The three of us were gathered around the granite island in Sanger's kitchen, and for the past ten minutes, Max had been trying to convince Sanger that drinking down a raw egg from a wineglass was a worthy execution of **11. Poisoning**.

We hadn't talked about Joel since driving out to the Hill Country. After leaving the W, we'd pushed aside the bad feelings and grabbed dinner at Tacodeli (it was my turn in the Sanger vs. Stevie Taco War). Then, with fresh minds and full stomachs, we'd decided we should complete our remaining death for the day. Sanger had swung back by my house so that I could pack a duffel for a sleepover and so that Max—who had plans with his gramps early the next morning—could drive out in his own car. We acted like everything was fine, like there hadn't been a blowout that afternoon. But Joel's outburst was still present, spread over the three of us like sticky chewing gum residue we couldn't be rid of entirely. And for whatever reason, that unshakable residue had turned Sanger argumentative.

"It's supposed to be about the effect," Sanger argued, "not the cause. Anyway, raw eggs aren't dangerous."

"There's always a chance they could be," Max said.

"Yeah," said Sanger. "Like, one in a million. You're the one who's been complaining about these deaths being lame, Max. Drinking down an egg is the height of lame. How does that even touch upon the awesomeness of Death by Poison?"

"Death by Poison isn't awesome," said Max. "It's brutal and ugly."

"Says who?"

"*Madame Bovary.*"

Sanger gave Max a look, just like the look she'd made when he'd said his favorite composer was John Williams.

"Prepper," she muttered.

Max squinted. "Is that a prep school slur? Because you do *not* want to open that can of worms, thou who art schooled at home."

"Both of you calm down," I said. "It's Max's list. If he wants to drink an egg, he can drink a freakin' egg."

"But I'm the Researcher," Sanger said. "My idea was way better."

"Your idea was to make Max eat another pepper."

"A *different* pepper."

"Yeah, funny I didn't go for a repeat of that pleasant experience," said Max. "You eat a ghost pepper, then we'll talk."

"Go ahead, then," said Sanger. "But I thought you were into taking risks. How the mighty have fallen."

I'd never told Sanger about what Max said to me in the car that night after the STA rally, about the car accident and exposure therapy. And I hadn't told her about the night after the fake drowning, when I'd asked Max to tone it down. How could I? Max told those things to me in confidence, in moments that were just ours. It would have been trite, *wrong*, to pass them on to Sanger.

Still, in that moment I wished that Sanger would magically know all that I knew. I wished she knew that the death list wasn't just Max's way of filling a school-free spring. I wished she knew that he was afraid of the things he was doing, more afraid than he let on. I wished she knew that the reason Max wasn't being such a risk taker this time around was probably because of what had happened at Barton Springs. He'd promised to calm down a little.

Max was ruffled by what Sanger had said. I could see it in his darkened expression as he studied the orange yolk sitting at the bottom of the wineglass.

"If you're going to make it an egg," said Sanger, "you should at least do it in style. Whip up a Prairie Oyster or something."

"What the hell is a Prairie Oyster?" Max asked.

"A cocktail," said Sanger. "Cures hangovers."

"All right," Max said, scooting the glass across the counter. "Then whip up a Prairie Oyster."

"I don't know what goes in a Prairie Oyster. Anyway, it would still be lame."

"Then what do you want me to do?" Max demanded. "You want it to be less lame? Fine."

He crossed to the sink, crouched, and threw open the cabinet doors. After rummaging for a moment, he came up with a bottle of window cleaner.

"Let's go crazy, huh?" he said, unscrewing the spray nozzle.

I shot Sanger a panicked look, but she was busy staring Max down, daring him to go on.

"Max," I said. "Put it away. That stuff can actually kill you."

"What if it's just a splash?" he said, tilting the bottle precariously over the lip of the glass. "Is that still enough of a gamble?"

"Both of you, stop it," I hissed. "There's a reason people make cocktails with raw eggs and not cleaning solutions."

"That's why this is so risky," said Max. "Right, Sanger?"

"Honestly," I said, and I grabbed the bottle from Max, its contents sloshing over my hand and his shirt, though not into the glass.

I slammed the bottle down hard on the counter and screwed the nozzle back on.

"Drink the egg, Max," I said. "Do it your way, and let's be done with it."

286 • KATHRYN ORMSBEE

This wasn't the way the death list was supposed to happen, especially now that we were down to our last handful. It was supposed to be fun and edgy and full of laughs, the way it had been before. Now it was a mix of moody glares and accusations of lameness. And *why*? We'd been having a great time just hours earlier, when Max had worn his makeshift wings and stood over Austin. Was it just Joel who had thrown things off?

"Well, go on," said Sanger. "Bottoms up, Maximilian."

It could've been in my head, but I heard Sanger inject Max's name with a venom she'd never used before.

Max looked between the two of us. He shrugged. "Then here goes."

He tossed the whole thing back in one go. He swallowed with an extra-loud gulp that sounded like something from a cartoon.

Sanger and I watched his reaction in rapt attention.

It wasn't much of a reaction.

He smacked his lips a few times, contemplative. Then he lumbered over to me and made a terrifying slurping sound. I pushed him away by the face, laughing.

"It wasn't bad?" I asked.

"It wasn't bad," he said, rubbing his index finger across his top row of teeth. "In fact, I think I liked it."

Sanger looked disappointed.

"Go on, Nicks," she said. "Photo."

"What does a victim of salmonella poisoning look like?" Max asked.

"Just pretend you're dead," I said. "You're a seasoned pro."

Max got down on the floor and crossed his arms over his chest, Dracula style. I leaned in close and snapped the photo.

Max opened his eyes. He stuck his tongue out at me. Then he leaned up and tickled me, hard, in the gut.

I lost my balance and toppled onto his chest, a mess of giggles. The Polaroid fell from my hand to the ceramic tile, and there was a cracking sound. Still, I couldn't stop giggling. Max kept tickling me, and I vainly swatted him off, and we were tilted on the floor in a jumble of limbs.

"Guys. YOU GUYS. CUT IT OUT."

When my face emerged from under the crook of Max's elbow, I saw Sanger crouched next to us. She was holding the Polaroid. She looked irate. Max and I disentangled.

"It's broken!" she shouted. "You fucking shattered the *lens*. I can't believe this. We've got four more deaths to go."

"It's not a big deal," I said. "We can just use a disposable camera for the last ones."

"It's not a big deal because it's not your camera," snapped Sanger.

"Hey, I *gave* it to you in the first place," I snapped back.

"It's my fault," Max cut in, appeasing. "I'll pay to replace it."

"That's not the point!" yelled Sanger, standing up and slamming the camera back against the tile. Its casing fractured, sending bits of plastic skittering. "It wouldn't be broken if you two could keep your hands off each other for, like, a minute straight!"

I staggered to my feet. "Hey, that's totally unfair. Max was just kidding around. He always is. Around both of us."

"You know what?" said Sanger. "Whatever. It's past Max's bedtime, and my moms will be home soon, so why doesn't he just piss off to the orange room. You can join him for all I care."

Max picked up the broken camera. Gingerly, he placed it on the counter.

"Or maybe," he said, "I'll drive myself home. You want a ride, Stevie?"

I looked at Max. I looked at Sanger.

"Well, go on, sweetie," she cooed. "Just make sure you use protection."

"Fine," I spat. *"Fine."*

I shoved past Max to the kitchen door and burst out into the night. He caught up with me at his car, where I was already impatiently tugging at the locked passenger door handle.

"I'm sorry," he said, unlocking the door. "Maybe she just needs time to cool down."

He slid into the driver's seat, but I stayed where I was, staring at the lawn. Floodlights illuminated the towering stone and latticework of Hamasaki House in all its Old World grandeur. The lights also hit the orange Realtor sign staked next to a plastic mailbox full of fliers, which informed interested parties that Hamasaki House was for sale, and at a price most interested parties couldn't afford.

I opened the car door and leaned inside.

"I think I should stay," I said.

"You sure?"

Max looked worried, as though I might possibly be walking back into the lair of a serial killer.

"I'm sure," I said. "Really. It's best if I stay. Anyway, my duffel is still in there."

He nodded slowly.

"Oh, hey!" he shouted, just as I was heaving the door shut. I caught it and stuck my head back in.

"Tomorrow," he said. "Don't forget. First real date. Seven o'clock. Wear something fancy."

"First real date," I echoed. "Seven o'clock. Something fancy. What do you mean by 'fancy'?"

Max shrugged. "Just—fancy."

"You're still not going to tell me what the surprise is?"

Max turned up the radio. He smiled blithely, clearly through with talking.

I watched him drive off down the cedar-lined road until his taillights smudged into the night fog. Then I went back inside.

I found Sanger in her bedroom. She was eating from a Tupperware bowl filled with popcorn and rainbow mini marshmallows—"popmallow," Sanger called it. The combination had been her favorite snack since I'd met her. She was watching the Home Shopping Network.

"Over that quick, huh?" She spoke with a full mouth. "You

know, they say that's a common problem for boys Max's age, but I really thought he could keep it together for longer than—"

"This isn't about Max."

Sanger made a noisy swallow, then grabbed another handful of popmallow.

"Look, I'm mad that you're moving too," I said. "But I'm not taking it out on the wrong people."

"Ooh. What's it like there, way up on the moral high ground? Clear skies? A balmy seventy degrees?"

I grabbed the remote control from the bed and clicked off the image of a rotating topaz bracelet.

"What the hell is wrong with you?" I demanded.

"You know, you wouldn't even care about Max if I hadn't hooked you two up."

"You said you're weren't jealous."

"I'm not jealous of *you*!"

It went quiet. Sanger and I looked at each other. Really looked. I dropped the remote back on her duvet. Sanger began to cry.

"Sisters before misters, right?" she whispered.

I crawled onto the bed next to her, and I wrapped my arms around her neck. I cried too. Something inside of me had been bunched in tight, and only now did it begin to expand, slowly but relentlessly. The funny thing was that I couldn't quite place where the expansion was happening—my brain or my chest. That sounds stupid, because there's obviously a big anatomical distance between your brain and chest, but that's simply how it was. In that moment I couldn't tell the two apart.

My best friend and I hugged, couched against the throw pillows. After a while, Sanger wiped a thin film of snot from her nose.

"And Joel hates me," she said, "which makes everything worse."

"He doesn't hate you, Sanger."

Sanger wiped her nose again. "Nothing's really turning out the way I planned."

"Yeah, I know."

Sanger said, "I'm going out of town tomorrow."

"What?"

"Moms are taking me to San Antonio to see Mam's relatives before we peace out of Texas forever."

"They just sprang that on you?"

"No," said Sanger. "I've known for a while."

"How long are you there for?"

"A week."

I said nothing. I shut my eyes.

"I'm sorry," said Sanger. "If we don't finish the list on time, I mean. I thought maybe we'd get ahead of schedule and it wouldn't be a problem. You and Max can do a few on your own. You have my blessing. Knock yourself out. I mean, we'll still have spontaneous combustion."

I still said nothing.

Since April, I had known Sanger was leaving. I'd known, but I'd done everything not to think about it, and I'd done a pretty good job. The list and Max and STA and all the life that sprang up in between had kept the move from my head. Even up until ten minutes earlier, I'd still thought in terms of June 1. That was when things ended, and we still had two weeks left. There were two full weeks before Sanger would pack up and leave for good.

So it was a shock, having seven days cut away like that. One week was so much more imminent and awful than two.

"You should've told me," I said, squeezing her shoulder. "I would've spent more time with just you. I wouldn't have invited Max to stuff. We wouldn't have even had to do the list."

"I like the list, though," Sanger said softly. "I like Max. I like you with Max."

"Then what do you want?"

"I don't *know*. I know things weren't awesome before. I think about last spring and the spring before that, and it's not like we did anything epic or that our lives have been easy peasy, but they were somehow better than now. I don't like *Now*. I think that's it. It's not that I don't like Max or that Mam got a promotion or any of that shit. I just don't like it all combined. And I'm like, maybe the future is just going to be a lot of crappy Nows all strung together. And I'm like, no wonder people jump out of buildings. No wonder they choose to end it. Like, maybe they're the ones who've caught on. And you

LUCKY FEW • 293

don't have to look at me that way, I'm not suicidal or anything. I'm just saying."

"It's just a crappy Now," I said. "It'll get better."

"I don't know that," said Sanger. "For real, Stevie, I don't. Maybe the whole deal with getting older is that it doesn't get better. Maybe the Nows get even crappier. Austin to Philadelphia, Philadelphia to Detroit, Detroit to Siberia. Some unavoidable downward spiral like that. Am I making any sense?"

"Not really."

That wasn't true. Sanger was making sense, just not a sense that I wanted to hear.

"I think I'm having an existential crisis," she said.

"What?"

"I've heard they're common in people like me. Affluenza. Quarter-life crises. It's because I'm rich and smart and have too much time on my hands. Oh God."

I sat up and gave Sanger a good looking-over. "Have you been drinking?"

She shook her head into a pillow. "Only thinking."

We sounded like some sick sort of Dr. Seuss rhyme.

Sanger got out of bed and washed her face in the bathroom. She turned the Home Shopping Network back on and tucked herself under the duvet.

"You don't have to stick around," she told me.

"Yes, I do. Unless you want me to drive your Fiat back home."

"Oh," she said.

"Also, I want to stay."

Sanger smiled, though not with her whole face.

"When do you leave tomorrow?" I asked.

"Noon."

"You can call whenever your relatives get too boring."

"Right."

I fell asleep during a floor polish demonstration, still clothed, my makeup on. In the morning, when I woke, I found that I'd left a mascara mark on Sanger's pillow.

I fetched a cold washrag from the bathroom to blot it out, but Sanger stopped me.

"Don't worry," she said. "Just leave it."

Eighteen

Mom dropped me off at the capitol late Saturday afternoon. It was the first time I hadn't hauled a poster with me to the Texas Rangers Memorial. There was nothing left to haul. Nothing left to protest. We'd won. This was our victory lap, and I meant to enjoy it.

If I wasn't busy enjoying something, I'd be busy thinking of Sanger in San Antonio and the fact that I wouldn't see her for another six full days and that seven full days after that I wouldn't see her again, period. Or I'd be busy worrying over how Joel wasn't on speaking terms with me. We hadn't really interacted since Joel had stormed out of the W Hotel; I'd slept over at Sanger's, and tonight Joel was meeting up with those incoming freshmen he'd met online. But our paths had crossed once that morning, at home, when we'd literally brushed shoulders in the hall. I'd squeaked out a shamefaced "hey." Joel had said nothing, all ice.

I was in desperate need of distraction. I needed to sit next to Maribel and hear about the most recent customer service fiasco at her bakery. I needed to toast STA's victory with paper cups, gathered around a meager potluck. I'd brought a bag of baked chips and a two-liter of root beer, because Mom had warned that ninety percent of people who attend an open potluck bring desserts, not drinks or salty things.

Mom was right. Even from yards away, I could see the over-abundance of brownies and cookies and a three-layer chocolate cake courtesy of Maribel's bakery. The food was spread out on a large patchwork quilt, but no one was eating. Everyone was on their feet, gathered in tight conversational bunches. The majority of the group was huddled around Leslie Cobb. I could just barely make out her face. It was tearstained.

"Stevie?"

I turned around.

It was Jessica Parrish. Her stringy hair was gathered off to one side in a braid.

"Are you here for that environmental rally again?" she asked. "Or were you looking for us?"

"Who's us?" I asked, but I had already caught sight of the group gathered farther down the capitol lawn.

I recognized several of the faces from the creationist rally the month before. I also recognized a fair amount of people from co-op, including Mrs. Weiss. I scanned the crowd for a banner. I found one—a wrinkled strip of blue butcher's paper being unfurled by two middle-aged men.

In black paint was the image of a male figure, identical to the icon on a public bathroom placard. A plus sign. The figure of a woman. An equal sign. Then the word "SACRED."

I closed my fists.

"Yeah, no, I'm definitely not here for you guys." I didn't bother softening the anger in my voice.

"Oh," said Jessica.

She seemed to be fumbling for the right words to say, for some socially awkward bow-out. I didn't have the patience for it this time.

"Have fun," I said in a way that conveyed just the opposite.

I stalked away from Jessica toward my own people. I'd momentarily forgotten the panicked concern I'd felt upon seeing Leslie Cobb's red, wet face. Now the panic came surging back in. I broke into Maribel's group, squeezing between six-foot college guys.

"What's going on?" I asked.

"It's a no-go," said Trevor. "Haven't you checked your e-mails?"

"Obviously not." I wanted to add that I'd been too busy faking death by salmonella and offending my cousin and bawling my eyes out with my best friend. "What's a no-go?"

"The bill." Maribel's voice was gravelly. "The bill went to the governor's desk yesterday. He vetoed it."

"But—but he isn't allowed to do that," I sputtered.

I was studying American government that year. I knew that the governor was most certainly allowed to do that.

"He's saying it's a deterrent to new businesses," said Trevor. "His advisors inform him that the threat to the watershed isn't overwhelming."

"No," I said.

"These things happen," said Maribel. "It's politics."

I threw my bag of chips to the ground. I tossed the two-liter after it.

"No," I said.

I had decided to throw a tantrum. Another one of the college guys, Nick, backed away from the group, hands raised.

"Calm down, firecracker," he said. "We can't change it now."

I fixed him with a fiery glare. "Yeah, you're damn right. *I* can't change anything. I can't even vote. And the one thing I can do doesn't even happen because of *one signature*. We got hundreds of signatures on that petition, and none of them matter because of just *one*."

That wasn't the whole of it. What I couldn't explain to Nick the college guy was that STA hadn't been about politics to me. It hadn't been about petitions and committee meetings and rallies. It was about a place. It was about sunbathing with Sanger. About diving practice and freestyle races with Joel. It was about swimming out to save a half-crazed guy named Max Garza. It was about nothing in particular, just a summer day spent coated in sunscreen, lying out with a book held close to my heart. It was anonymous me, thinking my clearest thoughts. It was Barton Springs I'd been fighting for, and all the memories sunk into its murky water and sprouting from its grassy bank. And that, all of that, had been dismissed by one stupid signature.

"It happens," said Maribel, squeezing my shoulder. "It's just one of those things."

"What is that even supposed to mean?" I shouted.

I left them. I stormed blindly across the capitol lawn, pulling my cell phone from my back pocket. I punched Mom's speed dial.

"What's wrong?" she greeted. "Did you forget something?"

I told her she needed to come back and get me. I told her about the veto. I started crying as I told her, and I got angry that I was crying, which made me cry harder. Mom told me she was turning the car around, that she'd be there in less than five minutes.

I didn't want to stay there with all the rest of the STA people. I didn't want nineteen-year-old idiots telling me to calm down or kindhearted Maribels telling me this was just one of those things. I wanted to go somewhere I could scream.

And then suddenly, without knowing how I'd fallen into their path, I was in the middle of the anti-gay rally. They were around me, all around, and they were walking toward the street, the same as I was. Their signs were held high, and I could smell heady perfumes and body odor. Then someone was tugging at my sleeve, and it was Jessica again, and she looked at me with wide-eyed concern.

"Are you okay?" she asked.

I cracked.

The sadness, the utter loss I felt suddenly formed a hard edge, turning to pure rage.

I shoved Jessica off.

"No!" I yelled, and I mean *yelled*. I hadn't yelled like this since I was a six-year-old. There was so much anger clawing up my throat, demanding release. And it did release, in one red-hot explosion of words that jetted off my tongue like cannon fire.

"No," I kept yelling, "I'm not okay, so stop asking! Would you just leave me alone? Would you just leave *everyone* alone? The schoolchildren and the scientists and the gays and the lesbians, and everyone in between—would you just leave them the fuck alone already? I mean, honestly, Jessica, why can't you act like a normal human being? Why do you have to go around giving homeschoolers a bad name? Why can't you and all your creepy clan just—just move to Alaska and secede from the Union and let everyone else in the world *live their lives*?"

There was pressure on my arm. Someone was grabbing me and pulling me off Jessica, because I was clutching Jessica's shoulders, and I was shaking her. I whipped around to face the intervener. It was a guy from co-op, a freshman. I didn't know his name, but I knew his face, and in that moment he looked at me as though I had metamorphosed into a wild dog.

"Don't touch her," he said, and he led Jessica away.

She was crying.

I had made Jessica Parrish cry.

Then I realized I was crying too.

I stood gaping after her, my mouth turning dry, my body shuddering. Then I became aware that there were dozens of eyes on me, the eyes of other protestors who had heard my shouts and who now stared at me the way the freshman boy had—like I was insane or possessed or just an altogether horrible human being.

I was in the wrong.

I'd done something wrong, and I could do nothing now but stand in the shame of it, under those stares, alone.

A car honked from the curb. Mom.

When I collapsed in the passenger seat, my tears had cleared up, but my head hadn't. Anger swelled within me, then ebbed out with a sour sadness, and the anger and the sadness did a twisted dance, driving me into a place that was beyond something as superficial as crying.

"What on earth is going on?" Mom asked. "Hon, are you that upset about the veto?"

"I don't know," I said. "I don't know."

I kept seeing Jessica's shocked, horrified face. I had been vicious to her, this girl I barely knew. I'd been so angry, my actions hadn't even felt like my own. But they had been mine, mine entirely. *This* was why I'd scored a sixty-two on that empathy test in ninth grade. This was it. I'd lost control, I'd hurt Jessica Parrish without even thinking about her feelings.

I shouldn't have yelled.

I shouldn't have, but I still wanted to. Not at Jessica. Not at anyone. I just wanted to *yell*.

Mom reached over and squeezed my elbow gently.

"Do you want to go?" she asked. "Or do you need to recoup for a second?"

"I want to go home," I said. "I think my sugar's low."

Mom didn't ask any more questions. She drove home.

I wasn't just playing the diabetes card; I really didn't feel well. My eyes were beginning to splotch, my head was arid, and my stomach felt flat. I fished a roll of wild cherry Life Savers from my purse and popped two candies in my mouth.

"Where are your glucose tablets?" Mom asked, glancing sidelong.

"At home."

"Stevie, how many times have I told you—?"

"I *know*. I wasn't planning on going all hypoglycemic today, okay?"

The Life Savers clunked in my mouth, impeding my speech, but not so much that Mom didn't cast me a concerned look.

"No one plans on 'going all hypoglycemic.' That's why you have to be pre—"

"I had *something*," I cut in. "What more do you want from me?"

"I want you to be careful."

I said nothing. I crunched into the candies and, after a few moments, swallowed the crumbly bits. I shoved two more candies in my mouth, lowered my seat to a reclining position, and tried to rein in the expanding weightlessness in my head.

When we got home, Mom stood by while I checked my sugar. The Life Savers had boosted it back up to a respectable enough range that Mom didn't hyperventilate, but she did force me to "take it easy." This directive entailed lying on the den couch while she sat across from me, shelling lima beans she'd purchased earlier that morning at the grocery.

"I feel like I haven't seen much of you lately," she said.

That was true. I'd been MIA almost every waking hour of every weekend for the past two months, presumably hanging out with Sanger and Max. The "presumably" didn't refer to being with Sanger and Max, just to the "hanging out" part, since I knew Mom's definition of "hanging out" didn't include faking drownings at Barton Springs.

"I'm trying to spend all the time I can with Sanger," I said, "before she leaves."

"Of course you are." Mom smiled a condoling smile that I didn't much care for. After a pause, she said, "So, a date with Max tonight."

I froze. I hadn't told Mom anything about the date with Max. I instantly went on the defensive.

"You said when I turned sixteen, I could—"

"I know what I said," Mom interrupted. "I stand by it. I'm not upset with you, Stevie."

I relaxed, just a little. When I was thirteen, Mom told me I could start dating at sixteen. At the time, I'd complained that the rule was a gross injustice. Then I'd proceeded to be generally disgusted with boys for the next three years, and the rule hadn't ever had any practical application. Not until now.

"How do you know about the date?" I asked.

Mom shook four freshly pried lima beans into a bronze pot, then discarded the shell into an open grocery bag.

"I have my sources," she said.

"What sources?"

I was already envisioning graphic scenes of how I would make Joel pay, that accursed eavesdropper.

"Well," said Mom. "Max."

"Max," I said. "Max told you about our date?"

"Yes."

"When? *How?*"

"Goodness, I don't remember when exactly. He came over while I was watering the garden. He was very polite."

"Why would he tell you about our date?"

"Why wouldn't he?" asked Mom, putting on the front of being flummoxed. "Better *he* tell me than the mailman. All I meant by it was that I hope you have a lovely night."

"Thanksss," I said suspiciously.

My suspicion was that Mom wasn't done talking.

My suspicion proved to be correct.

"Your father and I will be at one of Louie's concerts until *late*," she said, eyebrows bouncing on the "late" part. "But all the same, I expect you to observe curfew."

Curfew was midnight. Mom had never enforced it before

because I'd never had a real date before and also because any night I ever was out past midnight I spent at Hamasaki House.

"Okay," I said. "I will."

Mom still didn't look like she was quite through.

"I just . . ." Mom suddenly looked very concerned. "I just hope you remember who you are."

"*Mom.*"

All the irritability from earlier now rushed back into my system. I thought about the governor and about Jessica's face and about Sanger in San Antonio, and I thought, *If Mom gives me a sex talk right now, I will lose it. I will no longer be in control of my mental faculties.*

"That's all I wanted to say," Mom assured me.

But I didn't believe her, so I left her in the den and went to my room. I lay on my bed, pressing my nose into my pillow until it hurt, but it didn't hurt too much, and so I kept doing it. I felt something edging into me, something I'd been trying to block since I'd gotten inside Mom's car: that anger, and that sadness, and their painful dance. I didn't want to let it in. I couldn't. I blocked myself against it, using all the effort left in my spent body.

And I fell asleep.

I woke to the sound of a knock.

Mom was standing in the doorway of my bedroom, pink dusk light slatted across her face.

"Max said he was coming at seven," she said. "I thought you'd want to be up in time."

It was 6:25.

I thanked Mom, shut my door, and proceeded to panic.

Something fancy, Max had told me. I was supposed to wear something fancy. Accordingly, I went the extra mile with my makeup and chose the brightest red lipstick in my collection. I left my hair down. Then I put on something fancy, which was my little black dress and a pair of heels that matched my lips. There was a reason I didn't usually wear these heels: They made my feet ache after fifteen minutes of use. But I figured Max's surprise would entail sitting down. A restaurant. A movie. Nothing that would strain my feet too badly.

At seven on the dot, the doorbell rang.

"Hi," said Max when I opened the door.

He was wearing a tux.

He held out a box to me, and it took a stupid moment for me to realize what was inside it: a red rose corsage.

I looked at Max, processing.

"You know," he said, "your mom predicted you would wear a black dress. I figured a rose would be safe."

"What's going on?" I said. I felt electrified.

"Stevie Hart," said Max, "will you go prom crashing with me?"

Nineteen

Max had written out the itinerary on a yellow legal pad, which sat tilted on the dash of his car.

"And you thought Sanger was the only one capable of planning," he said.

He looked so insanely proud of himself. His face had been cracking with a smile since he'd showed up on my doorstep.

The itinerary read:

7:30 GROUP PHOTOS

8   DANCE THE NIGHT AWAY

10   STARLIT GAZEBO???

12   WILL TAKE YOU HOME AND NOT TO SLEAZY HOTEL

"Very impressive," I said.

"Right?"

"Out of curiosity, whose prom are we crashing?"

"You're not the only one with cousins."

"You have cousins in Austin?"

"Well, no," said Max. "My cousin lives in Waco, but my cousin's *friend* lives here in Austin. Luckily, this cousin has an excellent sense of humor. He says he'll pay me good money if I weasel into a Lady Bird High prom picture. His friend, Will, is our insider."

"How much good money?" I asked.

"Two hundred."

"*What?*"

"He's on my dad's side," said Max. "Two hundred bucks is like Monopoly money to them. Anyway, I don't plan on keeping the cash reward. I'm going to donate it all to Forever Springs of the Future or— Shit, what's it called?"

"Springs for Tomorrow Alliance," I said, slinking into a depression.

"Yeah. That. Are you okay?"

"We lost," I said.

"Lost what?"

"The governor vetoed the bill," I said. "I don't want to talk about it."

"I'm sorry."

"Don't say you're sorry," I said. "Just take me prom crashing. Prom crashing is exactly what I need right now."

So Max drove, and I admired my corsage in the passing streetlights of South Lamar. After a short distance, Max pulled into a parking lot. I blinked dumbly at the restaurant in view.

"Tanaka?"

Tanaka was this ridiculously swanky Japanese restaurant in South Austin. It was the place where celebrities ate when they were in town for SXSW or to shoot an independent film. It was the place people went to propose, the place where you could walk out the door having paid $275 for a bottle of sake.

"Don't freak out," said Max. "We're not eating here. But Will and his date are, and they're taking an intimate group photo with friends."

"So, your rich cousin has rich friends."

"The rich tend to stick together," said Max. "Just look at the presidential cabinet."

I snickered. It was the first political thing I'd ever heard Max say, and I liked him for it if for no other reason than that it was a general jab at the executive branch, and I took that jab to include shoddy governors.

"We *are* going to eat at some point, right?"

"Ah," said Max. "Yes. The Condition."

Over the past weeks, Max had picked up Sanger's habit of referring to my diabetes as "the Condition."

"I thought we'd grab some P. Terry's after we get our fill of dancing. Or is that too late?"

It was later than I would've liked. I didn't usually go that long between meals, and I'd already had a scare for the day. Still, Max was emanating pure joy about his prom-crashing plan, and I didn't want to ruin it.

"It's fine," I said. "But *right* after, or you're going to have one hangry date on your hands."

"Duly noted."

Max led the way to Tanaka's back garden—a flat stretch of grass lit by strings of white paper lanterns. For such a high-end restaurant, the landscaping wasn't anything special. Dad's work on Hamasaki House was much better.

The garden was currently occupied by a gaggle of high schoolers, all shrieking and laughing and attempting to line up in order of height. A professional photographer stood across from them, shouting commands that were largely ignored.

"Come on," said Max.

He crouched behind a thick row of honeysuckle bushes that ran behind the posing prom dates. My feet screamed in protest. Crouching in a dress was awkward enough, but the heels made it a veritable feat of nature.

"So this Will guy," I whispered, "does he know you're bombing his photo?"

"Hmmm?" said Max, as though he hadn't heard the question, which was all the answer I needed.

We lined ourselves up on the far edge of the row of prom dates, just behind the shortest couple. As we waited, I watched the guy's hand wander down his date's waist and clamp around her silk-clad backside.

"Classy, bro," Max snorted.

The line finally settled, and the photographer began shouting out *three-two-ones*, followed by flashes that cast the whole of the garden in blinding light.

"Okay," Max whispered. "On the next count of three, you and I are going to pop out. You have to jump. I mean, *really jump*."

"Hang on," I said.

I took off the heels. When I was through, Max gave me a tentative thumbs-up. I gave him an enthusiastic one back.

"Okay," he said. "Next countdown, we jump."

On the next countdown, we jumped.

I wondered afterward if we would've gotten away with it had Max not released a primordial scream whilst doing the jumping. The photographer would've caught on, surely, but there was no reason any of the giggling couples would've known we'd bombed their photo, not until much later, when they received the prints.

As it was, Max screamed, and the couple in front of us promptly shrieked in terror. The line of dates went scattering like insects whose nest had just been demolished.

Back under the cover of the bushes, I grabbed my shoes, and Max's yell to run was superfluous, because I was already flying toward the parking lot. The blacktop was warm under my bare feet. Something sharp bit into my heel, but I kept running, running, and I outran Max, and I threw myself into the passenger seat with a giddy squawk.

"You're my witness, right?" Max yelled as he slammed his door shut. "You're my witness to Cousin Emilio when I ask him to shell out that two hundred."

"I'm your witness," I said, breathless. "Now, *go!*"

Max pulled out of the parking lot at an infuriatingly sluggish speed. He even put on his right blinker as we turned onto South Lamar.

"Dude," I said. "Worst getaway driver *ever*."

"Safety is sexy," Max asserted.

"They totally could've gotten your plates."

"If we jumped the right way, then they have our *faces*. Anyway, so what? Photo bombing isn't illegal."

I thought about this. "It felt illegal."

"Good."

As Max drove us to Lady Bird High, I got my foot into my lap and inspected my heel for damages.

At the next red light, Max looked over.

"Are you hurt?"

His voice was drenched in so much concern that my chest felt close to bursting. But then, that could've just been the adrenaline still wearing out of my system.

I pulled a foreign object from my skin. It was the front of a minuscule, bronze stud earring.

"I'm fine," I said, just as blood began to prick to the surface. "My tetanus shot is up to date."

I opened the glove compartment, on the hunt for a napkin. My mom always kept a hearty supply of them in her car. Max did not. I was forced to get creative. I ripped out the back page from the car manual and used it to blot away the blood. There wasn't too much of it to clean up.

"Life fact of the day," said Max. "It is impossible to bleed out through your heel."

"Watch," I said. "That's how you're going to die now."

"Me? Die?" Max laughed. "Impossible."

· · ·

We parked under the clunky shadow of the Lady Bird High football stadium. Max turned to me with a solemn expression.

"This is where it gets dangerous," he said.

"I don't claim to know much about proms," I said, "but don't you need, like, a ticket to get in?"

"You've learned well from the movies, young padawan," said Max. "That's why I took precautionary measures."

He held up a spare key that had been sitting in his cup holder. He explained.

"They're holding the dance in the auditorium. Will is a tech for school productions. *This*"—he indicated the key—"will get us up on the catwalk."

"I thought you said Will didn't know about this."

"I said no such thing. I said he was our inside man."

"You're crazy," I said happily. "But don't we still have to make it through the front doors to *get* to the catwalk?"

I expected Max to have a snappy comeback to that. I thought he would say something like, "Leave it to the professionals, darling" or "I've got it *alll* figured out" or "Trust the one who went to a *real* school."

Instead, Max said, "Hmm." He frowned. Then he said, "Fuck."

"You didn't think about that?"

"Fuck," Max repeated. "Not exactly. But hey, I'm sure we can still slip past them. It shouldn't be a big deal."

"Security has got to be a kind of big deal," I said. "It's

prom. There could be pervs or gunmen trying to sneak in."

"Or homeschoolers desperate for their one and only prom experience."

"I'm not desperate, and you are not allowed to spin it that way."

"We can still get in," he said with renewed hopefulness. "And once we *do*, I'll sneak us up to the catwalk, and—"

"You have this all playing out in your head, don't you? A slow dance up in the lighting booth, right?"

"That can be arranged too."

I studied my bare feet and the bloodied instruction manual page, now crumpled on the floorboard.

"I'm sorry," said Max. "Maybe I didn't think it through entirely, but it's still a decent plan, right?"

"It's a great plan," I said. "The whole thing's great."

"So, what's that look for?"

For the first time that night, Max sounded nervous.

That feeling from earlier in the day—that awful cocktail of anger and sadness—had begun to resurface. I gave up trying to push it back down.

"What happened today," I said, "the whole veto thing? It really, really sucked. And it doesn't help that Sanger's gone, and the list is winding down, and June first is going to be here way too fast."

"Yeah, but number seventeen is a damn good way to go out, right?" said Max, grinning.

I crossed my arms. "You said you wouldn't talk about it anymore."

"I'm just trying to lighten the mood."

"I don't want the mood to be lightened."

"Okay." Max nodded. "Fair enough. No more mood lightening."

And then I said it. I finally said what I'd wanted to tell Max before, after his fake-drowning incident.

I said, "Number seventeen means it's all over. School and Sanger and Joel and *you*. It means it's all going to change."

"And *me*?" Max turned in his seat. I could feel his gaze tearing across my face. "How am I going to change?"

"It's just . . ." I waved my hands weakly in his direction. "You'll be in school. You're going to make a dozen new friends. Everyone is going to love you, and you're going to be busy with homework, and the list is going to be over, so presumably you're going to be cured of your death anxiety, and you won't need me anymore."

Max was silent. For a moment, I contemplated throwing open the door and running for it, shoeless and injured though I was. But then he spoke.

"That's bullshit, Stevie. All of it. You know that, right?"

My eyes met his. I was on the edge of crying, and to reply to Max's question meant losing it, so I just shook my head.

"It's bullshit," Max repeated, more emphatic. His voice was the deepest I'd ever heard it.

I shook my head again, and despite my best efforts, two tears came trickling out, hot on my cheeks. Max leaned over the console. He touched my jaw. Then my ear. Then my hair. Then he leaned in closer and kissed me.

I pulled back.

"It isn't bullshit," I whispered. "You're going to change."

Max fell back into his seat. He sighed. "Okay, I'm going to change. But so are you. That doesn't mean we're changing for the worse. And I'm *not* going to go off to school and forget about you. What kind of asshole do you think I am? What kind of kids do you think go to a summer Montessori school? Believe me, Stevie, I'll be dying to get out of that classroom. I'll be dying to be with you. *That's* not going to change."

"But everything's going to be different," I insisted. "Everything's ending, and I know that isn't always a bad thing. It's just that it's all ending without my permission."

Max said, "Life can be a real dick."

"Life and Time," I said. "Partners in crime."

"We don't have to dance, you know," said Max. "If you just want to sit here and philosophize—"

"No, I don't want to philosophize. I don't even want to *think*. But I'm not sure I want to dance, either."

Max tapped the steering wheel column one finger at a time, pinkie to index finger, index to pinkie.

"What's the name of the corporation?" he asked. "The one that's clogging up the spring water?"

"New Systematic Solutions."

It came off my tongue instantly, saturated with vitriol, the same way the words "Stalin" or "nuclear warfare" might. It tasted oily and foul in my mouth.

"And you know where this New Systematic Solutions is located?"

"Yeah, in the Barton Springs watershed. That's the problem."

"No, but where they're *actually* located?"

"Sure. Why?"

"Mhm," said Max. And again, *"Mhm."*

He started the car up and pulled out of the lot.

"Where are we going?" I asked.

I was already beginning to feel light-headed with a hypothesis.

"First," said Max, "we'll need supplies."

"Do you think they can refuse service?"

Max and I stood in line at Griffin Hardware, both of us with a couple spray paint cans in hand. I had chosen blue and yellow. Max had chosen green and red.

"Why would they refuse us service?" Max asked.

"Because," I said, "we're two kids who look like we're fresh from prom, buying spray cans late at night. It's clear we're up to no good."

"First of all, it is *not* late at night. It's barely nine o'clock.

Second, it's not like we're at a Liquor Barn. We don't have to show ID to buy paint. And they can assume anything they want, but they can't prove what our agenda is."

"We're going to get a dirty look."

"You can't be afraid of dirty looks," said Max. "Everyone gets at least a few dirty looks when they're on the verge of something epic."

As it turned out, the clerk was a guy not much older than either of us. He didn't say anything about our purchase, didn't make eye contact at all, and merely droned out the owed amount of $31.56. Max paid him with two twenties. We got back in the car, where I placed our purchases in my lap. I started the work of peeling away the plastic coverings that attached each lid to its can.

"Have you done this before?" I asked.

"Nope. How hard can it be?"

"I don't know. Aren't there some rules we should know? Also, I feel like you shouldn't be going five under the speed limit when we're being juvenile delinquents."

"We haven't done anything all that delinquent yet."

We discussed where we would spray. I'd ridden past the New Systematic Solutions building plenty of times before. There was a smaller office space that fronted the larger building, which was four stories tall and made of stucco. I wagered that the execs worked there, so I proposed we do our dirty work on that building.

Then we discussed what we would paint.

"It has to be short and sweet," said Max. "We might not have much time before security catches on. Maybe just a big 'fuck you'?"

"No. That's too good for them."

"Okay. A frowny face?"

I gave Max a look.

"What!" he said. "I never claimed to be the next Banksy."

"It has to *mean* something," I said.

"Or it doesn't. It can just be a defacement of property. You're overthinking it."

Max had a point. There wasn't a chance that two inexperienced graffiti artists with a narrow window of time were going to leave a grandiose, profound message on the office front of New Systematic Solutions.

"A drop," I said. "A drop of water. A reminder of what they're contaminating."

"Yes. Perfect."

"You don't think they'll tie it back to STA, do you?"

"They won't be able to prove anything," said Max, "*if* we don't get caught. And if our faces don't show up on the security tapes."

"Dammit," I said. "We should've bought balaclavas."

"If we had," said Max, "I think they *would* have refused us service."

• • •

Max parked two blocks down from the building. We put the spray paint cans in an old backpack that he rummaged out of his car trunk. We walked calmly down the sidewalk. He'd shed his coat and tie. I walked barefoot, challenging the universe to send another rogue earring my way.

The street was well lit, but we were on an off-road, and this was a business district after hours, so very few cars passed by.

"Are *all* these businesses polluting the watershed?" Max whispered, gesturing to the surrounding office buildings.

I shook my head. "It's how far back New Systematic Solutions built their warehouse and where they get rid of their waste. That's the problem."

"You sound so knowledgeable," said Max, linking his index finger around mine. "It's a real turn-on."

"Maybe we should've come later at night," I said. "There could still be workaholics inside."

"On a Saturday?"

"Do you think workaholics care if it's a Saturday?"

"That," said Max, "is part of the risk. Remember: two minutes, tops. That's how much time we've got. Then we make a run for it."

"Uh-huh." I was only half listening, too distracted by what Max had said earlier about security tape footage. I was getting paranoid. "Maybe this is a bad idea."

"Oh," said Max. "It is definitely a bad idea."

We walked across the parking lot that separated the New

Systematic Solutions office front from another office park con-
glomerate. There were still a couple cars parked in the lot.

"Not the wall," I said.

I stopped, jolting Max back with me.

"What?"

"I don't think we should paint the wall," I said. "Look. You
can see the cameras from here."

I pointed to the security cameras affixed to each brick corner of the building's first floor.

"Well, if we're quick—" said Max.

Then I told Max something he'd once told me:

"There's crazy, and then there's *crazy*. Even you know the
difference."

Max grunted. "So what do you suggest?"

I looked around the parking lot.

"How about the blacktop?" I suggested.

"What?"

"Sure," I said, getting excited. "At the front drive, where all
the cars come through. We can paint it there, like the stuff they
paint on the lanes at a highway interchange so you know what
exit you're taking. That way, it's visible, but we can do it out of
range of the cameras."

Max asked me to lead the way. I led. I took us to the cen-
ter of the parking lot, where the main drive connected to the
street. Max fished the cans out of the backpack.

"We're lucky there's not a breeze," he said.

I used the yellow paint. With it, I drew a massive outline of a single teardrop of water. When I was through, I was pleasantly surprised to find that it actually resembled what I'd set out to paint. It was big, too—long enough that, if I so desired, I could comfortably lie down inside it with neither my toes nor my head touching its edges.

"Now we fill it with blue," I said, but Max was already at work on something else with the green can.

"Max," I hissed. "I told you—"

"Shhh. You're messing with my vibe. I'm feeling really inspired here."

It seemed that Max's artistic muse had instructed him to spray a giant *F*, followed by a giant *U*, right under my drop of water. The damage was already being done, so I left him to it and returned to my own piece, blue can in hand.

Even without a breeze, the blowback of the paint occasionally flew up into my face. I shielded my eyes with one arm and blindly waved the can back and forth. Paint vapor singed up my nose and coated my sense of taste and smell with a chemical bite.

I coughed once, then again and again, deeper each time than before. My eyes were watering, burning.

"Hey," whispered Max. He touched my shoulder. "Hey, you okay?"

"Let's just go," I wheezed out, well aware I'd blown whatever semblance of cover we'd had.

Max nodded. He grabbed my can from me and shoved

everything into the backpack, and we made a run for it, hand in hand, even though no one was chasing us and there were no angered shouts or sirens. My heart was beating hard in my chest—so hard I wondered if a pounding heart had ever before fractured a rib cage. We ran the two blocks to his car. When I reeled into the passenger seat, I was breathless, my forehead beaded with sweat.

And then Max was kissing me. Over the console, we grabbed at each other's arms and, already breathless, made ourselves even more so. My throat produced weird, rumbling sounds that I would've been embarrassed by under any other circumstances but these. And somehow I found myself crouched on the passenger seat in my bare feet, practically throwing myself over the gear shift, and Max's head conked into his window, hard, and I asked if he was okay, and he laughed and said he was more than okay.

That was when I started to feel dizzy. I played it out for a little, convincing myself it was the dizziness of the moment, of Max's kisses, of the entire dizzying night. But I knew what this feeling meant. I'd experienced it several times before. Most recently, I'd experienced it this afternoon. With a reluctance that hurt me physically, deep in the gut, I pulled away from Max and fell back to my side of the car.

I put my hand to my head. I tried to wrangle in deeper breaths. My skin was damp and overheated, and my dress was sticking to my back.

"Stevie? What's wrong?"

I shook my pounding head.

"The Condition," I said weakly.

My arms, my chest, my words were trembling.

"Okay. Okay, what do we need to do? Am I supposed to stab you with an insulin pen?"

"NO!" I shouted. "No, no, that is the absolute *worst* thing to do. My sugar's too low, not too high. I need candy or juice or—"

Or my glucose tablets, which were at home in the kitchen, and not in my sequined clutch.

"I don't have any of that stuff," said Max. "Hang on, we'll go to—"

"Take me home," I interrupted. "Just take me home. Everything I need is there. Unless I pass out. If I pass out, you should take me to the hospital."

"Oh my God," said Max, cranking the engine. "Okay."

My eyes were closed most of the drive in a feeble attempt to pull my body back together. Still, I knew. I could feel it as he gunned the accelerator and in the way we turned corners. Max sped all the way home.

Max helped me to the front door, one arm threaded around my back and hooked under my sweat-soaked armpit. I was aware, even in the haze and the panic, that I must have looked a complete mess. I tugged the house key out of my clutch, but my hands were shaking too hard to align its grooved edge with the lock. Max took the key from me and opened the door.

He hurried me into the kitchen, opened the medicine drawer I directed him to, and unscrewed the cap of my glucose tablets. He placed one in my hand and watched as I chewed.

"Is that enough?" he asked. "Do you need more? What else can I do?"

He was, I realized, completely freaking out, and I felt guilty but not strong enough to make him feel remotely better. I just needed to lie down. I told him that, and he took me into the den.

He didn't walk me to the couch, he carried me. He picked me up like a doll and deposited me on the cushions and propped a pillow behind my head. Then he sat on the coffee table, gripping my hand, and asked again if I was okay, if I needed something, if he should call someone, if he should just shut up. I told him that a cold washrag would be nice, not because I really needed it, because he looked like *he* needed something.

And while he was gone, my vision blackened on the edges like a scalloped frame.

Twenty

I woke in a bright, white room. There was a nurse there, her back turned to me.

I struggled to produce words out of thoughts.

"Urrr," I said.

The nurse whipped around. She looked young, in her twenties, and her lowlighted hair was pulled back in a bun.

"Hi there," she said, smiling.

I rubbed my nose. I swallowed. I said, "Hi."

"Glad to see you moving. You were fluttering in and out there for a while. But no need to worry. The paramedics got right on it, and we've had you stable for some time. Just keeping you under observation. How're you feeling? Thirsty?"

Thirsty was a mild way of putting it. I felt like a desert carcass sapped of all moisture. I nodded, and soon the nurse was placing a Styrofoam cup in my hand. I clumsily positioned the straw in my mouth and drank in a blessed font of ice water.

"You're looking much better," the nurse reassured me. "Just got to watch that sugar."

I tried to remember why, before I woke up in this hospital, *why* I hadn't been watching my sugar. Within half a minute, my memory pieced itself together. I remembered now, waking up in a blur to a blaring siren and a bleeding color palette of movement. I remembered prom crashing. Spray paint. The car. The kissing. The kitchen. *Max.*

"Where's Max?"

"There's a doctor talking to your parents right now," said the nurse. "Why don't I go find them and tell them you're awake, okay? I'm sure they'll be so happy to hear that."

I watched the nurse leave the room. I kept inhaling my water, until all that remained was a bed of crushed ice. I tried moving my legs. They felt like cold elastic. I knew in my head that I should probably feel scared, feel panicked, feel confused. But all I felt was sadness that I was out of ice water.

The door opened.

"Mom," I said.

She burst into tears.

"Mom, it's okay. I'm okay."

Mom kept crying as she walked up to me and wrapped her arms around my back.

"Oh, thank God," she said. "Stevie, thank God."

I pressed my forehead against Mom's faux leather jacket. I told myself to feel something. I told myself to cry along with Mom. But I didn't.

"Your father's in the waiting room with Max," said Mom, once she'd recovered. "We haven't told Joel anything yet. And like an idiot, I didn't check my phone at the concert until way after Max had left a message, and I'm so sorry, sweetie. I'm so, so sorry."

"We've been taking good care of her!" sang the nurse, who was lingering by the door.

This served as a segue into Mom and the nurse talking about things like the glucagon injection that had brought me back to consciousness and the necessary two hours of observation that had nearly expired, and that, no, I hadn't just woken from the coma, that had happened on the ride here, and I was just sleepy from all the spent energy, and I really should consider wearing a diabetic ID bracelet. Then the nurse turned to me with helpful suggestions about eating habits and scheduling that I already knew by heart.

All the while, I kept telling myself to feel something, feel *something*. This was a big deal, I'd landed in the ER, I'd gone into a coma, this was a *big deal*. But I just kept crushing my straw against the ice in the bottom of my cup. And I just kept feeling nothing.

I asked if I could go home. It took some hemming and hawing and the nurse stepping outside to consult some Authority, but I was finally set free.

We emerged into the waiting room, and I was in Dad's arms before I even got a good look at him. He held me close, and I held him close back, breathing in the scent of smoke, fresh from Louie Wilson's concert.

"I love you, Steves," Dad said into the crown of my head.

And finally, I cried.

Maybe it was because Dad had called me by a nickname I hadn't heard in ten years. Maybe it was because I'd recently been in a diabetic coma. Maybe it was just the smell of smoke. Whatever the reason, I felt like a wreck. I wanted to go home and burrow into a twin-size hiding place for the next month at least.

But that wasn't a possibility just yet, and when Dad released me I saw Max sitting in the corner of the waiting room, bathed in ugly fluorescent light. He was staring at his phone. He didn't see me until I was only a few feet away. When he did, he jumped to his feet and folded me into his arms as though it were a reflex.

"God, I was so worried. I shouldn't have made you wait to eat that—"

I shook my head. I began to cry again.

Max kept his hand on my back. He said nothing, but I felt him there, felt his fingertips form a border to my spine.

"Stevie," he began, but I cut him off. I told him I didn't want to talk, didn't want to listen, didn't want to think.

So I did none of the above. I just *felt*, and what I felt was his fingertips pressing into my spine.

On the car ride home, I sat in the passenger seat, while Max and Mom sat in the back. At a stoplight, I finally registered that the reason Dad was driving us home was that Max and I had gone to the hospital in an ambulance.

No one said a thing until Dad pulled up to the driveway,

and Max got out and told us that if we needed anything, he was there. Mom told him thanks. I did too, though so softly I didn't think he heard.

"Come on, Stevie," Mom said, unbuckling her seat belt. "Let's get you inside."

"I'm sorry," I said, knowing I owed her several sorries for several offenses.

I was sorry I hadn't taken my glucose tablets with me. I was sorry for ruining a Louie Wilson concert night. I was sorry for the harrowing drive she and Dad must've made to the hospital. I was sorry for the bill they would owe the hospital, when our suppers already consisted primarily of ramen, eggs, and rice-based dishes.

I wanted to say sorry for all those things, a dozen times over. But I just said it once, and Mom told me there was nothing to apologize for, and she helped me get out of the car.

During the car ride, I had turned weary—in my bones, in my head. I was weary in a deep, all-consuming place that might've been my muscles but felt like something else, something beyond that, in a place that couldn't be drawn out in an anatomy textbook.

Even so, once I was in bed, the sleep didn't come. I spent an hour lying in the dark, my face turned to the wall. I called Sanger. She didn't answer. I called again. Again. I left a voice mail telling her to call me back. I sent her a text with the same message. Then I returned to the hellish silence of pre-sleep.

First I was too cold under the covers, then too warm, even without them. The sadness and anger from earlier that day—had that been this same day?—came waltzing back in, hand in hand, a grotesque pair of ballroom dancers.

I'd lost Barton Springs to a signature. I'd lost Sanger to Philadelphia. And I'd nearly lost myself to something as stupidly preventable as a diabetic coma. I felt the losses in the deep place, where the weariness was. It burned at first, keeping me from sleep. Then it turned into a mild ache, and the ache carried over past consciousness into restless dreams.

Mom woke me up for breakfast. Dad had left an hour earlier for a meeting with a potential client, someone the Sadler-Hamasakis had referred to him. If he got this client, Mom explained, it would mean a doubling of this month's wages. What she didn't say was that we would need a doubling of this month's wages to cover last night's events. I didn't have a clue what the ER visit and ambulance ride cost, but I knew it had to be pretty brutal.

Joel had spent the night with one of his new online college friends and still wasn't back. Mom had decided not to call him the night before, once she'd arrived at the hospital and been assured I was stable. I wondered if, with some convincing, Mom would promise not to breathe a word about the incident to him. Ever. But of course that was impossible. Joel was going to find out. I just didn't want to deal with him giving me sympathetic looks and tiptoeing around. I didn't deserve sympathetic looks and tiptoes. What had happened to me was the result of my own stupidity, not some unfair affliction from the powers on high.

I gave myself an insulin injection as I sat at the kitchen counter, watching Mom scramble eggs. Bacon was in the microwave, and biscuits were in the oven.

"I know you need your sleep," said Mom, "but you also need your energy, and we're going to stick to a better eating schedule from now on. You can crawl back under the covers when you're through."

I nodded, though I didn't feel like going back to sleep anytime soon. I'd already refused Mom's offer of breakfast in bed, determined to eat like a normal person who hadn't received an emergency glucagon injection the night before.

"Max came by earlier and wanted to know how you were doing."

Earlier? Earlier than—I checked the oven clock—9:13 in the morning? I wondered then if Max's night had been more sleepless than mine.

"Stevie?" Mom said, glancing up from her work at the stove.

I was crying, I realized. Blistering tears wound down my face. My throat was simultaneously freezing and on fire.

"I'm fine," I said, crying some more, willing my tear ducts to shut off. "I'm totally fine."

Mom flipped off the gas burner. She abandoned the eggs

and came to the counter, reaching across to take my hands.

"You don't have to be fine," she said. "What happened last night was really scary. You don't have to be fine after something like that."

"I know," I snuffled through the tears. "I just now figured that out."

Mom didn't ask me what I meant, and I was grateful, because what I meant wasn't something I could express in words. It was just a feeling, so great and all-encompassing that I knew its worth if not its language.

I got down from the kitchen barstool, and I crossed to Mom's side of the counter. I hugged her, and she hugged me, and the microwave went off, beeping in bursts of threes every minute, unheeded. Much later, when we were through hugging, the biscuits in the oven had burned.

"Hey."

Max had answered my call mid–first ring.

"I want to talk," I said. "Can you come over?"

"I'm there."

I had just taken a seat on the front porch when I heard Mr. Palomer's storm door clatter and saw Max jogging across the driveway toward me. The collar of his polo shirt was popped, but only on the left side. The laces of his Top-Siders were untied. I gave the shoes an ugly look. I didn't meet Max's eyes, even once he'd taken a seat next to me.

"How are you?" he asked.

"Not dead," I said.

"I was in such bad shape last night. Even after we'd driven home and I knew you were okay, I was—"

"I don't want to do it anymore," I interrupted. "The list. Number seventeen. Any of it."

Max was quiet for a long moment.

Then he said, "Right. Okay. We'll, um, we'll take a break."

I raised my eyes. I looked at Max. It wasn't a kind look.

"How can you think that way?" I asked.

"What way?"

"How could you *want* to fake all those deaths after what happened to you? Why would you want to put yourself through that again? I don't get it. I thought I did before, when you told me all the stuff about the car accident and your therapist. I thought that made sense. But I could've died last night, and there is nothing in me that wants to relive that. Ever."

"Okay," Max said slowly. "Well. You're totally allowed to feel that way."

I shook my head. "What's wrong with you, Max?"

"Excuse me?"

"I mean, what's really wrong here?"

Max cleared his throat. He got to his feet.

"I should come back later," he said.

He took the porch steps two at a time, but I didn't let him go. I raced after him. In the driveway, I caught hold of his elbow.

"You can't cheat death, you know," I said. "You can't show it up. And you shouldn't make fun of it. I mean, what were we even doing with your list? Joel was right: It's irreverent. All the people who really did die those ways, who didn't see it coming—it wasn't a checkmark for them, it was just their life. People actually die. They *die*, Max, and they don't come back."

"Look, I know you're really shaken right now—"

"This isn't about last night!" I shouted. "I just don't understand why you can't be grateful you're okay. Why can't you be happy that you didn't crack your skull in that car wreck and that you didn't bleed out at school and that you got a second chance? Because some people don't get them. Some people don't get a fucking second chance."

Max was silent. I heard a neighbor mowing his lawn a few doors down. I heard my own staggered breaths.

"You don't have to be fine," I said. "You don't have to come up with some sick list to make it all better. You don't have to fix yourself."

"Yeah, I do actually. I *want* to. Maybe there's some stuff I can't fix"—Max threw out his three-fingered hand between us—"but I can at least *try* to fix what's going on in my head."

"Well, you're doing it the wrong way."

"You don't get to say that."

"Yes, I do."

"I thought you understood this."

"I thought so too. But hey, I'm not empathetic. Maybe I never understood."

Max shook his head. He laughed, just once—a short burst.

"God, that is such a load of shit."

"What is?"

"This empathy card of yours. You're plenty empathetic, Stevie. You're the most empathetic person I know. You tried saving my life twice before you even knew me, when I was just some stranger. You've been worried about me every single death we've faked. You've been worried about Sanger and her moms and their move. You've been worried about Joel. You feel what we're feeling. I know you do. You're like an—an empathetic goddess. That's not what the problem is, so don't throw it out there like it's some kind of fucking explain-all."

"Okay, then what is it, Max? Since you're such an expert on mental health, what is my problem?"

"This," said Max, waving between us.

I narrowed my eyes. "Air?"

"Don't be a wiseass. *This*. This—this *judgment aura* you put up. It's like something clicks off in your eyes. I can see it. You suddenly stop seeing me as Max and start seeing me as some labeled faceless person you store in your brain. I see you trying to file me away, only that's not going to happen. You can't file me. Or what I'm dealing with. Or the list. Or what's between us. They're not things to be filed."

A siren wailed in the distance. Max formed his three-fingered hand into a pointer, and he directed it straight at me. "You don't get to tell me I'm doing it the wrong way when it's your damn filing system that's wrong."

"I'm not wrong," I whispered, taking a step back.

"No? So what're you saying?" asked Max, taking a step forward.

"I—I don't want to do the list."

"Yeah, and what else do you not want?"

Max's voice was so thin.

I thought, *This is how it's going to end.*

And I said, "I don't want any of it. Not right now. I just can't."

"Right," said Max. "Bye, Stevie."

He walked away, back to the Palomer house, skirting the wall of concrete flowers, just a flash of dark hair and peach-colored shirt. Then he was gone altogether.

Twenty-One

Sanger still hadn't called me back.

I sat cross-legged on my bed, looking out my window at the orange vinyl siding of the Palomer house. My phone was wedged in the space between left ankle and right shin. I was waiting.

As I waited, I looked, and I thought. I'd given up all other forms of activity. Earlier, I had checked my e-mails, and I'd found the one Leslie Cobb had sent late Friday night with the subject line "Tough News." I'd trashed it without opening it. Its message wouldn't tell me anything I didn't already know. The governor had vetoed our bill, effectively crushing our dreams and allowing New Systematic Solutions to dump its waste with no ramifications. And we would rally, cried Leslie's voice in my head, amplified by the almighty growl of a megaphone. We would call for new measures, we would not give up the fight! But I didn't want to be rallied. At the moment, giving up the fight seemed like the best course of action.

I tried reading *The Great Gatsby*, but things had taken a turn for the worse for Gatsby and Daisy and everyone in their little West Egg sphere, and I didn't want to keep reading, because

I knew that each paragraph was pushing the plot closer and closer to an unhappy conclusion. I could stomach a book like that in a good mood, but I wasn't in a good mood.

Something was growing inside my chest—a black and tendriled thing that had germinated deep down the night before and was now expanding.

The only word I had for it was "guilt."

When people talk about guilt, they say, "I feel guilty," like guilt is something that you produce, the same as you produce laughter or tears. But I didn't *feel* guilty. Guilt was happening *to* me. It was making contact with me the way a drill makes contact with a plaster wall. It was messy and relentless, and there was so much debris.

I should've watched my sugar. I shouldn't have worried my parents.

I should've heard Max out. I shouldn't have yelled at him after he'd ridden with me in an ambulance and he'd pressed his reassuring fingertips into my back.

I should've taken Joel more seriously, that day he'd gotten so upset about the death list. Because I understood now what he meant.

I shouldn't have made so many mistakes and, in spite of them all, pushed on like they meant nothing, like they weren't mine.

Guilt drilled in, and I lay on my bed, weighted down.

• • •

When the doorbell rang late that afternoon, I had an imbecilic thought. I thought that rather than call me back, Sanger had driven to Austin from San Antonio. That when I opened the door, we would hug and talk it all through on the front porch. I had that thought. It seemed the sort of scene that Frank Capra would write into my life, maybe, if he had the rights.

I didn't answer the door.

Mom did.

It wasn't Sanger.

"It's Jessica Parrish," said Mom, peering into my bedroom.

"What?"

I wore a stupid face of confusion. Jessica Parrish deserved an award for Last Person I Was Expecting.

"She heard you were in the hospital," said Mom, tapping the doorknob, her nail making a soft *ting, ting* against the metal.

My face went from stupid to suspicious. "She heard that from . . . ?"

Mom sighed. "I may have posted something about asking for good thoughts because you were in the emergency room."

"*Mom.* You know that stuff spreads like wildfire, especially with those co-op moms. Oh God, I'm probably on, like, their prayer request lists. They're probably holding vigils for me."

"Well, I'm sorry, Stevie, but I was terrified at the time. And I happen to think that every good thought and prayer counts."

"Can you tell her I'm sleeping? Or puking? Or something?"

"You're perfectly capable of talking to her, and I think it's very sweet she's come all this way just for you. I didn't think you even knew her all that well."

"I don't. That's why it's weird."

And I screamed at her in front of the capitol. That makes it weird too.

"She brought flowers."

"Holy shit, that makes it even weirder."

"Language, Stevie."

That was a reprimand, but it wasn't for my language. It was for my lack of decency as a human being. There was no getting out from under Mom's convicting glare. I slipped off my bed and padded after her into the hallway.

Jessica was seated on the couch in the front room, hands clasped atop her knee-length plaid skirt, blond hair brushed out and hanging to her waist. A bouquet of daisies rested on the coffee table. When she caught sight of me, she hurriedly got to her feet.

"Hello, Stevie," she said.

"Um. Hey."

"Jessica," said Mom, "would you like something to drink? Water? OJ?"

"No thank you, Mrs. Hart."

"Mhm. Well, I'm just going to do some things."

Mom left us alone.

I stared at Jessica. She remained standing, swaying slightly, her hands clasped so tightly in front of her that I felt sure she was going to break a finger.

"You can sit back down," I said, flapping a hand to the couch as I eased onto the edge of a rocking chair across from her.

"If you're not feeling well enough . . . ," Jessica began. "Your mother said . . . but I don't want to—"

"I'm sorry," I blurted.

Jessica stopped short. She looked shocked, which I guessed was owing to the fact that her well-behaved, well-groomed family was probably taught never to interrupt.

"I'm really, *really* sorry about all that stuff I yelled at you," I said. "At the rally?"

Unnecessary clarification, Stevie. Of course she remembers the time you went off on her like a raving psycho.

"Oh," said Jessica.

Then, mercifully, Jessica said something more than "Oh."

"That's okay," she said. "I heard what happened to the bill you were supporting. The Springs Alliance? I'm very sorry that happened."

"Yeah. Me too."

"I noticed you hadn't been at the co-op the past few weeks," Jessica continued, tugging at something under the daisy bouquet. "Then when my mother told me you were at the hospital . . . That must've been scary."

"Yeah," I said, frowning at the object she'd pulled from the coffee table and was now handing to me.

I took it, looked it over. It was a handmade get-well card, featuring a giant, carefully watercolored sunflower.

"Did you do this?" I asked.

Jessica nodded. "You always said really nice things about my artwork."

"Yeah, because it was really good," I said, eagerly grasping at a topic other than my emergency room visit. "*This* is really good. You could, like, sell these, you know? At the farmers' market, or even online. Or wait, do you do the Internet?"

"Yes," said Jessica. She was looking at me with an amused smile. "Of course we have Internet."

"Oh."

"The real daisies are my sister's," said Jessica. "Anna. Do you know her?"

I nodded, even though I had no idea who Anna was. All the Blue-Jean Jumper types at co-op sort of blurred together in my mind, a visual swirl of braids and Velcro shoes. I'd piled them into an easily forgettable, easily dismissible box.

"She grows flowers," said Jessica. "She's very good at it." Then, after a pause, in a softer voice, she said, "My grandfather—he's passed away now, but he had diabetes. I loved him very much. Sometimes he would tell me he wished he didn't have it, because he couldn't do all the things he wanted. But he was still the best person I've ever known."

I waited in awkward silence for Jessica to continue. I waited, dreading that she would launch into a bout of heavy moralizing, or invite me to her church, or quote an inspirational poem. But that was it. And as her words washed over me, I felt weirdly good about them. It was like Jessica Parrish and I shared something, something we both understood inside and out. And right there in the front room, she wasn't a Blue-Jean Jumper and I wasn't a Normal Type.

I remembered then something Max Garza had once told me. *Death is everyone's common ground,* he'd said.

I looked at the watercolor card in my hand. And I thought, maybe sunflowers were a good common ground too.

Joel came home while I was in my bedroom, door shut. I heard Mom corral him into the kitchen and tell him in a low, but not low enough, voice what had happened to me. When he asked to see me, she told him I was sleeping.

Mom brought me dinner in bed. The day had worn down my defenses, and I decided I was okay with being treated like an invalid for a little while, if it meant avoiding contact with Joel. But eventually nature called, and I was forced to venture out to use the bathroom.

When I emerged, I felt a warm breeze tickling down the hallway. The den's screen door was open, and Joel sat on the patio stoop, his back to me.

He said nothing when I sat down beside him.

"If you're menstruating," I said, "I'll go away."

Joel smiled in the direction of his feet.

"Aunt Carrie should've called me," he said. "I would've come home right away if I'd known."

"Yeah, well, that would've been stupid. I wouldn't have wanted to talk to you. I was all distraught and emotional and would've thrown stuffed animals at your face."

"I'm glad you're okay," he said.

I pounded my chest. "Invincible."

"No, you're not."

My smile faded.

"No," I said. "I'm not."

"Stevie. What happened—it wasn't about that death list you were doing, was it?"

"It had nothing to do with that. Actually, that's what makes it so funny."

"You think it's *funny*?"

I rubbed my palms along my cheeks, sighed. "No, that wasn't the right word."

"I talked to Max," said Joel. "After the W. He told me what the list was really about. I think I get it now. Partway, anyway. I'm sorry I was an ass."

I shook my head. "We were the asses, Joel. You were right: It was super insensitive."

"Maybe. But I've been super sensitive lately. Bad combination."

"I guess."

I didn't press it. I knew very well how Joel had been over

the past weeks—his weird new habit of lingering, the fight on the lacrosse field, the blowout at the W. If he hadn't talked about what was bothering him before, I figured he wouldn't talk about it now.

I was wrong.

Joel handed me something. It was a letter, stamped and postmarked, but unopened. A thin yellow sticker marked RETURN TO SENDER ran across the front, but I could make out, written just beneath the sticker's edge, the name of Joel's dad and, beneath that, a Montreal address.

"What did you send him?" I asked.

"You can open it. I don't care anymore."

I opened the envelope. Inside was an invitation to Joel's graduation party. Beneath the details of the where and when, there was a message written in green Sharpie: *Hope this gets to you. Come if you want.* A confident-bordering-on-smug Joel stared up at me from his enclosed senior portrait. A less-than-confident Joel let out a long sigh beside me.

"I didn't know you were in touch with him," I said, handing the card back.

"I wasn't," said Joel. "Not until January. He gave me his e-mail back at the funeral. So I decided to do it one night— just write him and see what happened. And he wrote back. And we kept on writing. Like, all the time. Twice a day. And he was great. Really funny, sent me these links to great bands and shit. Then one day he just stopped. I kept writing for a while. Then I tried sending something snail mail. And that's what I got back."

"You don't think," I ventured, "something could've—?"

"I found his home phone number. I called. He answered. He's fine, he's just an asshole. I mean, I should've known he would be. He's a classic Dick Dad stereotype. But I don't know. You like to think you're going to be the exception."

I thought of Val, on instinct. A memory that had flown around in my brain, never to roost properly, returned to me.

"Val said something to me once," I said. "About you having a pen pal."

"She caught my inbox open this one time, saw a bunch of messages from the same address. She thought I was cheating on her."

"Why didn't you tell her the truth?"

Joel shrugged. "I didn't want to. She was just some two-week girlfriend. I didn't owe her an explanation about my dad. So then we broke up, and she got Aaron on her side. I guess they spent a while trying to crack my Gmail password, because one morning I woke up and my account had been hacked."

"So they found out you *weren't* cheating," I said, trying to inject some hopefulness into the conversation.

"They found every fucking thing I'd ever written to my dad, Stevie. Really personal stuff. Embarrassing stuff. They read it all."

"You don't know that."

"Yeah, I do. Because I know Val, and I know Aaron. They were probably drunk-laughing at it all night long."

"The lacrosse game," I said, realization driving in. "Your fight with Aaron. That's what the fight was about?"

"He was freakin' quoting my letters *at* me. He'd been doing it for a while, just trying to get a rise out of me. And I finally let him."

I stared at the invitation in Joel's hands. The invitation his dad would never see, the picture he'd never stick on his fridge. I hated that man. I hated him so much. And for all the awful amount of feelings I'd been brewing those past few days, it felt good to have an object to angrily funnel them on.

"I just didn't want your parents to find out," Joel said. "I didn't want them to think I was ungrateful or, like, they weren't doing a good enough job."

"No, I get it. You don't owe anyone an explanation."

"Yeah."

We didn't say anything for a long time after that. A breeze blew over the smell of gasoline from the carport.

I laughed a little. Then I said, "Are most people like us, Joel?"

"How do you mean?"

"I mean—I don't know what I mean. I guess I'm afraid I'll get to college and find out I've been doing it all wrong."

"Doing what wrong?"

"Life."

Joel said, "That's not going to happen."

"It's just," I said, "something happens to you, right? Something bad, or something big. It changes you. And afterward, there's this part of you that normal people without your experience will never understand."

"Are you talking about the diabetes?" he asked softly.

I shook my head. "It doesn't matter what I'm talking about. It could be lots of things."

"Because I feel that way about Mom."

I said nothing, too afraid to break the moment.

Joel said, "No one gets that. People can be nice to you, and they can love you, but they can't *get it*. I think that's something you've got to work out for yourself."

I thought of Max. I thought of his list. I thought of Sanger and her popmallow and her neon poster boards. I thought of car accidents and moving vans and funerals and dick dads and diabetes. I thought my head would burst from thinking.

"I think you're right," I said. "But I think some people *can* get it, in a way. I mean, everyone goes through shit. And I think sometimes, if your shit is similar enough, you can understand each other. Maybe if you're lucky, you find a person or two like that. But 'lucky' isn't the right word for it. It isn't luck. I don't know, the gas fumes are really strong out here."

We fell back into silence, thick and punctuated only by a chorus of cicadas.

In the silence, Joel put his arm around my shoulders. In the silence, my bare foot nudged his.

He said, "I'm lucky you're my cousin, you know? Even if 'lucky' isn't the right word for it at all."

I kept my phone on ring that night, even after I'd turned off my bedside lamp. I had the wild hope that Sanger would finally call me back in the middle of the night.

She didn't. I slept the whole night through.

Twenty-Two

In the morning, I went walking.

It was raining pretty hard, but I was desperate to move, to breathe air that wasn't filtered. So I walked.

I didn't give myself a destination. I didn't take an umbrella. I just walked until my ponytail was sopped through and my socks squished in my sneakers. Headlights slung around rainy corners, tires splattered water onto the sidewalk—cars carrying people carrying Monday tasks on their shoulders. These people were going to work and to school, but I was just going. I went, and I went, rounding culs-de-sac, cutting a path through my own private claim on suburbia.

For a while, I entertained the crazy idea that I would walk all the way to Barton Springs. Because I needed to be there. I needed to sit anonymous in the rain—me, my thoughts, and a deserted pool. Eventually, I thought better of it. I couldn't go to Barton Springs. Not now. It would only depress me, make me think of failure. So I just walked on in the rain, no purpose, no destination.

As I walked, I found myself thinking about Max. He had become a well-worn groove in my mind, and for once I stopped fighting his presence and just let my thoughts play out. I let myself remember all the things I'd shouted at him in the driveway, and all the things he'd said back.

I'd told him that night in the ER had nothing to do with it.

But that night had everything to do with it.

We had been so careless these past two months. We'd been brushing elbows with Death for weeks, but in the end Death hadn't come for Max. Death had come for me.

I was angry with Max for that, even if it wasn't fair. I was angrier with myself, even if that wasn't fair either. But more than anything, I was angry at Death. And in that moment, when I was angriest with Max, I understood him the most too. I understood, for the first time, what Max had told Sanger and me on the bank of Barton Springs. I understood what he'd meant by calling Death a sick bastard that deserved to be screwed over.

I stopped walking then.

"I get it," I said out loud, the rain trickling over my lips and touching my tongue. "Seriously, Max. I get it."

He'd told me I didn't lack empathy, that my problem was something else altogether.

I was beginning to get that, too.

Since her visit, I'd been thinking a lot about Jessica Parrish.

Jessica wasn't what she protested. I knew that now. Jessica wasn't defined by evolution or gay marriage any more than I was defined by stream pollutants. And she wasn't her cause any more than I was STA. I'd stereotyped her the same way I hated to be stereotyped—lumped her in with the worst and most unflattering of her kind. And I hadn't just judged her in my head. I'd done it out loud, in the meanest possible way.

Max was right: I, Stevie Hart, had judgy face. Judgy mind. Judgy heart. Whatever you wanted to call it. I'd yelled at Jessica Parrish because, in that moment at the capitol, she was just a label. A faceless person I wanted to hurt and not a living person who was all manner of complicated and indefinable and whose sister Anna grew sunflowers.

Max was right about that, too.

I didn't walk the rest of the way home. I ran.

I came home soaked and frenetic with energy. As I passed the mailbox, I saw him. He was in the driver's seat of his car, headlights on and wipers swishing. He caught my gaze, and we held it there, for just a moment. And I wanted to say, "Seriously, Max. I get it." I wanted to say it all over again. But I couldn't. I got it, but I was still angry.

I let the gaze loose and went into the garage. I heard Max drive off as I unlaced my shoes.

I took a hot shower. Afterward, when I sat down at my desk, trig textbook open, I saw that I had one missed call.

Sanger.

She'd left a voice mail, but I didn't waste time checking it. I called her back.

"Stevie?" she answered. "You *cannot* leave enigmatic

messages like that. I thought you were *dead*. Is someone dead? Just tell me now."

"No one's dead," I told Sanger.

Then I told her everything, beginning with Joel and the hospital, then winding back to prom crashing, and back further still to the governor's veto, and ending, hesitantly, on my fight with Max.

Sanger said very little as I spoke. She produced grunts and gasps and threw out the occasional expletive, but she made no real commentary until I was through.

"Are you okay?" she asked.

"No," I said.

"I wish I were there."

"Aren't you going to say something like, 'I go away for one day, Stevie'?"

"It doesn't bode well for the coming year," Sanger admitted.

I asked the question then, before I lost the nerve. It was the question that had been sawing into my brain since Sunday.

"Is this what it's going to be like all the time? Once you move?"

"I sure hope not," said Sanger. "It sucks."

"I wish you'd never shown me *Mr. Smith Goes to Washington*."

"You mean, you wish you'd never thought of yourself as Jimmy Stewart," Sanger said. And then, "I'm sorry, Stevie. Really. I know how much you cared about the bill."

"It wasn't the bill I cared about," I said.

"Yeah."

"Why didn't you call all yesterday?"

"That. Ugh. Melanie hid my phone. I was going berserk, too, because she's on this kick now where she flushes things down the toilet. Last week, Uncle Jim said she flushed this really expensive ballpoint pen. Also some of her sister's headbands. Cousins are *whack*. You're lucky Joel isn't."

"Well. What's your definition of 'whack'?"

Sanger sighed. "I never got to kiss him."

"Trust me. Five years out, you're going to look back on that fact with relief."

"Maybe," said Sanger. "Or maybe it'll rip me up inside and turn me into a great poet. Either way, I guess I win. Thank Joel for that sometime, would you?"

The rain picked up outside and pinged hard against my window. Thunder growled in uneven stutters. With a mechanical pencil, I drew a line down the length of my trig book cover.

"I'm sorry I wasn't there." Sanger's voice dipped into softer territory. "I feel like shit."

"Don't," I said, though the night before I'd come up with a dozen different tirades I'd launch on Sanger when she finally called back, all with the express intention of making her feel like shit.

"I'll make it up to you when I get back," she said. "We'll make the last four deaths absolutely—oh. Nope. Never mind. Guess that's over. Dude, Nicks, you really burned down the whole barn, didn't you?"

"Yes."

"Did you mean to break up with him?"

"I don't know," I said. "I don't even know. I just needed space to think."

"You didn't use *that* line on him, did you?"

"No. Worse ones."

"Damn."

"I'm sorry I ruined the whole deathscapade thing. I know it meant a lot to—"

"Shut up, Nicks, right now. Sisters before misters, always and forever."

"Still a stupid phrase."

"Still a true one. Are you crying?"

"No."

"You made this snotty sniffle noise."

"Cedar fever."

"Nicks, I hate to do this, but we're going hiking with the cousins. Moms will kill me if they see me being asocial."

"I'm really glad you called," I said.

"Yes, well, I'm watching Melanie like a hawk now— That's *right*, Mel, youuuu." I heard a peal of uninhibited giggles in the background. "Take your allergy meds, okay?"

"Okay."

"I'm running back to you just as fast as I can."

I was smiling when I hung up, but I knew then, for certain, the answer to my question.

After Sanger's move, this *was* what it was going to be like. All the time.

Twenty-Three

As a going-away present, I bought Sanger a new Polaroid camera. Its purchase didn't require so intensive a regimen of saving as when I'd been in fifth grade, just the sacrifice of an expensive pair of sandals I'd had my eye on for the summer. Tucked into the hand strap was a creased construction paper heart with a glitter border. The sticky note inside the BFF card read: *Send me a pic a week.*

I gave it to Sanger as the movers were hauling the last of the boxes from the garage. Hamasaki House was empty, completely empty, and I refused to go in one last time. It wasn't really the Sadler-Hamasakis' anymore. It belonged to a family that was moving in from Oakland the next week.

"So impractical," Sanger said upon receiving my gift. "It's not like I'll have any friends to take pictures of. Should've bought me a pair of mittens. Gloves? What the hell do they even call them? I'm not meant for the North."

She said it while she was hugging me, and while she was crying.

"You're supposed to take pictures of your new life," I explained. "I expect a lot of selfies."

"You're such a sap," Sanger said, pulling out of the hug. "You're almost as bad as Max."

I thought at first that it must've just been a slip, that Sanger hadn't been thinking when she said his name. But then I took a good look at her face. She was staring at me, unblinking, *challenging* me. She'd meant to say it.

"He came by yesterday," she told me. "Dude was more serious than I've ever seen him. He didn't even smile, but he was still really nice and grateful about me helping with the list."

"Oh," I said.

I leaned against the side door of the Fiat, my thoughts turning murky. Why was Sanger doing this? Why was she making things awkward? These were our last moments together, and I didn't want them ruined by the taint of Max Garza, even if what Sanger was saying was softening my insides. Of course Max had come to see her. Of course he'd been nice and grateful. Of course, and why was I still angry with him?

Was I even angry with him at all?

"Stop it," I said. "It isn't going to work."

Though it already was, and Sanger knew it. She was smirking an ungodly smirk.

"You miss him, Nicks," she said. "I can tell."

"Did he put you up to this? Did he ask you to, like, talk to me?"

"What?" Sanger looked affronted. "*No.* I am no man's puppet."

"I was really awful to him," I said. "I was—"

"So suck it up and apologize. Goddammit, Nicks, I didn't go to all the trouble of shoving you kids together only for you to toss it away. You're so *ungrateful*."

"You didn't shove—"

"Oh, come *on*. Like you would've gone along with Max's plan if I weren't there. I had to play the effing BFF card on you. Do you even know what you've got with him? Do you know how ridiculously rare it is to find that? I told you, he's like *us*. He's a fringe schooler. He's someone who *gets* it. And you act like that's nothing."

"He's crazy," I said feebly.

"So are you." Sanger flicked my shoulder, hard. "I'm not saying you've got to have his babies; I'm just saying, Max Garza should be in your life. You need someone left in this place who understands you, stupid."

I rubbed my shoulder, looking ahead at the bright red sign in the lawn that read SOLD. And I had a thought.

"You did it on purpose," I said slowly. "You knew you were moving, and you wanted to find me a—a replacement, for when you left. That's what you were doing, wasn't it?"

"That is," said Sanger, "both preposterous and totally, um, totally off base."

But I was looking at her, and I knew I was right.

Sanger shrugged violently, as though trying to shake off an unseen bug. We stared at the SOLD sign in a gaunt stretch of silence. Sanger started to laugh.

"Like Max could ever replace *me*," she said. "I'm your Duckie, remember? You told me."

"I know," I said, smiling. "I know you are."

"Okay. Now come on, let's use this camera. I do not want its first exposure to be the Philly skyline."

She slung her arm around my neck, and I wormed mine around hers, and Sanger took a selfie of us leaned against the back of the Fiat.

She gave it to me to keep.

Later that week, I got a picture in the mail. It arrived in a brown manila envelope. There was no return address, no letter inside. It was a six-by-eight glossy photograph of a half-dozen formally dressed teenage couples, all lined in a row. In the upper left-hand corner, just over the strapless shoulders of a grinning girl, were two red-eyed, blurry faces—mine and Max's.

Tucked in the bottom corner of the envelope was a check from Emilio Garza III made out to Springs for Tomorrow Alliance in the amount of two hundred dollars.

I put the photograph back in the envelope and shoved it into my lowest desk drawer, the same place I stored Sanger's dream journal. I mailed the check to Leslie Cobb.

Joel met with Coach Whitt for a coach-parent discussion about the Austin Christian incident, after which he was allowed to continue playing lacrosse. From what I could tell, though, he and Aaron never really made up. The Wolverines ended the season with eight wins and four losses. At the start of June, Joel and I received joint ownership of Mom's sedan. Joel attended summer registration for UT-Austin. In some ways, things went on like normal.

In other ways, they didn't.

Mom made me sign a pact of sorts promising to carry my glucose tablets at all times. She asked a lot more questions about my eating schedule and my sugar levels. Dad began actively seeking new summer clients to foot the ambulance bill. Whenever possible, we ate family dinners together at the table. On weekdays, Mom made us sit down together for lunch, too.

There was a tension between Joel and me. It wasn't a bad tension, but it was palpable—a warm wax that settled between us and clung to our words and actions. It was a carefulness that hadn't been there before. We didn't snark and fight with each other as much as we used to. We weren't as blunt, but in some ways we were more open.

One early evening, we drove out to the food trucks on South Congress. Joel got a kebab and I got a plastic cup of pad thai. We set ourselves up at one of the picnic tables. Joel told me he was thinking of majoring in communications. I told him he had plenty of time to decide.

I insisted on window-shopping. We ducked into a costume shop, then a bookshop, then a store filled with unrelated knickknacks and that Joel and I joked was going through an identity crisis. I bought a key chain to send to Sanger. It was shaped like the state of Texas, with a glittery heart positioned over Austin. It was kitschy and bright yellow, so Sanger would love it.

On our way out of the knickknack store, we saw none other than the elusive Lemur Dude. Joel went gape-mouthed. I squeezed his elbow and jumped up and down. Lemur Dude was riding his orange Vespa southward. A green-blue kimono fluttered around him. He was wearing the straw hat, but he passed too quickly for us to make out if there really was a lemur nestled inside it. Not that Joel and I doubted. Lemur Dude's lemur was just something you had to believe in.

"I did it," Joel said. "I saw him."

I said, "Lucky you."

The second Saturday of June, we held a small graduation party for Joel at our house, which consisted primarily of extended relatives drinking punch and eating mini pretzels and exchanging pleasantries. Every so often, a new relative would kiss Joel's cheek or slap him on the back and tell him how pleased they were by Joel's decision to be a Longhorn. They said how proud they were of him.

I was proud of Joel too, in a way I didn't know I could be before that spring. But it wasn't a kind of pride I could tell him about like the relatives did, out loud, and with a smile.

I was in the kitchen, pouring an orange soda for my nanna,

when I saw him through the window. He was walking back to the Palomer house, his hands in his pockets, sunglasses propped on his head. I handed Nanna her drink, and then I ran out the back door to stop Max before he got inside.

I called his name, crossing through the succulent garden to the back patio, where Max had stopped and stood staring at me. He looked antsy, as though a play were about to start and he wasn't in his designated seat.

"I didn't see you in there," I said.

"Yeah, I just popped in. Left a gift."

"Did you even get to talk to Joel?"

Max shrugged. "I see him around. No big deal. Anyway, it seemed like a family thing."

He turned to his patio door.

"I have something for you," I near-screamed at him.

Again, he paused.

"Can I just—go get it?" I asked. "Is that okay?"

"Sure," said Max. "Sure, I guess."

"Okay. I'll be right back. Just hang on."

I ran to the house and into my room, where I retrieved Sanger's dream journal from my bottom desk drawer. I returned outside in long, awkward strides, the journal clutched to my chest. I felt unusually young. Max, on the other hand, looked unusually aged, sitting there on a patio chair, his eyes closed up at the cloudless sky.

"Hey," I said, and he opened his eyes.

I handed him the book.

He smiled humorlessly.

"I had a feeling," he said.

"It was your list to begin with. You should be the one to have all that."

After a moment, he said, "I got one again. One of those dark funks. You know, after . . ."

He didn't finish, and he didn't need to. After my own near-death experience, he meant. After I'd chewed him out. I nodded weakly, waiting for him to go on.

"Yeah, so I was in one of those funks again. And at first I thought it was the same kind as before. About Death, you know? And I drove out to Barton Springs that day we got all that rain, and I sat out there, and I was looking at the water, and I was thinking about all that STA shit, and how that place you loved so much was going to eventually be run over by all this toxic sludge from douchey corporations. It was really bleak. And then I got it—what I'm really afraid of."

I frowned. "Death," I said. "You're afraid of death."

Max shook his head. "I mean, maybe. But it's not just that. I was thinking about what you said when we went prom crashing, about things ending without your permission. You remember saying that?"

"Yes."

"Yeah, well, that's when it clicked. I got it. That's what I'm afraid of: things ending without my permission. And yeah, death's part of the problem, but it's bigger than that. And maybe I've been going about it all wrong, you know? Maybe I don't need exposure to death. Maybe it's just exposure to, you know, *life*. Which is technically happening all the time. So, in a way, I've been getting a dose of exposure therapy without even trying. Does that make any sense?"

"Yes," I said, not because I understood completely, but because I understood enough.

"Anyway," said Max, curling his fingers around the binding of the dream journal, "that's what I've been trying to tell my therapist. She's going to get a *kick* out of this list when I show it to her."

"I thought you weren't seeing your therapist anymore."

Max shrugged. "I started up again last week. She's not as bad as I thought. After I told her about Dark Funk Number Two, she said I have to find a way to be okay with things ending without my permission, or whatever, but that there are some things that don't have to end. Things you can fight for. And I've just got to figure out what's what. Like Barton Springs. Stuff like that, it's worth saving. Stuff like that, we can do something about."

I nodded. Carefully, I sat on the deck chair across from him. I said, "You're worth saving too."

Max just looked at me.

"I forgot that for a little while," I said.

"I felt like what happened to you was my fault."

"It wasn't."

"Sanger said you needed space."

"She told you that?"

"She's a smart girl, Sanger."

"You were right too, you know. About the empathy thing? About my filing system? You were totally right."

"Look, Stevie."

I leaned closer, the deck chair tilting forward with the press of my weight.

"Yeah?"

"Look," Max said again. "It wasn't all just about showing up Death, or getting over Death, or any of the other stuff I told you. I guess I liked the adrenaline, too. And toward the end, I just liked—being around you."

"Max."

I reached across the distance between us. I caught hold of his right hand, and I rested my thumb over the puckered skin of his two fingerless knuckles. Max flinched, but I didn't. I didn't flinch at all.

Slowly, Max shook his head.

"Sanger's right," he said. "You are a total sap."

I laughed. "She only says that about people she loves."

"So," said Max, looking down at our touching hands. "I had this idea."

"Okay."

"I was thinking, now is the perfect time to enjoy Barton

Springs in all its splendor, before it's overrun by that toxic chemical sludge."

"I agree," I said. "Though STA is going to stop that from happening. Eventually. Leslie Cobb is already concocting a new plan."

"Eventually," Max echoed. "But worst-case scenario, we'd better make the most of what we've got."

"We should go sometime," I said.

"How about now?"

I hesitated. I said, "Not today, but sometime."

"All right. Sometime. Soon. I know where you live."

"Oh, come on, don't be a creep like that."

Max smiled, but it wasn't a creepy smile. It was oddly peaceful, a little like the way I'd first seen him, when I thought he was dead in the succulent garden.

I went to Barton Springs that night, on my own. I could go now, free of bad feelings, because the failure of what had happened was fading and the hope of what could be was on the rise. I could be there like before, my anonymous self and my clear thoughts. I sat high up on the grassy bank. The sun had begun to set, and the swimmers were greedily using up the remaining dusk light, punching in and out of the water in a chaos of glass-shard sprays.

Earlier that day, during the party, I had texted Sanger.

Do you think we're lucky?

It had been more than five hours since then when, as I watched the swimmers, my phone went off.

Sanger had texted back.

You mean, to be alive?

I texted, *I guess. Yes.*

Sanger said, *Well we ARE alive.*

And ten minutes later, she said, *Nicks. We're the luckiest damn people I know.*